T0277115

"Busse enchants in this stunning introduction to her new series, The Nordic Wars. *Winter's Maiden* is a compelling, imaginative exploration of purpose, truth, and consequence with some haunting, dark undercurrents. The story and its characters linger long after the last page. Absolutely enthralling!"

— **RONIE KENDIG**, award-winning author of The Droseran Saga

"With its rich worldbuilding, engaging characters, and intricate plotline, *Winter's Maiden* captivates from page one. Though Brighid struggles with loss and finding her place in the world, hope relentlessly steps into her life, steering her toward the right path. I am always on the lookout for novels with nuanced female warrior protagonists, and Brighid is one both teens and adults will relate to. I'm anxiously awaiting book two!"

— **HEATHER DAY GILBERT**, RWA Daphne Award-winning author of The Vikings of the New World Saga

"This book is amazing! I am a fan of Nordic-inspired fantasy, and this book has everything I love: rich setting, unforgettable characters, and a world so real I feel like I'm there. I highly recommend *Winter's Maiden*."

— **S.D. GRIMM**, author of *Phoenix Fire*

Books by Morgan L. Busse

Follower of the Word
Daughter of Light
Son of Truth
Heir of Hope

The Soul Chronicles
Tainted
Awakened

The Ravenwood Saga
Mark of the Raven
Flight of the Raven
Cry of the Raven

Skyworld
Secrets in the Mist
Blood Secrets

The Nordic Wars
Winter's Maiden

The Nordic Wars | Book 1

WINTER'S MAIDEN

MORGAN L. BUSSE

Published by Enclave Publishing, an imprint of Oasis Family Media, LLC

Carol Stream, Illinois, USA.
www.enclavepublishing.com

ISBN: 979-8-88605-138-4 (printed hardcover)
ISBN: 979-8-88605-139-1 (printed softcover)
ISBN: 979-8-88605-141-4 (ebook)

Cover design by Emilie Haney, www.EAHCreative.com
Typesetting by Jamie Foley, www.JamieFoley.com

Printed in the United States of America.

To all the strong women in my life.

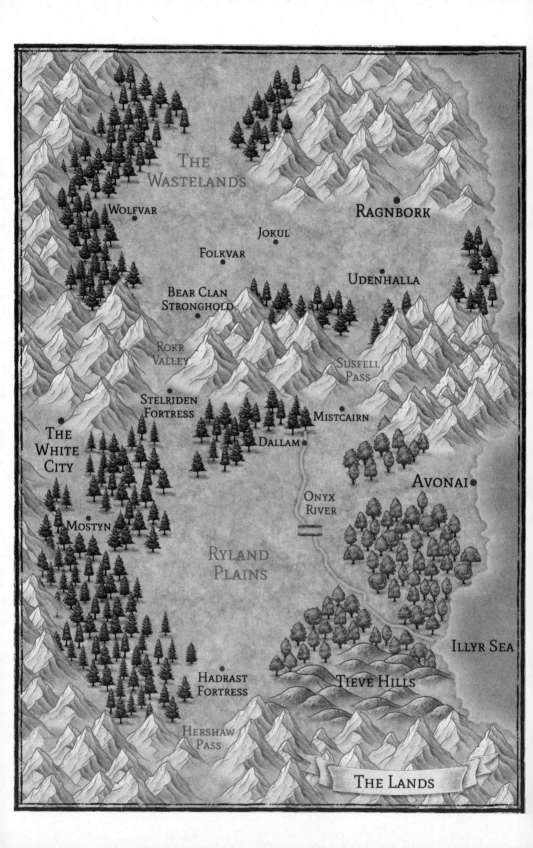

1

Winter covered everything in white like a blanket of wool beneath a rising sun. Despite the fire burning in the nearby firepit, nothing seemed to warm the decrepit cabin. Elphsaba murmured words of encouragement to the young woman clinging to a rope that hung across the rafter as she labored to give birth.

Elphsaba knew nothing of the woman: not her family, not where she was from, not how she came to be in this place. All Elphsaba knew was someone had come to her two nights ago and told her that her services were required. That was all she needed. Her job was to usher life into the world. Or at least try.

The woman let out a gasp followed by a long moan. Elphsaba licked her lips. Nothing was going right. A lot of blood collected in the hay beneath. And the young woman had been in labor for too long.

Elphsaba began to hum an old birthing song to comfort the woman and maybe instill a little more strength into her. But she was fading fast and could barely hang on to the rope. While she continued to hum, Elphsaba knelt and checked the woman's progression.

Finally.

She wiped the side of her face with her sleeve, keeping her hand away from her grey hair. Despite the chill inside the cabin, sweat covered her body. The baby was finally coming. "Good, good," she said and looked up. "You're almost done. Just a little more." For the last two hours she feared the mother would not have enough strength to finish the birth.

A few minutes later, the babe came. Elphsaba caught the child. Wet and sticky, but beautiful just the same, as new life always was. With a sudden suck of air, the babe let out a cry that echoed across the cabin.

Elphsaba laughed. "It's a girl!" She held the baby up. "Strong and healthy."

The woman sank to her knees, one hand still holding the rope, her head bowed. "Is he here, yet?" she asked weakly. Her blond hair was plastered to her face, and there was a pale hue to her cheeks. "A message was sent, right?"

"Yes, it was." By the same man who had retrieved her two nights ago. Elphsaba lowered the babe and began her ministrations. Whoever this woman was, it was clear that if she had family, they would not have accepted this birth. It wasn't the first time she had helped deliver an illegitimate child. And usually these stories did not have happy endings.

After the child was free of her mother, Elphsaba wrapped the little one in a long piece of cloth she had prepared. Elphsaba glanced back at the hay where the woman continued to kneel. More blood. Even as she watched, the darkening pool spread, and a shadow passed over her heart.

Elphsaba crouched down with the baby. "Do you wish to hold your daughter?" A small part of her hoped the woman would. The bonding might help. She had seen miracles happen the moment a mother held her child.

At first the woman didn't move, then she jerked her head side to side. Elphsaba swallowed her disappointment. "Are you sure? She's a beautiful little thing—"

"No." Her answer was forceful, and she refused to look at the baby.

The baby quieted and seemed content to curl her fingers over the edge of the wrappings. Elphsaba sighed and placed the tiny girl in a wooden box near the firepit and readied for the next part. There was still more to be done. A birth never ended with the baby.

She frowned again as she faced the woman. More blood. "Bolva," she muttered.

She helped with the afterbirth, then grabbed a few strips of cloth to try to staunch the bleeding. The blood was flowing freely. But why? There was a tear, but not that large. And the woman had been delivered of everything inside her. It was possible her labor been too long and arduous for what little strength the young woman seemed to have. Or perhaps there was something deeper . . .

The door to the cabin slammed open.

"I received a message to come here," a man said from behind her.

"Shut that door," Elphsaba snapped as a cold wind blew through the room.

The woman glanced up toward the front of the cabin, seemingly unaffected by her body's bleeding. "You came," she whispered.

The man looked around. "Where is it? Where is the baby?"

"In the box." Elphsaba had no time for this. She needed to find the reason behind the blood if possible. She searched, using every bit of knowledge she had from years of midwifery. There wasn't a visible tear. Internal, then?

"A girl," he said a minute later with a hint of disgust. "Of course it would be a girl."

Elphsaba glanced over. The man was tall, straight, and lean with the dark-blue military attire and cloak of the Rylanders. He was handsome in a rugged way with a small scar along his left eye. So the woman's lover was a Rylander?

The woman's breathing grew shallow and rapid, and her skin paled to match the snow outside. Elphsaba worked to remove the flow of blood and discover the source. She had been a midwife almost all her life, and she knew what this blood meant if she didn't stop it soon. "Bolva," she gritted again.

"What's going on?" The man roughly placed the baby back in the box. The babe began to cry.

"Rylander filth," Elphsaba muttered, then said, "The mother is not doing well."

"What do you mean?"

Bah! How thick was this man? The mother let go of the rope and collapsed across the hay. "No, no, no." Elphsaba was covered in the red life force from the woman. "At least hold her hand!" she yelled.

He hesitated, then came forward. She could see his face grow white from the corner of her eye.

He reached out, then held his hand aloft. He shook his head, his eyes wide. "She-she's gone."

Elphsaba moved around the makeshift straw bed. There was nothing in the woman's face now, no pain, no relief, no joy. He was right. She was gone.

"I never wanted this." He took a step back. "Any of this."

Elphsaba turned and glared at him. "Where do you think you're going?" He took another step back toward the door, his face as blank as stone. "I need help with the woman."

"She's dead. There's nothing I can do about that."

Elphsaba gritted her teeth. "But she will need to be burned, and her ashes scattered."

"Do it yourself."

Elphsaba snarled. "I am an old woman. I cannot carry the body alone and burn it."

He glanced away, but she noted a brief expression of pain on his face. Perhaps he cared a little. "She's gone now."

"And what about the baby? Your flesh and blood?"

He paused. "If it had been a boy . . ."

"A boy?" Elphsaba stepped forward and raised her fist, still covered in blood. "Bolva! What difference does it make? The babe is healthy and strong! If you don't claim the child, she will grow up without family or clan."

He turned toward her again, his stone face back in place. "If it had been a boy, I could have raised him as my son, and he would have been welcomed into my family despite his mother's heritage. But there is no place for a girl."

He spun around and headed for the door.

"Then what do I do with the baby?" Elphsaba shouted at his back with her fingers clenched.

"Keep her. Or leave her on the mountaintop. I don't care." Then he stepped through the door and into the winter chill.

"Rylander filth." Elphsaba spat on the floor. "Coward." The baby's cries were desperate now. Elphsaba sighed and reached for the last bit of clean cloth by which to clean her hands. "Don't worry little one, I won't leave you for the wolves." She placed the cloth down and reached for the baby. The child was beautiful. A strong, healthy, *Nordic* girl. She glanced at the dead woman in the bed. She didn't even know her name, or the name of the Rylander. She didn't know if the woman harkened from one of the five clans or if the Rylander had a family name. There were no Marks of Remembrance on her skin, nothing to point out who she was.

In the end, it didn't matter. Elphsaba kissed the baby's forehead. She'd never had a child of her own. Never bonded, never had a family. But maybe fate was giving her one last chance before her life came to a close.

She nodded to herself and held the baby close. She would raise the child as her own. There would be no leaving the babe at the foot of the mountains.

"Brighid," she murmured as she gazed down at the perfectly formed face. "I will call you Brighid. For you are strong. And you will be a Nordic who will stand shoulder to shoulder with the greatest of our people. I will see to that."

2

Brighid stilled the needle in her hand where she had been creating interconnecting circles with a deep-red-colored thread along the edge of her new wool dress. She glanced over at Elphsaba as the old woman sat a few feet away in the sunshine. It had always been just the two of them for sixteen years.

The home they shared was small and cozy with a thatched roof, a warm bed covered in furs, and two goats who currently enjoyed the foliage near the edge of the woods. A cool breeze swept through the trees, causing them to sway with a lovely swooshing sound. Far beyond the rolling green hill stood towering mountains, capped in snow that never melted even in the midst of summer.

Her eye caught Elphsaba's hands. A small sun-shaped symbol was inked onto her wrist, her Mark of Remembrance for her family. It was the only mark she wore. Brighid's eyes then traced the multiple folds in her skin. "Elphsaba, I have a question. What makes your skin wrinkle like that?" Elphsaba had always had wrinkles, but they seemed more pronounced now.

Elphsaba laughed. "You're always asking strange questions, ever since you were a little girl." She lifted her fingers and stared at them. "I suppose it's because I am old and they have worked hard. So my skin is tired."

"So my skin will also grow tired someday?"

"Yes, if you live long enough."

Brighid stitched a few more circles, her mind churning over more questions. She looked up again. "Why are your eyes green? And why are mine blue?"

Elphsaba smiled. "Because the world is full of color. And because my mother's eyes were green."

Brighid set down her needle and touched the edge of her cheek. Her eyes were the color of a summer sky. She hesitated, then asked, "Does that mean my mother's eyes were blue?" She waited to see if Elphsaba would answer.

The older woman stilled and gazed at the faraway mountains. Anytime Brighid brought up questions about her parents, Elphsaba grew quiet, like she did now. Then she would say, "When you are older, I will tell you." But she held a different expression today on her withered face, a pensive look coupled with a glare.

Was she finally going to say something?

Elphsaba took in a deep breath, and the look washed away into a sad smile. "When you are older, I will tell you."

"But why not now?" Brighid asked before she could control her tongue.

Elphsaba appeared taken back.

Brighid held her ground. For some time now, a fire had started to burn inside her, a discontent with the way things were, a desire to know who she was and what her future held.

Elphsaba opened her mouth, then closed it. Brighid leaned closer, her heart beating faster. Finally she would have some answers. Who were her parents? Why did she live with Elphsaba—who had years before confessed they were not related? Was she part of one of the Nordic clans? Did she have a heritage?

"I'm sixteen winters now and of age. When will I be old enough?"

Elphsaba stood. "You are right. It's about time you knew. And it's time for me to test you as an apprentice."

An apprentice? Brighid sucked in a breath, the blood leaving her face. Not that. She only wanted to know who she was—

A young man crested the hill. "Hala!" He raised his hand and waved. "You are needed!"

Brighid glanced at Elphsaba, then back to the young man still making his way to their cabin. Her chest tightened. If he was here for Elphsaba's skills . . .

Elphsaba had already disappeared into the cabin. Brighid slowly bundled up her dress and placed it in the basket beside her. *It's time for me to test you as an apprentice.*

She curled forward as a heaviness filled her chest. She hated birthings. The cries, the pain, the smells. Even more than that, she could feel death. Always had, since she was young. Death lingered in the doorway of every birthing, waiting for its moment. Sometimes it came like a winter wind, taking souls with it. Sometimes it slinked away without prey, but still it hungered. She hated how it felt. It terrified her to her very core.

How can I become her apprentice? Her hands began to tremble. She'd known this day would come. Like every young woman, she needed to work. But how could she take on such a critical role when the presence of death paralyzed her?

She caught the young man staring at her, and a silence filled the air. Brighid turned away. She could hear Elphsaba gathering her things inside.

What if she was sick? She pressed three fingers to her forehead. She did feel a little warm. But deep down, she knew she was perfect in health. And she was honest, too honest sometimes. Elphsaba had once said she was as honest as the eagle, and Brighid had wondered if that was a hint, that she was part of the clan of the Eagle. But Elphsaba hadn't said anything more.

Seconds later, Elphsaba appeared with a small pack slung over her shoulder. "Brighid, come. And you, young man, lead the way."

The boy—for he didn't appear much older than Brighid—nodded and turned back toward the hill. Elphsaba and Brighid followed. She could barely keep up with the firm, quick steps of Elphsaba. The woman might be old, but she was still fast, although lately she had started to complain of pain in her fingers and legs.

Triangular wooden homes dotted the handful of hills, their thatched roofs reaching toward the ground. Smoke curled through an opening in the middle from the firepits within. Long green grass covered the hillsides, and tiny white flowers were beginning to appear everywhere.

With each step, Brighid's stomach twisted tightly, and not even the beauty of this summer day could make her relax. Elphsaba glanced her way, but if she noticed her pale face, she didn't comment.

The boy led them along the narrow dirt path and took a right where the path split. Up past an old pasture where a couple sheep currently munched on the grass was a single home, jutting out of the side of a steep embankment. A muffled cry echoed from within, and Brighid missed her step.

"How long as she been this way?" Elphsaba asked as Brighid caught her balance.

"Since dawn. But Mother didn't want to call for you until it was close to time. Father is in Jokul."

Elphsaba nodded, her lips grim and her fingers tight around the cord of her pack. Black spots appeared across Brighid's vision as she followed Elphsaba toward the door. The boy glanced at her with pity, then fled down the hill. If only she could follow him.

She clutched the edge of her sleeves as they entered the dwelling. A year ago she had been summoned during a birthing when Elphsaba needed more clothes, and she'd barely kept her mind. It wasn't uncommon for a girl her age to begin learning a trade if there were no bonding prospects. And as a clanless one, Elphsaba had no one to match with Brighid, nor would any clan possibly want her. But what would happen to her if she couldn't overcome this fear of death? What then?

The interior was dark and smoky. A woman held onto a rope that hung from the rafter, hunched over as she panted. Brighid could already feel death. It was here, standing in the doorway, like always.

"Brighid, attend the fire and clear this smoke."

Brighid did as she was told. Elphsaba talked to the woman in hushed tones, broken when a minute later the woman gave out a low moan. Brighid squeezed her eyes shut and gripped the kettle.

I can't do this. I can't do this. She bit her lip and sucked in a long breath through her nose until she had shoved all thoughts and feelings into a small, tiny corner of her mind. Then she finished clearing the smoke and stoking the fire.

Just as she completed her work, Elphsaba called her over.

"Yes, Elphsaba?" She kept her gaze away from the woman in labor.

Elphsaba narrowed her eyes and started explaining what was happening and what to expect next. Brighid nodded at the right places and even managed to utter a few words.

"Now watch me. I'm checking on the position of the baby." Elphsaba turned and talked to the mother. The woman seemed disoriented. Did she know what Elphsaba was saying? Then Elphsaba placed her hands on the distended abdomen.

Seconds later, the woman cried out, and Brighid wanted to join her. Elphsaba began to sing in the old tongue, a song of life and healing, and something about the Word, which seemed to comfort the woman. Brighid didn't understand most of the lyrics, but the song was one Elphsaba often sang at birthings to help the mother.

Elphsaba peered over her shoulder. "Now you do it."

Brighid froze. She wanted to shake her head and back away, but she wasn't a coward. At least she hoped she wasn't. But she could feel it, the tug between life and death. First toward life and warmth. Then toward death. Death was cold, colder than the deepest winter. And she sensed it edging its way into the cabin.

Her hands started to shake. Which would win? Death . . . or life?

"Brighid?"

"I . . ." She took in a deep breath. "Yes, Elphsaba?" She stepped next to the older woman and reached out her fingers. The cabin grew chilly. The woman's skin was hot and sweaty. Brighid recoiled.

"Feel, like this—"

The woman gripped the rope, let out a deep moan that made the hairs on Brighid's body go rigid. Fear took hold of her mind. The shadows in the cabin spread to every corner. She whipped her head around and checked behind her, almost expecting to see a dark apparition.

"Brighid, is everything all right?"

"Yes, yes," Brighid blinked. Elphsaba watched her for a moment, then showed her again how to feel. Brighid touched the mother, and seconds later, her teeth chattered. Elphsaba checked the woman, then started singing. It seemed to calm her. Brighid let the melody wash over her, but it couldn't take away the frigid feeling inside her soul.

"That's it," Elphsaba said softly. She gazed up at the woman. "You're doing well."

The woman smiled weakly, her light-brown hair wet with sweat. Then her eyes went wide.

Brighid's hand stilled. In that one moment, everything hit her: the smell of blood and sweat mingled with hay, a moan surging into a cry, and the feel of death pressing into her mind and body.

She jumped away from the bed, her palms raised. "I can't—I can't do this!" Then she twisted around, stumbled past the firepit, and fled the cabin.

Brighid ran outside, leaving behind the cries of the woman. She reached the edge of the yard and hunched down, wrapping her arms around her knees. Even the sun could not extinguish the chill, hunger, and gaping void of death she felt around her.

She began to rock back and forth. *I don't want to be a coward, but I can't do this. Why can't I do this? Why am I like this?*

Maybe she should have told Elphsaba that she could feel death. But she was afraid to. Afraid of so many things. From the corner of her eye, she spotted the boy, and her face flushed. Fear was not the way of the Nordic people. She was already a clanless one, she didn't want to be labeled a coward. It was the most dishonorable title a person could hold in the north.

Brighid slowly rose to her feet while finding that corner again inside her mind and shoving all of herself inside. She brushed her face, tugging the errant hairs back behind her ears, and turned toward the cabin. She would not enter. She would wait outside, like she had always done.

But what about the next time?

Her throat tightened. If she didn't learn Elphsaba's trade, what would she do?

She shook her head. She would figure that out later.

Brighid stopped near the door but didn't enter. A bird sang in the trees nearby, and beyond the hills, she could see the towering peaks of the Ari Mountains. She let out a long breath. There was no feel of death out here, just life. From the tiny white flowers to the swaying trees. The sun's continual warmth drove away the chill from minutes earlier.

A baby's cry echoed inside the cabin, and Elphsaba cheered. Brighid sagged against the cabin and closed her eyes as death slinked away empty-handed.

Life, and not death, had won today.

3

Later that evening, Elphsaba and Brighid sat outside their cabin and watched the sun set to the west. Neither said a word until Elphsaba finally broke the silence.

"What happened this morning?"

Brighid swallowed, not wanting to relive the birthing. Shame still held her in its tight embrace.

"Brighid?"

She wanted to wring her hands, but that would only give away the fear in her heart. Instead, Brighid lifted her head. "It was a moment of panic. It won't happen again."

Elphsaba watched her, but Brighid refused to fidget under her gaze. It was a lapse in emotion, and it wouldn't happen a second time. She couldn't let it happen. Her only future lay in working with Elphsaba, so she needed to find a way to overcome this ability to feel death. If she didn't, it would be her undoing.

Elphsaba let out a sigh. "I've wondered for a while now, and today confirmed my thoughts. Brighid, you do not have the hands of a healer."

"*What?*" She jerked her head so hard a sharp tingle swept up her neck.

"Daughter, I have lived many winters, and I know many things. It is not a bad thing if you don't have the hands of a healer. Many don't."

Brighid held out her palms as if expecting to see Elphsaba's words carved into her skin. Was that why she could feel death? Because she didn't have the hands of a healer? Did that mean others were like her? "But then, what will I do?" She looked up. There were few options for a girl like her.

Elphsaba gave her a small smile. "I had hoped we could work together, but that is not your path. I can see that clearly now. But you are not alone. I will help you find your calling. Together." She turned her gaze back toward the sun as it slowly disappeared beyond the Ari Mountains. "And we might find it in Ragnbork."

"Ragnbork? Why Ragnbork?" She'd never been to the capital city of Nordica, nor any city for that matter. She'd spent her whole life wandering the mountains and wastelands of the north with Elphsaba.

Elphsaba sighed. "I've been thinking about moving back for a while now. It's getting hard to deliver babes with these feeble hands of mine. I believe Ragnbork will provide better opportunities than these small villages. For both of us."

Brighid took a closer glance at Elphsaba. More than wrinkles, her fingers were red and swollen. They did appear tired. Brighid looked away and swallowed. If only she had been stronger today. What good were her own hands if she couldn't help the one woman she loved as a mother?

"I know what you're thinking, and that path will lead nowhere."

Brighid glanced up and blushed. Sometimes she wondered if Elphsaba was a mystic with the way she seemed to read her mind.

"Instead of dwelling on who you are not, we must discover who you are."

"And what about my parents? They might provide a clue to who I am."

Elphsaba paused. "Yes. It's about time. But not until we reach Ragnbork."

There was hardly anything to pack over the next few days. Living for years on end by traveling from one remote village to the next meant whatever they owned had to be carried on their backs.

Brighid finished rolling her new wool dress and placed it on the furs and small book she had carefully wrapped for the journey. She had worked on shoes over the winter, so both she and Elphsaba had new boots for the trip.

"Brighid, can you help me braid my hair?"

Brighid looked up. Elphsaba had never asked her to do her hair before.

Elphsaba gave her a sad smile. "My fingers do not want to work today."

A shadow passed over Brighid's heart. Elphsaba's condition was worse than she'd thought.

She walked over to where Elphsaba sat in a rickety wooden chair and touched the coarse salted-grey strands. First, she parted the hair, then started the braid from the nape of the neck and made her way around Elphsaba's head. When she reached the other side, she wrapped the end in a leather strip and tucked it into the braid. It was the usual style for older women. Whereas her own hair . . .

Brighid touched one of the twelve tiny braids woven through her golden strands. Each held beads at the end, beads she had crafted and painted robin's-egg blue.

"Thank you, Brighid." Elphsaba rose and turned. Brighid frowned. Was it her imagination, or did Elphsaba appear smaller? It seemed the woman was aging before her eyes, and it brought a mixture of sorrow and fear to her heart.

Brighid shook her head and finished packing. If death were truly here, she would feel it. Instead, there was only a quiet stillness as Elphsaba bundled her things. The goats would stay, and a young couple had offered a small sum for the cabin.

Elphsaba let out her breath and hefted the pack. "Time to go. Henrik is waiting with his cart. He's taking supplies to Jokul and offered us a ride."

Brighid glanced around the one-room home once more. They had spent only a year here, attending to the women of this area. Not enough time to build many friendships. That was the usual way of things. She lifted her pack and left the dwelling.

The sun was bright and the sky clear as the two women headed over to the cart that waited at the edge of the hill. Henrik waved as they approached. Jokul was a full day's ride from this area. After Jokul, it would take almost three weeks to reach Ragnbork, unless they were able to secure another means of transportation. If only they had enough money for horses. But personal transportation was for those with means, and a midwife and her adopted daughter made very little, despite having sold their home.

Henrik helped them settle in the cart between small barrels of seed and crates of dyed wool. With a quick shout, they started forward, pulled by two shaggy mountain horses. After a half hour, they reached the bottom of the hills where a vast forest spread toward the next mountain. A single dirt road wove between the trees. The air smelled like life, and Brighid sighed at the comforting scent. Then she burrowed next to Elphsaba and closed her eyes, lulled by the gentle motion and warm air.

The cart lurched and a loud huffing followed by a growl sent Brighid wide awake. "Wha-what's going on?" She blinked as Elphsaba made her way to the back of the cart. Brighid looked over her shoulder to see why they had stopped. Henrik spoke with someone near the front.

A man sat astride the largest bear Brighid had ever seen, with five brutish men surrounding him. Brighid's eyes went wide, and she twisted around to get a better view. He was dressed in dark leather with light fur along the collar of his cloak. His wheat-colored hair and beard were carefully trimmed. One of the men standing nearby had a line of runes inked along his cheek. Another wore nothing but a leather jerkin on his upper body, his bare arms covered in tattoos of mountains and stars.

The bear huffed, and the man spoke in a quiet voice while patting the giant animal along its shoulder, which seemed to calm it. The horses were skittish near the beast, but Henrik had them under control. The man looked up from the bear.

"Where are you heading today?"

"Jokul, Hjaren Bard," Henrik answered as he patted the closest horse.

The man glanced at Elphsaba, and she walked around the cart. "And you, hala?"

"Ragnbork, Hjaren Bard."

Hjaren? Brighid sucked in her breath. The man was the son of the clan leader. The Bear Clan. The wastelands were under the Bear Clan's jurisdiction, and many of the villages were members of the clan. But never had she met one of the leaders.

Bard's gaze shifted and caught sight of Brighid. His brow wrinkled for a moment, then his face went smooth. "And the girl?"

"She is with me," Elphsaba said.

"Your . . . daughter?"

"A girl I've taken in."

Bard studied Brighid while his men shifted as they waited. "I see. You shouldn't have any trouble as long as you stay on the roads. May the Great Bear watch over you."

"Yes, Hjaren," both Elphsaba and Henrik said.

"Come, men, let us continue our hunt." Bard spoke a command to the bear, and they started west with the five men in tow. Brighid wondered what they were hunting as she watched them disappear into the trees. Elphsaba climbed back into the wagon and sat down beside Brighid.

"I never thought I'd see him again," Elphsaba said quietly. Henrik let out a click with his tongue and the horses started again.

"Who?" Brighid asked.

"Hjaren Bard. He is the son of Gurmund, the Hjar of the Bear Clan."

She wanted to ask how Elphsaba knew the man, but there was a faraway look in her eyes, so Brighid closed her lips. Elphsaba was also clanless Maybe she had delivered for his wife. Or maybe she delivered the hjaren himself. She was old enough.

Brighid eyed the trees again where the bear, his rider, and the men had disappeared. How did Bard control that massive beast? By words? Yes, it had to be by words. There was no bridle, no reins. The man had spoken to the bear, and it obeyed. Did the bear only obey Bard? Could anyone else ride one? She suspected not.

In any case, it was a beautiful beast, full of strength and power. But not one she would want to meet alone in the woods.

They arrived in Jokul that night and stayed in a small inn. The next day Elphsaba found a traveling merchant who was willing to take them all the way to Ragnbork for a couple coins. Elphsaba counted out the money. How much would they have left once they reached the city?

The next two weeks were spent mainly on the road. Brighid practiced reading during the day with Elphsaba's help, and night came with a warm fire and the stars as their companions. They met other travelers and heard the latest news in Nordica. The last winter had been brutal, and the crops were not growing as they should, leaving the Nordic people searching for other ways to prepare for what seemed like another harsh winter.

One night, five other travelers joined them around the fire. Most were quiet as they ate small round biscuits filled with fruits and nuts—common fare when traveling. The biscuits were good for weeks or even months, but the taste left something to be desired.

Brighid nibbled on hers as an older man named Vind started speaking. His long grey beard bounced across his chest as he spoke, and his eyes reflected the firelight, almost burning with the same intensity of his words.

"Rylander filth stole the best of my sheep during the night a couple months ago, and the Nordic warriors did nothing about it. When I went to take my retribution, Hjar Gurmund's men stopped me." He broke a stick and threw it into the fire. "Our clans are allowing the south to cross our border, trample our land, and steal our livelihoods."

"Aye, that happened to me as well," another man said, a woman nodding next to him. "Name's Asp, and this is my wife, Ingrid. We're from the border. Rylander bandits came during the night and took my flock. When I petitioned to Hjar Gurmund, he promised to send men, but by the time they arrived, the Rylanders were back across the border. Ingrid and I finally decided to move north near Ragnbork to seek protection from the capital."

"I thought about going west first and seeking refuge with the Wolf Clan," Vind said. "At least the Wolf Clan is protecting their own. But then I heard that's all they protect: their own. I hope Ragnbork is different."

"But you're part of the Bear Clan, are you not?" Elphsaba said.

A few others scowled around the fire. "Aye, and was proud of it, until now." Vind poked the coals with a stripped branch.

A younger man with only the beginnings of a beard spoke up. "There are political complications that make it hard for Hjar Gurmund and his men to take the action you speak of. There are treaties in place that must be followed."

Ingrid snorted. "Even if the Rylanders break those treaties and cross our borders?"

Her husband huffed next to her. "Doesn't seem so complicated to me. A man steals my stuff, and I take it back—and then some."

The younger man looked up. "And that would lead to conflict or even possible war with the south."

Vind stood and raised his fist, his grey beard brushing his chest. "Then bring it! When did the Bear Clan become so cowardly? We bow to no one!"

Brighid nodded while others cheered their assent. She remembered Hjaren Bard, Gurmund's son, and his men from a couple days ago. Maybe the Bear Clan was finally doing something about those trespassers. It was possible they were hunting Rylanders at this moment.

The young man spoke again. "Even if we stop the border crossings, it won't help our crops."

"But it will make me feel better," Vind said and laughed. The others joined in, even the merchant.

Elphsaba crossed her arms and shook her head.

"But what if we need the Ryland Plains and Avonai to help us get through another winter?" The young man asked. "Creating bad blood between our people will not help us receive aid if we need it."

The others quieted, and Vind glared at the young traveler. "Boy, how old are you? Not more than twenty winters, I imagine. You're just a cub. There's always been bad blood between our people. Always. The south would rather see us starve than trade with us. The only reason the clans made treaties was so we would appear more 'civil.'" Vind spat into the fire. "Civility has never been our way. The north is harsh and winter is cruel. Only those strong enough can live here in Nordica. This land is not for civilized people. Never forget that."

A sense of pride swelled inside Brighid's chest. Yes. Only the strong lived here. And she was one of the strong. But she was still curious about those who lived in the south. The Rylanders and the people of Avonai. What were they like? She stared into the fire. How were they different?

"Why won't they trade with us?" Brighid asked the next day as the cart lurched across the dirt road toward Ragnbork.

Elphsaba's lips thinned. "There has always been enmity between our lands. The people of the south think they are superior and that we are barbarians."

"Barbarians?"

"Aye. Because we live differently than they do." She tapped the sun mark across her wrist. "We choose to remember our ancestors with marks on our skin, we wear fur, and we live with our animals. Our clansmen follow the ways of the bear, the wolf, the eagle, the owl, and the stag. We have no king. Instead, our clan hjars rule in joint council. And"–she sighed–"we are poor."

"So we cannot afford what they offer."

"And they are not willing to negotiate."

Brighid gazed around at the trees and green meadows. The Ari Mountains stretched high to the sky to the south while the land grew flat as it traveled toward the north. What could the south possibly be like if the people there despised the Nordic way of life? What did they wear if not fur and wool? Where did they keep their animals if not in or near their home? Did they choose not to remember their ancestors? Were they willing to let the people of the north starve just because they were different?

Brighid sighed. She didn't understand. A dark, heavy feeling filled her chest. Maybe she didn't want to meet those of the south after all.

4

Ragnbork. The capital and pride of Nordica. Towering walls stood along the first rung of peaks along the Keshmin Mountains. A winding road wove through barren rock and sparse grass up toward the massive gates at the top. The walls themselves were at least twenty men high. Brighid had never seen such a monstrous construct. What might the city look like behind the massive walls?

The trek to the top took an hour, and by the time they reached the gates, the sun had fully risen. A horn blew as they approached and with a loud creak, the thick gates began to open. Runes were carved into the wood, words for strength and protection. Was there any power in those words?

A crowd waited along the field outside the city, anxious to enter Ragnbork. Among them were at least a dozen carts, one prestigious entourage, two groupings of warriors, each from a different clan by the coloring of their leather and mail, and perhaps fifty or sixty families, some with livestock in tow while others had only packs on their backs.

A minute later, the gates fully opened, and the crowd surged toward the entrance. The merchant gave his horses a quick whistle, and they started forward.

Brighid stared in wonder as they approached the arched entryway. Guards dressed in green and chainmail patrolled the walls and checked those wishing to enter the great city. As the cart approached the gates, one guard moved forward with a quill and rolled scroll.

"Reason for your visit to Ragnbork?" he asked.

"I'm here to sell my wares," the merchant replied.

"Place of origin?" the guard continued, writing down the information.

"Jokul."

The guard spotted Elphsaba and Brighid. "Hala," he said as he approached the back of the cart. "Reason for your visit?"

"Looking for work."

"Occupation?"

"Midwife."

The guard scribbled down the words and then looked at Brighid. "Is the girl with you?"

"Yes."

"Place of origin?"

"Folkvar, in the Wastelands."

"You have come a long way, hala."

"Aye, and I'm ready to rest in the city of my ancestors."

"Clan?"

"Clanless."

The guard's face darkened, and he wrote down her answer. "You'll go left once entering the city to report to the census. They will give you instructions on where you can go as a clanless one."

Elphsaba bowed her head while Brighid frowned, puzzled by the sudden change in the guard at the word *clanless*. Their clanless state never seemed to matter in the villages they entered. All the people wanted was the healing and protection Elphsaba provided as a midwife. She wanted to ask more but chose not to. Now was not the time and certainly not in front of the guard who appeared decidedly colder toward them.

The guard backed away and waved the cart inside.

As they entered, the heavy feeling vanished. Ragnbork was the epitome of nature and beauty, strength and dignity. Buildings of stone with wooden pillars and rafters stood along the cobblestone street. More runes were carved into the poles and over the doorways. After a couple blocks, the street widened into an open area, displaying the rest of the city in its splendor.

The city was built inside a basin on top of the Keshmin Mountains, which provided protection from both nature and man. Waterfalls cascaded down the mountainsides into the city over the moss-covered boulders, then wove through Ragnbork and its streets. Curved bridges connected the cobblestone paths over the flowing mountain water. Towering buildings made of stone and wood lined the upper terraces, with many more homes and shops spread around the city.

And the people . . .

The streets were filled with the people of Nordica. Brightly colored wool clothes, tattoos of every size and shape, hair braided in an array of designs, men with beards that reached their chests, children running through the crowds in laughter.

"Ragnbork is incredible," Brighid said as she took in the ancient city.

"Aye, it is. One of the oldest cities this side of the world. Not even the harshest winter can take out Ragnbork. It has withstood storms, darkness, and even the Great War itself."

The merchant glanced back with pity. "I'm afraid this is where we part."

"Come, Brighid." Elphsaba led the way to the back of the cart and both women disembarked. Elphsaba paid the merchant, and his cart rumbled away along the cobblestone until it disappeared into the crowd.

"Now we must register at the census."

Brighid tightened her hold on her pack and followed Elphsaba left in the direction the guard had instructed. With each block they passed, the buildings grew more decrepit and dirty, and the road narrowed between the structures. Women with stained and faded wool dresses stood outside small doors. The children were grimy but still carefree. A wolfhound bound alongside a small boy, letting out deep barks as the two dashed down the street.

Brighid wrinkled her nose at the smell of squalor.

"It's the city's refuse. This particular stream carries it out of the city." Elphsaba pointed to a stream running toward the walls a block away.

Brighid made a face. Even she could tell that this part of the city was not as nice as everywhere else. These people were no doubt clanless. Many did not wear Marks of Remembrance on their faces or arms, no clan crest, nor jewelry. Clans meant everything to the Nordic people. To be born outside of a clan was to be born outside of Nordic society. But having grown up in the Wastelands, that hadn't been as important as survival. That appeared to be different in Ragnbork, which explained why the guard from earlier had reacted the way he did. Her excitement from minutes ago diminished in light of this new truth. Was this what her and Elphsaba's new life would be like? If so, why did they move here?

"It's changed," Elphsaba said under her breath. Brighid looked around again. So maybe it hadn't always been this way.

A block later, Elphsaba stopped to inquire about the census office. An older lady, haggard and weary, pointed down the road. "You're almost there. But you won't find a welcome reception. Too many clanless moving to Ragnbork, and the clans are not happy about it."

"Even for a midwife?" Elphsaba asked.

"Well, we could always use another one."

"Thank you." Elphsaba and Brighid started along the street again. Brighid wrinkled her nose as they passed a pile of refuse, and for a fleeting moment, she wanted to go back to the Wastelands, to where the air was clear and the mountains were all around her. Not this dingy, dirty place. But—she glanced at Elphsaba—she would not leave her. She would never leave her. When the time came that Elphsaba could not do birthings anymore, Brighid would find work. If only she had the hands of a healer . . .

Brighid looked at her hands again. What were they good for? What had they been made to do? If not a healer, was she a crafter? A baker? Brighid laughed at that one and dropped her hands. Certainly not that. Her bread always turned out dense and burned.

"What are you laughing at?" Elphsaba asked.

Brighid chuckled. "Nothing."

The census office was a small wood-and-stone structure surrounded by dilapidated log buildings, cracked cobblestones with weeds growing between the crevices, and leaves from last autumn still scattered.

Elphsaba approached the door and opened it. Inside was a small table and chair, a firepit, and a shelf loaded with scrolls. The windows let in very little light, and the room smelled like old smoke. A tall man stepped out from a doorway in the back. His hair was the color of the sunrise, with grey streaks along his temples. His beard reached his chest and was braided with a bead at the end.

He approached the table and sat down. Without looking up, he reached for a scroll, grabbed a nearby quill, then dabbed it in an inkwell. "Names?"

Elphsaba gave them.

"Purpose for coming to Ragnbork?"

"Work," Elphsaba said.

"Occupation?"

"Midwife."

The man raised his head and studied Elphsaba for a moment. Then he went back to writing. "And the girl, is she your apprentice?"

"No. She is my daughter."

"And what will she do here?"

"We are not sure yet."

He looked up again with a scowl on his face. "We have no room for someone who doesn't work."

Elphsaba pulled herself up to her full height. "She will. But we haven't yet discovered her gifting."

"Her gifting?" He laughed and wrote something down. "Nobody cares about a clanless one's gifting. Only that they work."

"That is not the way of our people."

"Well, *hala*, times have changed."

Brighid sucked in her breath. Never had she met someone who treated an elder with such disrespect. She opened her mouth to say something, but Elphsaba answered first. "Searching for one's purpose will never change. Or else there is no reason for life."

He waved his hand and continued writing. Brighid took a step forward as a hot whooshing filling her veins. A sudden strange red haze filled her vision. Her heart started thumping hard, each beat drumming with whispers of *fight, fight, fight*—

"No, Brighid," Elphsaba said softly and touched her arm. That gentle gesture cooled the abrupt heat in her blood. Brighid took a long, even breath, and the red haze faded, bringing the room back into focus. She blinked, still feeling Elphsaba's touch. What was that? For one moment, she had been ready to pummel the man. The violence of that thought chilled her. Had the long journey put her on edge?

He finished writing on two small pieces of soft skin and passed them to Elphsaba and Brighid. "Your papers. Lose them and you will be exiled from Ragnbork. You are required to show them to any Ragnbork soldier or clan member if asked."

Brighid slowly took the tiny leather piece. Glancing down at the scribbles, any trace of that lingering heat melted as she read her name and lack of occupation. All her life narrowed down to a couple words. Was that all she was worth?

5

They spent the first night at an inn on the border of the clanless section and the rest of Ragnbork. The next day they searched for a more permanent dwelling. Elphsaba found them a room with a firepit, cupboard, and a couple cracked mugs and wooden plates. They bought hay for sleeping on, and Brighid laid out their blankets across the pile. Elphsaba secured two bags of oats, a jar of animal fat, and dried berries.

Brighid looked over the food. She couldn't bake, but she could make travel biscuits. Apparently that would be their fare until Elphsaba found work. *I also need to find work,* she thought. *But what kind?*

She lay down next to Elphsaba later that night. She still hadn't any idea what she should do and was too tired to think.

During the next few weeks Brighid ventured out on the streets, but all she found for work was a couple errands that brought in less than a handful of coins. Elphsaba connected with nearby families who were expecting babies and was out almost every day. There was indeed a need for midwives. But Brighid worried every time Elphsaba came home. She appeared more and more tired. How long could the older woman keep working?

And they still hadn't talked about her parents, despite now being in Ragnbork. If her parents were from a clan, perhaps that connection could help them now. But wouldn't Elphsaba have said something earlier?

"Elphsaba," Brighid said quietly as she put away their few dishes into the cupboard one evening. No answer. She turned and found Elphsaba had already crawled under the furs and was fast asleep.

Brighid let out a long sigh. She doubted Elphsaba was purposely forgetting, she was just exhausted. Brighid walked over and tenderly tucked the furs beneath Elphsaba's chin.

She could wait. She didn't want to trouble Elphsaba when the older woman was doing everything to keep them alive. Besides, if that connection could have helped them, she was sure Elphsaba would have followed up years ago.

Winter came, bringing a bitter chill that nothing could keep out and many in the clanless district died. Brighid felt it every night when she curled up next to Elphsaba for warmth. Death weaved through the streets, taking both young and old. The sound of unending coughing through the walls from the other occupants. The smoke from the pyres across the city.

Despite the cold, Brighid left their home each morning and took every job she could find: cleaning stables, running errands, washing clothes. But honest work was sparse in a city bursting with new occupants every day. Clanless gangs started to roam the city, spurred on by hunger and lack of employment. She took to carrying a knife in her boot. Other girls her age started bonding, but no young man was interested in a girl who had no family and no future as a midwife.

She was . . . nothing. And deep down, that hurt.

Days after midwinter, Elphsaba came home one evening looking even more tired than usual. Dark circles filled the space beneath her eyes, and her wrinkles were more pronounced. She appeared thinner beneath the billowing wool dress. When she went to move the pot from over the fire, she let out a cry.

Brighid ran to her side. "Did you burn yourself?"

"No." She held her hand to her chest. Her fingers curled over like twisted claws. "My hands hurt so bad."

"Let me see," Brighid said.

Elphsaba hesitated, then finally extended them. Brighid bit back the gasp inside her throat. Elphsaba's fingers appeared like gnarled tree branches with swollen joints and redness. How could she grasp anything with these hands? Why hadn't Brighid noticed how bad they had become?

Elphsaba took in a breath. "I almost dropped a babe today. I don't know if I can do this anymore. If I injured a child, I could never forgive myself. And the family would go after not only me but you as well."

Brighid began to gently knead the fingers. "Can we get ointment for your hands?"

"There is nothing available for the clanless. Winter was hard, and there are few medicinal herbs to be found. What little there is the healers are keeping for those who can afford to pay."

Brighid scowled as she reached for the animal lard, dipped her fingers in and drew out a dab. Once again the pang of their meager existence hit close. She worked the fat into Elphsaba's fingers. It wasn't much, but maybe it would help. She paused briefly over the small sun mark on Elphsaba's wrist, then went back to working the grease into her skin. "Can we leave the city and find herbs ourselves?"

Elphsaba laughed sadly. "The ones I know of grow near the border, at least a week's ride from here."

"Oh." Her mind began to feverishly think through all their possibilities. Maybe she could try to assist Elphsaba again. The very thought of a birthing made her feel suddenly nauseated and cold. Bolva! Then what? She paused her ministrations and pinched her lips together. No one wanted a girl of sixteen winters. There were too many people in need of work. One man had showed interest in her a few days ago, but it wasn't for work or bonding.

"What are you thinking about?"

"Hm?" Brighid looked up and realized she had stopped massaging Elphsaba's hands. She bowed her head and resumed the kneading. "Work. Money. How I can help you."

Elphsaba gently drew her fingers away. "Thank you, daughter."

Brighid dropped her hands and clenched them across her lap. "I wish there was something more I could do."

Elphsaba smiled. "You've done much for me, more than you'll ever know."

"But you can't keep going to birthings!" She stared at her palms. "If only I could help you. These hands of mine are good for nothing—"

"No." The terse reply made her look up. "Never say that." There was a deadly seriousness in Elphsaba's expression.

Brighid turned away, ashamed.

"I'm sorry, Brighid," Elphsaba said moments later. "I wanted to care for you until you reached adulthood or found a man to bond with. That was my hope." She let out a sigh. "But I also know I am beyond my prime. Many women do not live to see the number of winters I have. I thought by moving here we would find more opportunities. But Ragnbork has changed. All of Nordica has changed. And I'm not sure how to guide you anymore."

Brighid brushed her fingers along the top of Elphsaba's knuckles. "You've always cared for me. Thank you."

"Yes," Elphsaba replied with a faraway expression. "Ever since you were a baby."

Brighid paused. Was she finally going to tell her about her parents?

Elphsaba must have caught the look of anticipation in her eyes. She shuffled toward the bed. "Come, sit down. It's time I told you about your own birth. I should have shared when we first arrived in Ragnbork, but then I became so busy trying to keep us alive. I'm sorry, daughter."

Brighid rose from the ground stiffly, her mind whirling with questions. Would she finally learn who she was? And where she came from?

They both sat on the straw bed and faced the fire burning in the firepit. The watered-down soup was forgotten.

Elphsaba started quietly. "First, I don't know who they were. I don't know their names or where your mother came from. You're father, however . . ."

"Yes?"

"He was a Rylander."

Brighid blinked, unsure she had heard her right. "A-a Rylander?"

"Yes. He was wearing his regiments the day you were born. The blue of the White City. Tall, with dark hair and a scar that ran through his left eye."

"And my mother?" She was afraid to ask.

"Your mother was Nordic, as Nordic as you or I. Young, barely eighteen winters I wager."

"I'm a Nordic . . . and a Rylander?" Her pulse raced and her lip trembled. That was even worse than being clanless.

"Yes."

Elphsaba continued, "I have no idea how she came to be connected to the Rylander or why she was alone that day. But I believe she was part of a clan, perhaps even part of a main family, even though she wore no crests or marks on her skin. And if so, a union between a Rylander and a clan family would never be accepted. I believe she made her way to the border, hoping the Rylander would take her in."

Brighid wanted to hide. Maybe she didn't want to know where she came from. She'd always thought she'd been born to a poor family that couldn't afford to keep her, or a young woman who found herself with child. She had heard enough about those births to know they happened often. But this . . . this was not what she had expected. No wonder Elphsaba never said anything all those years when she pestered her for an answer.

She was the daughter of two lands that hated each other. And no clan to claim.

Brighid sucked in a breath. "What happened to them? To my . . ." She couldn't finish. She couldn't say *mother* or *father.*

"Your birth was difficult and long. By the end, your mother barely had any strength left. I did what I could, but I could not save her."

"Did she . . . want me?"

Elphsaba's face tightened, which gave Brighid all the information she needed. Her heart felt like a small pebble inside her chest. "What about my father?"

Elphsaba shook her head. "He was like many men I encounter in those situations. They are willing to accept a boy born outside of a bonding. But not a girl."

So if she had been a boy, she would have been wanted. Her tiny, shriveled heart exploded, piercing every part of her body, mind, and soul. It was a grief deeper than she had ever experienced. It took her breath away and left a gaping hole in her chest.

Not wanted.

Not by her mother. Not by her father. Even worse, a father from the south. "No wonder you didn't want to tell me when I was younger."

"It was a truth you weren't ready to carry. So I carried it for you." Elphsaba reached for Brighid's hands, her fingers cold and slick from the lard. "But if you think for one moment you were not wanted, banish those thoughts from your mind. You were the most beautiful thing I had ever seen. I knew from the moment you were born that *I* wanted you. No matter how complicated that made my life, no matter what it cost. I wanted you. My little Brighid. My beautiful *strong* Nordic daughter."

I wanted you.

Elphsaba's words rang in Brighid's ears. She swallowed the lump in her throat, then peered into the older woman's face and saw love in her eyes. Elphsaba's hand left hers, and a moment later, those gnarled fingers brushed her cheek. She had been crying and didn't even know it.

"I wish your story were different. That you had a home and a clan. That I could give you more. That is why I waited to tell you. I didn't want to see the grief I see now in your eyes."

Brighid gripped the hand near her face. "No. This is enough for me. *You* are enough for me." It still hurt that the ones who had created her didn't want her, but she had love, which was more than many had. "I only wish I could give you more. I wish I had the hands of a healer so I could work with you."

Elphsaba chuckled. "Do not waste your life wishing to be who you are not. Instead, let us continue to find out what kind of hands you were given. There is a reason for every birth. We will discover yours."

Tears continued to stream down her face at Elphsaba's gentle smile. "I love you," she whispered.

Elphsaba's smile widened. "I know. And I love you too. You're the daughter I was never able to have."

Brighid leaned against Elphsaba's chest. Silent tears fell across her cheeks for the child who was never wanted by her own blood, and for the hardships she and Elphsaba had endured. But at least they had each other.

After a few minutes, Brighid lay still, her head tucked beneath Elphsaba's chin.

Elphsaba ran her fingers through Brighid's hair and hummed that same song she sang at birthings. Something about the Word and life and beauty.

"Your name means strength."

Brighid sat up and looked at Elphsaba, her song now gone.

"That's why I named you Brighid. You are strong. Never let anyone tell you otherwise. We will find a way through this. Because you are strong, my daughter."

Brighid slowly nodded and wiped away the wetness across her cheeks. She knew the truth now. She knew who her parents had been and who her mother truly was: Elphsaba. It was her turn to find a way to take care of the woman who had raised her. She would live up to her name.

She would be strong.

6

Brighid softly kissed Elphsaba's forehead before slipping out of their small hovel one early morning late winter. The old woman slept most days now, spending more time in dreams than in reality. But whether dreams or reality, she still needed to eat, and their cupboard had been bare for days. Brighid had caught a rat yesterday and roasted the flesh, but it was only a few mouthfuls, and she was too ashamed to tell Elphsaba where she had gotten the meat.

Today would be different. She pulled the hood of her worn cloak over her head and moved quietly along the streets. Snow fell from a grey sky above, covering the clanless district in a white blanket. If she squinted hard enough, the filth of this area appeared pretty. Almost.

A mound moved beside one of the small stone houses, sending a fluttering of snow across the street. A ragged face appeared from beneath. The man's beard was grizzly and covered most of his face. His eyes were sunken and his nose red from the cold. A wind suddenly sprang up as he reached out gnarled fingers from beneath the mound of snow-covered blankets and coats.

"Food," he said in a raspy voice.

Brighid stared at his proffered palm, a chill running down her spine. It was here. The shadow that had become a perpetual presence in the clanless district. Death.

"I don't have any," she whispered. Her own stomach rumbled at that moment as if to confirm her words.

His eyes turned downward, and he pulled his arm back into the shivering mound.

Brighid swallowed the thick lump inside her throat, the hollowness in her chest expanding. She closed her eyes and turned away from the man. Death was near, its claws extended and ready to welcome another soul into its embrace.

I'm sorry. I'm so, so sorry.

She hurried past the man, almost breaking into a run. *I hate this! I hate this place! I hate living like this! Why?* She clenched the edge of her cloak. *Why does it have to be this way?*

Hot tears threatened to trickle down her face, but she held them back and gritted her teeth. No crying. She rubbed her face with her free hand. Death stopped following her. It had found its victim. She felt its cold presence fall away as she passed the barricade between the clanless district and the rest of Ragnbork.

She hurried along the wider streets, cleaner and free of homeless sleeping alongside dilapidated houses with wooden doors that could barely close. With each step, her resolve hardened. She had to save Elphsaba. And she had a plan.

After twenty minutes of making her way along the streets of Ragnbork, dodging guards and being careful not to slip on the snowy cobblestone, she reached her destination. Across the street with cheery warm lights shining through warped glass and a row of golden-brown loaves on display, was a small bakery.

Brighid slipped into a narrow gap between two buildings and waited. Snowflakes continued to fall gently across the city, and she pulled her cloak closer to her body.

Elphsaba would be horrified if she knew what Brighid was about to do. She shoved away feelings of guilt as she stood there. No work was to be found, especially for the clanless. She had to do something. She would fight death itself if she could save Elphsaba.

She pressed a hand against her midsection. There seemed to be very little between her stomach and spine. She patted her midsection and watched the baker move about his kitchen, working the oven, pulling more bread out. Eventually he would have to leave, to relieve himself or run an errand. And she would strike.

Minutes ticked by, and the snowflakes melted across the tip of her nose and cheeks. The occasional person walked past, and Brighid would duck between the buildings where the shadows covered her and wait. A woman entered the bakery and spoke with the baker for a few minutes, then left with a couple loaves. Brighid's mouth watered. What would it be like to simply walk in and buy whatever she wanted?

She blew on her chilled fingers and stomped her feet. Each second that passed, she wanted to turn and run home. She didn't want to be a thief. But then she pictured Elphsaba buried beneath the blankets and furs, and her heart became panic-stricken, fueling her with determination.

She looked up and her breath caught in her throat. The baker was gone. One more glance, then she dashed across the street. The snow fell harder, filling the air with a cold whiteness. She knew a bell rang when the door opened, so she barely pushed the door until the bell fell back with a quiet jingle. She only had this one chance, so she went for the first two loaves nearest her. The bread was still warm.

Brighid hugged them to her chest and ran out. Down the street she flew, tucking the loaves inside her cloak. More blocks, then she squeezed by the barricade. The heat felt good against her chest, and the yeasty smell made her lightheaded. It took everything inside of her not to start tearing into the loaves—

Something caught her foot, and she went sprawling along the street. Her knees slammed into the cobblestone, sending a painful crack up her legs. One loaf left her grip and tumbled up against a building. Brighid hugged the other one and started crawling when a voice broke the wintry silence.

"We've been watching you." A young man stepped from the alleyway. He was taller than her, lanky with a pinched, hungry look to his face. His cheekbones stuck out at sharp angles, and his stringy brown hair fell past his shoulders like thin twigs.

She glanced back. Two others gathered around her, a ragged group of outcasts. Bolva! An eljun. She hugged the bread closer to her body and dove for the other one.

"Oh, no you don't!" A hand gripped her collar and jerked her up to her feet. "That bread's for us."

Brighid twisted hard to her right and broke the young man's grip. "No, it's not. I took it. It's mine."

A fist came flying toward her face. Brighid swerved right, and his knuckles grazed her cheek. Before she could think, she returned his punch with one of her own. Her hand tightened right before catching his jaw, and her fist connected with his chin, sending his face flying back.

That one movement felt as normal as breathing. And so did dropping the bread to the ground and bending her knees, fists up and ready.

He came back swinging. She dodged the first two and caught his exposed midsection. He let out a loud *oomph*.

Her body hummed with a powerful rush, and a fire burned deep inside her, fueling her, making her skin tingle with anticipation.

He came at her again. This time she didn't move fast enough, and he caught her in the nose. Her vision went dim for a moment as her nose exploded in agony. Something wet trickled across her upper lip.

Her eyes cleared. She licked her lips. Blood. Instead of terrifying her, it emboldened her. She brought her hand across her face and wiped the blood away, then smiled. In that moment, it felt like she could fight anything. Even death itself.

The man's eyes narrowed and he took a step back. Brighid advanced, her smile stretching until it was more like a snarl. "Come on," she taunted. "You said you wanted the bread. Come take it!" All the years of fear, fighting to survive, and hunger converged into one powerful emotion inside her. It overwhelmed her like a tidal wave, demanding release. She couldn't hold it back. And she didn't want to. Not anymore.

"Get her!" the young man yelled.

All three rushed her. A strange red haze settled across her eyes. She punched, kicked, and fought like a wild animal. She could hear their yells and even screams from behind her red visage, but it didn't stop her. Nothing could. This need to fight poured out of her, and even if she wanted to, there was no stopping it until her body was empty.

Time had no meaning in this state. She had no idea how many minutes had passed until her vision came back and she found the three men on the ground groaning. Snow continued to fall gently across the street, piling up along the sides of the buildings. The snow beneath her boots was pink from blood. Somewhere deep within her mind she could feel where her skin had split from the blows she had delivered and more blood had spread across her face.

One of the young men finally struggled to his feet, his face swelling and his eye turning black. He spotted her and flinched away. "St-stay away from me!" He stumbled down the street. The other rose to his feet and joined him. Their leader still lay on the ground, dazed.

"Now," she said, breathing hard. "I am going to take *my* bread. And you are not going to follow me."

He tracked her with his gaze, never making a sound or movement.

Brighid collected the two loaves, now soaked from the snow, but still edible, and started for the clanless district. Every nerve tingled, ready to engage if the man behind her decided to follow. But he never got up. After a couple blocks, she let out a long breath, feeling every kick and punch she had received. *Bolva*, she groaned. And yet . . .

Her body was still humming with energy from the fight. It was like she had been made to fight. Every move, every thought worked in perfect harmony. And it was exhilarating–

A figure stepped out near the wall that separated the clanless district from the rest of Ragnbork. Another young man. Brighid tightened her hold on the bread, her lips curling over her teeth.

He causally approached her with a smirk. His dark curly hair reached his shoulders, and his cheek bore a Mark of Remembrance in the shape of an arrow.

"I saw what you did back there."

Brighid followed him with her gaze. "So what? Are you also going to fight me?"

He laughed and sauntered closer. "No. I was impressed. Falko is not easy to take out in a fight. I'm amazed that a little thing like you left him on his back. But you do realize there will be repercussions. He won't accept what you did to him. Falko's temper is as short as a day in winter. You might want protection."

She scoffed. "Are you offering such protection?" She knew eljuns protected their own for a price. And that price was usually steep for a woman.

"I am." He stopped in front of her. "Join my eljun."

"No." Brighid started for the district again.

"That was a fast answer." He fell into step with her.

"Why are you following me?" she asked a few seconds later.

"I'm not. But if you ever change your mind, my offer stands. Go to the house with the black door and ask for Roldar. Say you're the breadfighter."

He turned and disappeared down the street. Brighid watched him until he vanished out of sight, then stood there beneath the falling snow. She wasn't interested in joining an eljun or in the man's offer. Despite him being impressed with her fighting skills, she knew how most women were treated in an eljun, and she wasn't about to give herself to him. She would never concede to that, no matter how bleak life became.

She had Elphsaba. That was all she needed. And come this spring, she would find work again. This was only temporary. But to make it to spring, they had to eat. And she would do what she had to and make sure they lived. Both of them.

7

"What happened to you?" Elphsaba was sitting up in bed.

Brighid paused by the firepit. She fought the urge to touch her cheek. She had washed her face and knuckles with snow, but she couldn't wash away the bruises and cuts. She studied the fire burning in the firepit. "I got into a fight."

"A fight?" Elphsaba slowly moved her legs around and stood.

Brighid dropped the bread and lurched toward her, ready to catch the older woman. Elphsaba waved her back and brushed off her dress. "Who did you fight with?"

"A couple of boys."

"An eljun?"

She paused, then said, "Yes."

"Why?"

Must she add lying to her list of transgressions? Brighid squirmed under Elphsaba's intense stare.

"Does it have to do with the bread?"

Brighid worked her jaw. "Yes."

"And where did you get the bread?"

There it was, the one question she didn't want to face. Her heart throbbed and her cheeks flushed. Could Elphsaba see her guilt? No. She made a fist. She would never let them starve.

"Brighid?"

Brighid rounded on the older woman. "I took it, all right? We've hardly eaten in days, and there is no work to be had. I tried everywhere: the stables, the inns, I even went to the other districts hoping someone with means would want to hire a maid. Instead, all they wanted was—"

Angry tears filled her eyes, and she gritted her teeth. Men were beginning to pay more attention to her, and one even offered to pay for a night with her. The amount would have bought food for a month, but the cost . . .

She pressed her palms against her eyes. She wouldn't cry. Not here, not now. She had to be strong. Elphsaba was fading every day. Brighid had to be strong for both of them.

"Brighid . . ."

She felt Elphsaba touch her arm, and it took everything inside of her not to burst into tears. "It was wrong. I know it was wrong to take the bread. I was desperate." She slowly lowered her arms, barely holding in the storm swirling inside of her.

"Come here, daughter." Elphsaba led her to the small hay bed they shared and pulled her down so they could sit side by side. Brighid gripped her fingers in front of her, her hunger momentarily forgotten.

"Thank you for taking care of me."

Brighid glanced at Elphsaba. That wasn't what she'd expected to hear.

"You did what you thought you needed to do for us." She reached for Brighid's fingers. Her own were so bent and swollen she could barely grasp anything. "But I don't want you to become a thief. If I have to, I will beg—"

"No! Never!"

Elphsaba smiled sadly. "It hurts my pride, but it will provide, even a little bit. And if it saves you from wrongdoing, I will do that."

Brighid's nostrils flared. This wasn't fair! Were their only choices begging or stealing? Or worse? Her muscles quivered, and a feeling of fight and desperation came over her. "Don't beg. At least give me two more days to find work." Elphsaba frowned and opened her mouth, but Brighid cut her off. "Two days." She held Elphsaba's fingers tighter. "Please."

Elphsaba let out a long breath. "Fine. Two days." She murmured something about the stubbornness of Nordics, but Brighid didn't care. She would double her efforts. Surely she could find something. *Please help me find something*, she whispered inside her mind.

"But I have one request."

Brighid nodded.

"You will pay the baker back for this bread."

Brighid paused. Her eyes wandered to the firepit where the two loaves lay. She cringed. The bread was probably worth three days of work. But—she bowed her head—it was important to Elphsaba. She could do that. For her. "Yes."

"And the next time you think about doing everything on your own, please talk to me." Brighid turned toward Elphsaba. The old woman gave her hands a weak squeeze. "We must fight together. You and me. You don't have to carry the burden alone. All right?"

Brighid swallowed as another tear threatened to trickle down her face. "All right. I will."

Maybe one of the old gods had heard her yesterday because the next morning Brighid found work in a clothier in the eagle district. The woman running the shop didn't care about the bruises and cuts across Brighid's face because she would be in the back of the shop working. The woman had noticed the stitching on Brighid's wool dress and been impressed. She wanted someone who could sew a few dresses with the same design until her sick daughter could return to work.

It was temporary but Brighid was willing to do whatever she could to keep Elphsaba from having to beg. And working in a warm back room was bliss compared to mucking stables or taking care of livestock.

As she embroidered the edges of a wool-strapped dress, her thoughts returned to the young man from yesterday. Roldar. And his offer for her to join his eljun.

She pressed the needle into the grey cloth. Eljuns were almost like clans for the clanless, and they were growing in power. They brought protection, food, and a place to live, all for the price of one's freedom. Members did whatever the leader wanted or desired.

She pulled the string and started another loop. How desperate would a person need to be to give up their heart, soul, maybe even their body? Her stomach clenched at the last thought. Was it possible Roldar would let her in on her fighting skills only? Or would he demand more if she joined?

She let out her breath and continued with the stitch. Well, they weren't at that point. Not yet. She had Elphsaba to take care of, and there wasn't one eljun that would take in an old woman. Eljuns were made of young people full of fire and life. Sometimes to the point where it felt like they would set Ragnbork ablaze. She'd overheard from others that even the clan leaders were discussing the roaming eljuns.

Brighid trudged every day through the snow that had accumulated along the streets. After three days, she went to the baker and left a couple coins on the counter. She didn't dare confess what she had done. The penalty for thievery was twenty strikes to the hands, and that would be worse than the bruising and split skin from the fight. At least she could still sew with these injuries.

Winter finally left and spring came. Brighid no longer had a job at the clothier, but at least it was warm. Elphsaba never left the bed. Death hadn't come for her, at least not yet. On clear days, Brighid went outside the city and searched for edible plants or offered to run errands for merchants entering the city. She was taller now, her figure filled out, and her hair reached the middle of her back.

"You've become such a beautiful young woman," Elphsaba murmured one night as Brighid prepared a squirrel she had caught and a few spring greens. They were down to one meal a day, but at least it kept hunger at bay. Elphsaba lay with her silver hair spread around her head, her face gaunt and her skin as thin as an onion peel. The firelight twinkled in her eyes as she watched Brighid prepare their food. "I always knew you would be."

Brighid smiled back, then continued preparing the meat. The last fortnight had brought more people into Ragnbork, and there were whispers of discontent. Many families slept outside wherever space could be found. The clanless district was bursting with people, and more came every day, driven to the city in hopes of food and work. But there was none to be had. She was lucky Elphsaba and she had this tiny hovel, at least for now. Her smile slowly faded. What happened when the district became so crowded that the stronger took from the weaker? What if they were forced from this place—

"Have you received any offers of bonding?"

Her head snapped up. "*What?*"

"You're seventeen winters now. Prime age for bonding with a man and starting a family."

Brighid laughed. "You're not serious, are you?"

Elphsaba laughed as well. "No. Just curious. It would be nice to see you settled before I pass beyond the veil."

Brighid dropped the knife, and it hit the dirt floor with a soft thud. "Bolva," she whispered as she retrieved the knife.

"You know it's going to happen, Brighid. I won't be here forever." Elphsaba sighed and looked up at the ceiling. "There is no escaping death."

Brighid plunged the knife into the washing bucket, her lips tight. Why did Elphsaba have to bring that up? She knew death was inescapable. She wiped the blade forcefully and went back to mincing the meat. She felt it come and go all the time.

"Brighid, we should talk about—"

"Don't talk about death!" Brighid slammed the knife down on the board and breathed heavily through her nose. The pot bubbled nearby. She lifted the board and swiped the meat into it. "Just. Don't."

"Ignoring it won't make it go away, daughter."

"I don't want to talk about it!" She dunked the knife and board in the wash bucket. The fire crackled in the firepit, and steam rose from the soup pot.

"I almost bonded once."

Brighid rubbed the board down, but curiosity broke through the fog of anger clouding her head. Elphsaba rarely spoke of her past or her family.

"He was a hunter. Lived in the deep forests of the wastelands. At one point, he even worked for the Bear Clan."

Brighid remembered Elphsaba had some tie to the Bear Clan and even the son of the hjar.

"We were set to say our vows at the autumn festival. But he never returned from that last hunt."

Brighid finally looked up. Elphsaba had a distant gaze in her eyes. "He was a kind man and didn't care that I was clanless. I'd never met a man like him. Resembled a bear, too, with his black beard and hair. Big, like one of the Bear Clan berserkers. I sometimes wonder what my life would have been like if he had lived. But then I wouldn't have you." Elphsaba turned with tears in her eyes. "I'm not afraid to die, daughter. The Celestial Halls have been calling my name, and I am ready to answer when it is time. But I fear it is you who is afraid of death."

"I am," Brighid said, then clamped her mouth shut. She turned away and grabbed the wooden spoon hanging from a hook near the firepit. She stirred the soup, her heart racing. "Very afraid," she whispered.

A silence descended upon the small room. Brighid could barely breathe. Her lungs refused to expand, and when she ladled the soup, her hand trembled so badly she spilled a spoonful across the dirt floor.

She forced herself to pause. She couldn't afford to lose any of this precious broth. Focusing on that, she finished dishing up dinner for both of them and brought a bowl to Elphsaba. The older woman struggled up until she was sitting and reached out.

"Tastes wonderful," Elphsaba said after taking a sip.

Brighid lifted her own bowl. Bland. With only bits of meat and greens.

The two sipped quietly. A minute later, the food was gone. So much work for so little. Brighid took their bowls and washed them. She still hungered, but the edge had been taken away.

Elphsaba lay down again. Just sitting up seemed to take everything out of her. Brighid took a moment to spread out her senses. She couldn't feel death. She let out a long breath and her shoulders sagged. But it wouldn't be long, and then . . .

No. I won't go there.

Brighid tidied up the room, checked the fire, then crawled beneath the covers next to Elphsaba. There was no warmth to be found in the bed. Only the slow breathing of her mother. Brighid shifted over onto her side, her back to Elphsaba, hoping maybe her body heat would warm the older woman. Darkness spread across the walls with only the dim orange light from the fire for light.

"Brighid?" Elphsaba said seconds later.

"Yes?" Did Elphsaba need help going out to relieve herself?

"You don't have to be afraid."

Oh. That. Brighid burrowed deeper beneath the covers.

"When I go, I will close my eyes, and when I open them again, I will be across the veil. Just like that song I sang at birthings." It was a song of life and healing and the Word. The only thing that seemed to help when death came to visit during birthings. "Remember that song when I go. And don't be afraid."

Brighid pulled the top banket over her head. No, the only thing that would help her was if death no longer existed. Only then would she not be afraid.

Brighid felt death before she opened her eyes. Its frigid presence filled the small room, snuffing out any warmth to be found under the furs and blankets.

She threw the covers back and twisted around to look at Elphsaba in the dim light of dawn. Elphsaba barely breathed, just a soft exhale every couple of seconds.

"No, no, no!" Brighid got up on her knees. "No, please."

She grabbed Elphsaba's frigid fingers. "You can't leave me!" Tears burst from her eyes, and she couldn't catch her breath as sob after sob racked her body.

"Get away!" she screamed and waved her arm through the air. "Why do you have to take her? She's all I have!" She gripped her own throat in a tight hold. "Don't take her from me," she whispered. "Don't take her!"

Fingers barely brushed her knee. Brighid paused, her face hot and salty. "Elphsaba?"

Her hand moved again, just slightly. Brighid grabbed it and held it to her cheek. Her whole body trembled. If only death was corporeal, then she could fight it. She would throw everything at it and stop it. But it was invisible and moved like the wind, coming one moment, leaving the next.

Never had she felt so helpless. Until now, she could at least provide food and find wood for the firepit and rub Elphsaba's aching limbs every night. She could do *something*. But now . . .

More tears gushed down her cheeks, and her nose began to run. Moans escaped her throat as she rubbed those small, gnarled, frozen fingers against her cheek.

"I love you. I can't live without you."

"Love . . ."

"What?" Did Elphsaba speak? Brighid could barely see through her swollen eyes.

"Love . . . you." The last word came out as a sigh.

It was done. Death had come and gone, stealing away the one person she had loved with her whole heart and soul.

Brighid continued to hold Elphsaba's hand, rocking back and forth on the bed. The sun rose, and she could hear the rustle of people outside. But she didn't want to move. She couldn't move. A small voice in the back of her head told her there were things to do and arrangements to be made. But it was too much right now.

She wasn't sure when she collapsed on the bed and fell into a cold sleep, but when she opened her eyes, it was near noon. Full sunlight trickled in through the small gaps between the hut's rocks and boards, and the noise of everyday filtered through its walls. Life went on, even after a visit from death.

Brighid turned and looked at Elphsaba. She was gone. Was it like she said it would be? Did she close her eyes, then open them in a new place? Was she now walking along the Celestial Halls? Wherever she was, she had taken Brighid's heart with her. Only a cold lump remained in her chest.

Brighid slowly sat up, her body stiff. The fire had long since died, and the cupboard was bare, like always. Not that she felt like eating. She felt like nothing. Numb. That was what she was.

She finally crawled off the bed and shrugged on her cloak. It was time to visit the deathkeeper. She would find a way to pay for the pyre, but a place in the mountain sepulchers would not be possible. She would take Elphsaba's ashes outside the city and scatter them in the wind. Elphsaba would probably prefer it that way.

The sun held no warmth as Brighid made her way along the broken, narrow streets of the clanless district. She walked past the barricade and northward, toward the mountain basin in which Ragnbork was built. She had never been to the sepulchers before or searched out the deathkeepers. Elphsaba did not believe in the mountain gods, and Brighid was skeptical of any belief. But they handled the business of death, and so to them she went.

No one noticed her as she passed each clan district. She had never traveled this far into Ragnbork before. Ahead rose the Elding Citadel, home to the ruling clans and fighting arena. The massive structure was made of stone and wood with steep rooflines, a vast staircase leading up through curved archways, and a rounded side building that housed the arena. Along the staircase were carvings of the five clans. The road split at the bottom of the citadel, and Brighid slowed. Which street led to the sepulchers?

The street area bustled with people on their way to the citadel for business, those seeking audience with the clan leaders and trade. Brighid pulled her cloak tighter and searched for a sign.

A man bumped into her and bowed. "Forgive me." He was taller than Brighid with brushed-back hair the color of dark mead. His clothing consisted of leather and fur, and the brooch on his left shoulder was engraved with an eagle. As he lifted his head, his eyes caught Brighid's. "Are you lost?"

"I'm looking for the deathkeepers."

"Deathkeepers?" He straightened. "To the left of the citadel." Then he bowed again. "May the Eagle be with you."

Brighid bowed in response but didn't answer. She had no clan, so she had no patron. She could feel the man's eyes lingering on her as she turned left, but the gaze was not condescending or lustful. Perhaps there were still decent people left in this world.

The sepulchers were built into the Keshmin Mountains. Lit torches guided the way through the shadows cast by the high cliffs. A dozen pyres were built near the carved door that led into the mountain—three were currently burning, surrounded by weeping families. Brighid hesitated as she drew near the half circle where the pyres were located. Figures dressed in black robes wove between the pyres, chanting in a strange language. Death was not here, but she could feel traces of it lingering in the air like an invisible, icy fog.

As she drew closer, one of the deathkeepers turned and approached her.

She took a step back. His eyes were a milky white. Dark swirls were inked into his clean-shaven pale face, and snow-white hair escaped his hood.

He paused only a few feet away. His gaze was to the right of Brighid, but she knew he could see her, or at least feel her. "Death surrounds you, Nordic daughter."

Brighid fought the urge to rub her arm. "Yes."

"You are"—he lifted his chin as if searching—"clanless."

"Yes," Brighid replied.

"And yet not."

Brighid frowned. What did that mean?

He closed the distance between them. He would have been taller than Brighid save for the stoop in his back. He raised his hand, his gaze still to her right, and brought a finger to her face. "Yes, you can feel it."

This time she rubbed her arms. The air grew colder. She wasn't sure if it was from the shadow cast by the mountain or being near the rites of death. Or maybe it was the words the deathkeeper spoke.

"You feel that which cannot be seen. And someday you will hear the words that cannot be heard—"

"My mother died," Brighid said, interrupting him. The deathkeeper was spooking her. "I need her body retrieved and a pyre built."

He dropped his hand, the trance gone. "Please give the information to my acolyte. It will be done."

"What is the cost?"

"Nothing for you."

"Wait, nothing?"

He turned away. "I will let my acolyte know."

"But why?"

He never answered. Why would she not be charged for the burning? Not that she would complain.

Brighid turned and quickly left the deathly area after sharing the location of her home with a young man in black robes. The acolyte never asked for payment, so she went on her way.

The deathkeeper's words continued to worm their way through her mind, bringing a momentary reprieve from her grief as she headed back home. Did he know her secret? As a deathkeeper, did he also feel death? Did that mean her future might lie in the sepulchers?

Brighid grimaced and drew her cloak tight. Even if death did not dwell there, the victims of its work did. But maybe it would help her not be afraid?

The very thought of attending the pyres brought on a cold sweat. No, that would never be her calling. She hated death. It took and never gave back.

A lump grew in her throat, and her eyes burned. But Brighid held back her grief. The streets were crowded with people. This was not the place to wail. She would bare her heart again once she reached home. She would allow herself one day to cry. Then she would put her grief away and move on.

9

The first thing to go was Elphsaba's hands. Brighid wanted to look away, but she forced herself to watch the pyre. The sun mark on her skin disappeared into the flames, followed by the rest of her.

The deathkeepers moved around the pyre, chanting their scriptures. There were no other grievers. It had just been her and Elphsaba. Three other pyres burned, each with at least a dozen mourners. Brighid noticed only for a moment, then focused on Elphsaba again.

She was empty. All her tears and heart had been spent, leaving only a husk of herself behind. The sun rapidly made its way toward the horizon, taking with it what little warmth it had given the day.

Fire burned. Time moved. The sun finally set. Flames settled across the body as they continued to do their work. Torches were lit. Darkness took over until eventually the deathkeeper who had spoken to her earlier that afternoon came to collect the ashes. He gathered only a couple handfuls and secured them inside a small, unadorned ceramic jar, then placed it in her waiting hands.

It was done. All that had summed up Elphsaba's life was now burned away.

Brighid stared down at the jar, something finally moving again in her heart. She didn't want Elphsaba to be forgotten. She would get a Mark of Remembrance. Usually one received a mark for family members or clans. Elphsaba was the only family she'd ever had. She didn't need a clan symbol, so she would use the one Elphsaba had etched into her wrist. The sun.

The next day the wind sent Elphsaba's ashes flying over the valley toward the sea in the east. Brighid watched the remnants take flight, then turned and headed back into the city. She had a small pouch of coins in her cloak from selling their few blankets and the cupboard from their home. She had heard about a master in marks who lived in the bear district. Though she had traveled through parts of Ragnbork, she hadn't visited that district. It lay to the north, past the sepulchers, against the Kenshim Mountains and behind the Elding Citadel.

Brighid made her way through the massive gates and along the streets that led toward the middle of the city. Her boots were worn thin, and a hole in one place on the bottom sometimes caught on a stray cobblestone. The sun shone bright overhead, and the weather was warmer, almost warm enough to go without a shawl.

She'd managed to tame her unkempt hair into braid that hung over one shoulder. Elphsaba would want her to live: to make sure she ate at least one meal a day, brushed her hair each night, and took care of the little things that meant she was alive. And she would. But she didn't have the strength yet. Grief had sapped the very marrow from her bones. Only a grim determination to let Elphsaba's ashes fly and receive her mark kept her moving.

At the citadel, she turned right. A familiar path, one she had traveled yesterday. But when she reached the sepulchers, she passed the stone enclosure and continued. The next district was built almost entirely from stone. Only the rafters and rooflines were made from wood. Images of the bear were engraved on doors along with runes of strength. She passed an open-air blacksmith, stables, and a butcher shop displaying the latest domesticated meats. At the end of the street, set against the mountain wall, was a large longhouse with two bears carved in wood, standing on their hind legs, towering over the door.

Brighid paused. Something about the massive bears tugged on her soul. A presence of strength and defiance. Nothing could get past them. Maybe not even death. Elphsaba hadn't been part of the Bear Clan, but they'd lived in bear country and served the people of the Bear Clan for many years. Perhaps that was why she felt a sudden kinship with the bear.

A small wooden building caught her eye to the right. Above the door hung a sign with the symbols for *master* and *mark*. There. The place she was looking for. She slowly opened the door and peered inside. The room was small and smelled like ash. A work bench stood along one wall beneath an open window. Shelves lined the other wall with small boxes and inkpots stored on top. Another door was in the back.

As she entered, the other door opened, letting in bright sunlight. An old man walked in. His hair was grey and grizzly, and his shoulders were almost as wide as the door. His face and arms were covered in marks, giving him a fierce appearance. His light blue eyes lit on Brighid, and he stopped. "Aye. Mornin' miss. What can I do for you?"

Brighid stepped fully inside, firmly gripping her small pouch. "I'm here for a mark."

He named his price and Brighid agreed to it, showing him the coins in her pouch.

He walked over to the bench. "Where and what type?"

"Sun mark. On my face."

"Sun? Your face?" He studied her for a moment. "All right." He grabbed a rolled leather toolkit, then crossed the room, past the firepit, and picked up a box with circles carved into the sides. Lastly, he reached for an inkpot. "Follow me."

The master led her out back where a table and two chairs stood beneath an awning next to his shop. Another workbench was set up with tiny ceramic pots and a wooden bowl of full of ash.

"Take a seat here." He indicated the first chair. Brighid sat down and watched as he unrolled the leather toolkit. A dozen long needles, two scrappers, and a piece of charcoal. "What is the mark for, if you don't mind me askin'?"

Her gaze lingered on the needles. "My mother."

"That is a good mark to receive. And the sun?"

"It was her mark. I wish to have the same."

"A symbol of light and life." He opened the inkpot. "Any clan mark?"

Brighid looked away. "No clan."

The master nodded, but there was no condemnation on his face. Some of the tightness across her body loosened. She was tired of feeling lesser because she didn't belong to a clan.

"I'm assuming you wish to have the exact mark?"

"Yes."

"Can you draw it for me?"

"I think I can."

He passed over the piece of charcoal. "Go ahead and draw it on the wood."

Brighid paused. She could read, but she had never learned to write or draw. It couldn't be much different from the images she created for embroidery. She took the charcoal, closed her eyes, and pictured the sun on Elphsaba's wrist. For a moment, she saw the pyre, but she pushed that memory aside and chose a more pleasant, earlier one. Then she began to draw.

It was a simple design. A circle with lines extending beyond like rays. When she finished, she set down the charcoal and looked at the master.

"It is a nice, simple design. Where on your face would you like it placed?"

"Here." Brighid traced her left eye. It was considered the most prominent spot to place a Mark of Remembrance, usually reserved for a most beloved.

He studied the mark, then her face. "What if I did a half circle, like a rising sun? It would follow the contours of your face and eye better."

A rising sun? She liked that idea. Like rising from the ashes of night into a new day. "Yes."

"Then let us begin." He took the charcoal and etched the design around her eye. For the first time, a sense of unease settled across her body. No doubt it would hurt. But it was a ritual of bravery and strength to receive a mark. And she would be brave.

He finished the drawing, placed the charcoal on the bench, and reached for the narrowest needle. Her heart beat faster, but she remained still.

With two fingers, he drew her skin tight, then he placed his other hand in the crease of her nose and cheek and started the process. A hundred pricks in rapid succession with little pauses in between for dips in the inkpot. It hurt. She wanted to suck in her lips and gasp, but it could ruin the design. So she went deep inside herself. A bird sang nearby, and she let its song fill her mind, blotting away the master's touch and the constant pricks.

The bird stopped and another bird began. The hum of conversation floated through the air from the street on the other side of the shop. A soft warm wind blew. Then it was over.

The master sat back and cracked his neck. He eyed her face, then gave her a gruff smile. "You did well for your first mark."

"Thank you."

"And you chose a good design to honor your mother."

Brighid smiled softly at that, the first time she had smiled in days. She wanted to touch the area but knew it wasn't a good idea.

"Now, to care for your mark." He pulled out a pot and a small square of thin wool from his box. He dipped his fingers inside and drew out honey. He gently dabbed her face with the sweet stickiness. "Keep honey on your mark for two days, along with a thin piece of wool." He picked up the square, unfolded it, and placed it gently across the left side of her face. "Do not touch the mark. Let the honey heal it."

"Thank you." Brighid reached for the pouch and counted out the agreed-upon coins, then placed them in his calloused hand.

He stood. "Be proud, daughter of Nordica. Be proud of the mark you wear and the person you wear it for."

Brighid stood as well, her heart swelling. "I will."

"It will give you strength for the times ahead."

She believed him. Already a fierce desire to live had taken over her heart. She was proud of who she was. And of the woman who raised her. This mark would serve as a reminder when grief came, when hunger came, when the snow fell and everything grew cold. It would remind her to live.

Not even death could take that away.

10

Summer brought jobs but also more clanless immigrants. Then winter came, and even those with skills could find no work. Brighid sold the last of her belongings until all she had was her thick wrap. A week later, she was forced to sell her one-room home.

Brighid took the coins from a family of four. It was hardly anything, and certainly not what Elphsaba had paid for the space, but she had nothing, and the coins would see her through another week. As she walked toward the doorway, a piece of her heart seemed to tear away and flutter to the ground. An icy wind caught her as she exited and took her breath with its chill.

The door shut behind her. She gripped her cloak tight against her thin body as she stood on the street. How was she going to survive? No work, no home, nothing. She wanted to collapse onto her knees and cry, but that would do nothing but make her colder.

Death seemed to taunt her. She always felt it slithering between the buildings, snatching souls during the middle of the night. It wanted her, she knew. She drew herself up, thrust out her chin, and started down the street. Death would not have her. It would never have her. She would fight it with everything she had. No matter what, she would survive.

The thought chased away the chill as she crossed the clanless district. People filled every corner and alley. Fires blazed in the middle of the streets, keeping the homeless warm. A baby cried in a woman's arms, and the haggard mother tried to comfort the babe. Children huddled close to parents, shivering like pines in the wind.

Brighid stopped near one of the fires and blew on her fingers. The fire spit and crackled as snow made contact with the red flames.

"What are the clans doing about this?" A man muttered. "Are they really going to let us starve?"

"I heard a group is going to march on the clan districts. It's not right to keep us locked in this district just because we do not belong to one of them."

Another man snorted. "We should start our own clan."

"Some have," an old man said darkly. "They're called eljuns."

"Those aren't clans. They're violent malcontents."

"At least they're working together to survive!" replied a young man.

"It is not our way to turn on one another," the old man replied.

"Humph, someone should tell that to the clans."

"Tell me more about the group that is going to march," the young man asked the man beside him. The conversation continued as Brighid stepped away. Unrest was growing. She doubted the group planning to march would make the clans fearful, but the eljuns seemed to pose an actual threat. She remembered her encounter with them a year ago. And Roldar's offer. Since then, his eljun had grown to be the most powerful in Ragnbork. Was she desperate enough to go to him? Desperate enough to do anything he asked of her? Even give her own body?

Brighid suddenly felt ill, and she placed a hand against her middle. The snow crunched beneath her boots. She wasn't sure which she feared more: death or the eljuns.

What if one day she had to choose?

It was the coldest night Brighid had ever experienced.

Her fingers and toes were slowly losing feeling, and her face burned from the chill. She sat huddled next to the city wall in the farthest corner of the clanless district. The full moon shed its pale light across the city like a funeral veil. The few fires that burned were too crowded for even a child to stand near. She wrapped her arms tighter around her knees in an effort to keep all of her body under her cloak. But gaps allowed the cold gusts through. Her heart clenched at the chill.

Would this be the night she finally died?

Even now, she could feel death weaving through the streets, brushing unseen fingers along the backs of the unsuspecting and carrying their souls away.

She dropped her head and pressed her face against the fabric of her cloak. *I don't want to die.* She squeezed her eyes shut. *I don't want to die.* Despite what Elphsaba said before she passed—that death was merely opening one's eyes in a new world—Brighid didn't believe her. Death couldn't possibly be so peaceful, not when its presence was full of bitter cold and darkness. The very thought of dying sent her mind reeling and a shot of adrenaline through her heart—

The snow crunched to her left. Her head shot up, and she glanced to her right. A small group made its way along the narrow street. She breathed faster. "Bolva," she whispered. Eljuns.

She struggled to stand, but her frozen body refused to move. The eljuns drew closer. *You need to move! Now!* She finally stood and twisted around.

"Well, what do we have here? A loner."

Brighid recognized the voice. She peered back, and in the moonlight, she caught sight of the leader's face. Sharp cheekbones, stringy brown hair, and a pinched, hungry look. Her stomach gave a jolt. Falko. Head of the now second-strongest eljun in Ragnbork. Did he recognize her?

His eyes widened, confirming her fears. "You! You're that little vixen that gave me this." He ran a finger along a scar on the side of his face. "I think I owe you." His cheeks stretched wide into a nasty smile. "Get that girl!"

Brighid turned and ran. She slipped once in the snow, caught herself, and dashed down one of the alleyways. Her lungs burned from the frigid air, and her side cramped. She entered an intersection where a fire burned low and people huddled around it. No one looked her way, not even when five others burst from the alleyway. No one cared.

She sucked in a breath, glanced ahead, then right. She ran again. If she could make it to the district over, maybe she would find a guard on patrol. But that was a slim hope, and even slimmer that he would help her. The real power on the streets were the eljuns, and they knew it.

"Not now," she huffed, pressing her palm against her throbbing side. Lack of food and shelter had made her weak, but she wouldn't give up without a fight.

Something gripped her cloak and pulled her back. Instead of losing her balance, Brighid slammed her foot down and pivoted, a fist already formed. She caught her assailant in the jaw and sent his head reeling to the side and his body staggering back. One of Falko's lackeys.

His hold loosened, and she tore away, leaving behind the fabric still grasped in his fingers.

A familiar red haze settled across her vision. It burned toward the back of her skull and entered her body, spreading heat to her limbs. Her lips turned to a snarl, and her fingers curled as the rest of the eljuns caught up. Every heartbeat pumped with the desire to fight. Only a small fraction of sense within her mind told her to run. She hesitated, the bloodlust pumping through her veins.

Then the nearest eljun dove for her.

Everything went red.

Her body moved with a hidden strength. Fists against flesh, fingers along skin. Her legs connected with ribs and thighs. She could see nothing, hear nothing. It was as if she were possessed.

After a minute, the haze dissipated. Brighid sucked in her breath and feeling returned to her body. Blood covered her knuckles. Five men lay across the street in the moonlight, groaning or knocked out. Falko sat nearest her. He stared up at her as he gripped his eye. "What *are* you?"

"Someone you shouldn't mess with." Her words sounded firm, but inside she quivered. She turned and headed down the street, leaving behind the moans and whimpers of the men. She could feel the blood, now cold, across her skin, and tenderness in her muscles.

What in the Abyss had she done?

Her hands began to shake as her boots crunched across the snow-covered street.

What have I done?

"What am I?" she whispered as she held up her palms. No one

should be able to put down five young men. Especially not a girl like her. "Am I a monster?"

She stumbled into the wall, then fell to her knees and heaved. Nothing came up. There was nothing there to begin with. What kind of strength was this that took hold of her and turned her vision red? She curled into herself. "Elphsaba, what is wrong with me? Who am I?" she bowed her head and cried. "Why aren't you here? I need you!"

Rustling sounded behind her and she gasped. Quickly wiping her eyes, she turned and stood. Three men and a woman. More eljuns?

"I knew I recognized that hair and face. The moonlight only makes it more beautiful." The man in the middle stepped forward. He had an arrow-shaped mark on his cheek. Dark, curly hair surrounded his face.

Roldar.

Bolva! Was every eljun out tonight? Brighid stepped back and felt along the wall behind her. She wouldn't fight again. The very thought of it sickened her.

"She's the one I told you both about from a year ago. The breadfighter."

The young woman next to him snickered at the nickname, and Roldar grinned.

"Her fight just now was impressive," the taller of the other men said. "Wild, powerful. Reminds me a little of the Bear Clan berserkers. Never seen a woman fight like that."

They had watched her fight? And hadn't *helped*?

"So, what'll it be?" Roldar casually walked toward her. The moonlight glistened off his curls.

"What do you mean?" Brighid asked darkly as she inched away along the wall.

"Will you finally join my eljun?"

"Why? Why should I join you?"

He shrugged. "Food, shelter, warmth. Protection." The others joined Roldar from behind. "In many ways we are a clan to the clanless. Even family. And right now that is what many people need. Living alone in Ragnbork is a death sentence. If not from hunger, then exposure. Or other eljuns."

"I can hold my own."

"I know. I saw. But I also know you have no place to go."

A shiver went down her spine. "Have you been watching me?"

Roldar laughed and the others joined him. "That's what I do. I watch people. And I don't invite just anybody into my eljun."

Brighid took another step away, but she couldn't deny there was some truth and appeal to his words. But she also knew of their dark reputation. "What would you expect of me?"

"First, don't run. I can tell you're about to do just that."

For one second, she thought about ignoring him. But where would she run? There was nowhere for her to go. Only snow and death waited for her. The time had come to make a choice. Brighid stopped. The heat from the fight before faded from her body, leaving her chilled to the bone. Snow started to fall again, gentle and quiet along the narrow street.

Roldar reached past her face. She flinched as he tugged one of her small braids over her shoulder. "You do whatever I ask of you." His finger trailed her jaw.

Her eyes narrowed and her lips curled. "Let me be clear. I am no man's. And I never will be. If that is your condition—that I do whatever you ask of me—then my answer is no." There. She had drawn her line.

He raised an eyebrow, his hand hanging in the air near her face. "Never?" He shrugged and stepped back. "Fine. Then fight for me."

Brighid eyed him. Could she trust him? More than anything, she wanted to live.

She worked her jaw. She could fight. She didn't know why, but it had saved her twice now. And he wanted that ability. Was it worth giving to him in exchange for her life?

"All right. I'll fight for you." She held up a finger. "But that is all." She could hear Elphsaba's voice in the back of her head telling her this wasn't the way to live, but Elphsaba wasn't here anymore.

Roldar smiled. It reminded her of a cat with a mouse. But she was no mouse. If he dared to ask for more, he would discover that. "We shall see." He continued to grin as he motioned her toward his other companions. "Welcome to my eljun."

11

Five chairs encircled the massive firepit inside the Elding Citadel council hall. Ancient stone and lumber towered over the room, coming to a curved point near the ceiling. Here the clans of Nordica had held council since Ragnbork came into existence. And here they would meet today.

Gurmund, Hjar of the Bear Clan, sat alone in his chair. The embers burned and flickered in the firepit as he waited for the other clan leaders to arrive. He had already been in Ragnbork for a month and was tired of the city. Some of the other clan families thrived on the people and culture of Ragnbork, but his heart longed to be back home in the Northern Wastelands. For the open space, the mountains, and the untamed wild of his ancestors' lands. The letter he had received from his wife yesterday did not help temper his longing. She spoke of the daily affairs, the deep snow, and asked how their son, Bard, was doing.

Bard walked into the council hall at that moment and spotted him near the firepit.

"Father, how long have you been here?" he asked as he came to stand beside the chair.

"Since sunrise. A letter arrived yesterday from your mother. She sends her love."

"Everything well back home?"

"As well as it can be." He could read between the words Ana had written. There was more unrest, especially with how harsh this winter was. But she was a strong woman, and he knew she would take care of things in his absence.

He turned and studied Bard. His son resembled him at that age, with golden hair kept trim and a body solid from hard work. Except for his eyes. He had Ana's eyes. Light blue, like the sky on the horizon. "When do you plan on leaving?"

"Later this afternoon. A fight broke out along the border, and I volunteered to quell it."

Gurmund cursed under his breath. "Why isn't Lord Rayner keeping his country in check? Doesn't he know if these scuffles continue between the Ryland Plains and Nordica that war could follow?"

"I believe it was our side this time," Bard said quietly.

"Over what?"

"Food, I'm assuming."

Gurmund placed his chin on his steepled fingers. He wanted to keep a clear head on the matter, but it was growing more difficult. The people of Nordica were starving, and Lord Rayner and King Erhard refused to trade. The other clan leaders weren't making things easier. There had always been a rift between the north and the south, a difference in culture and beliefs. But that rift had turned to an intense hatred in the last hundred years. Some had even argued they would rather starve than have anything to do with the Ryland Plains or Avonai. Fools! The ones who would pay for such obstinacy were the people of Nordica. The women, children, and poor. Pride be hanged! Trade needed to start, and both sides needed to compromise. He sighed and dropped his head. He seemed to be the only clan leader who believed this.

"Thank you, son." Gurmund lifted his head and glanced at Bard.

"If it saves lives, I'm willing to go."

Gurmund laughed. "Who would have thought the Bear Clan would be the ones trying to keep the peace in Nordica?"

Bard grinned. "It would seem we have left our bloody ways behind us."

Gurmund sighed. "Maybe." If war did break out, the Bear Clan would be the first riding into battle like they always were. They possessed brute strength—the Vilrik—and their bear companions.

Their warriors were feared even more than those of the Wolf Clan. But how many would die? How many families would be ripped apart? Maybe he was getting old, but he desired peace more than war. Though not at the expense of starvation. War, it seemed, was inevitable.

The fire crackled as Bard left. Shortly after, the other clan leaders began to arrive in the council hall. Frieda entered first. She was a brawny woman with grey streaks in her honey-colored hair that she wore in one thick braid over her shoulder. Instead of a wool gown, she wore a fur-lined leather vest and britches, thick boots, and a fur cloak made from blue foxes. For many years she led the Stag Clan with her husband, and when he passed away, she continued leading with a firm, steady hand.

"Gurmund," she said in a low throaty voice.

"Frieda."

She took the seat across from him and sat with a quiet groan. The tips of her Mark of Remembrance poked out above her collar, five tips representing her clan and her late husband.

Seconds later, Bodin entered with his barred owl companion, Aisling, riding on his shoulder. Gurmund saw rather than heard him approach. Bodin was the epitome of the Owl Clan, silent and mysterious. In the fashion of his clan, ash was smeared around his eyes, causing his blue-grey eyes to stand out. His long, straight hair shined like a copper pot. His beard was kept short with a bead woven through each side of his mustache. A half dozen Marks of Remembrance lined his exposed neck, chest, and arms. He nodded to Gurmund and Frieda, then sat without a word.

All three quietly stared into the fire until Adrian walked in. "Greetings, friends," he bellowed, his deep, warm voice echoing across the council hall.

Gurmund snorted as he looked up. Adrian had recently taken on the mantle of leader of the Eagle Clan when his father passed away two winters ago. He was young, not more than thirty winters, with a boisterous, cheerful disposition and sunny golden hair. But Gurmund also knew the young man was strong. His burly muscles bulged beneath his tunic as he moved toward his seat. He could go toe to toe with a Bear Clan berserker. Not many could.

"Wonderful morning, eh?"

Frieda shook her head as a smile played along her lips while Bodin and his owl watched the young man with impassive expressions. Adrian didn't seem to notice. He held his hands out toward the fire and let out a happy sigh.

"Nothing like a fire on a cold morning."

"Indeed," Gurmund said.

Adrian grinned at Gurmund. "How's Bard doing?"

"He's heading to the border."

"He is? More skirmishes?"

"Yes, along our side."

Adrian pursed his lips and nodded. "If anyone can settle a skirmish, it's Bard and Amro."

Gurmund paused. Adrian knew the name of Bard's bear? The two men must be closer than Gurmund thought. Bard never gave out his bear's name.

Frieda stood and walked over to the pile of wood sitting in the corner, grabbed a log, and brought it back to the firepit. She placed the log on top and used a poker to position it better.

Adrian sat down. His eyes continued moving, as did his finger that currently tapped his knee. A minute later, he shifted in his seat and peered at the main door. "What is taking Volka so long?"

"I'm not sure," Gurmund said, a crease forming along his brow. The leader of the Wolf Clan was never late for council meetings. Usually Volka or Gurmund himself arrived first in the hall.

Volka was nearing thirty winters, around the same age as Bard and Adrian. But unlike Adrian, who was on friendly terms with Bard, Volka had nothing to do with either. He usually remained with his clan and interacted with the others only when needed.

Gurmund leaned forward and pulled on the tip of his beard. He had heard disturbing rumors about the Wolf Clan and their dealings with their own border along the Ryland Plains. While the Bear Clan tried to keep peace and honor the treaties despite what the Rylanders did, the Wolf Clan had taken a more violent approach. At least, that was what those fleeing to Ragnbork were saying.

He let out a sigh. He would need to inquire about it during this meeting.

The doors opened and Volka appeared, flanked by three other people. His long black hair was brushed back, ending in a small braid behind each ear. Marks of Remembrance covered one eye and were etched across his exposed chest. His eyes were a vivid blue, like the glaciers of the far north. He wore the pelt of a black wolf over his dark leather attire. If anyone embodied their clan's symbol, it was Volka. His presence and mannerisms reminded Gurmund of the famous black wolves of Anwin Forest.

"I appear to be late." His voice did not sound apologetic. "But I have good reason. I have brought guests today. I believe they could prove useful in our conflict with the south."

Frieda scowled and gripped the arms on her chair. "This hall is for clan hjars only, not acquaintances, friends, or allies without prior approval. I did not receive a message that there would be others today. Did you?" She stared around the firepit.

Bodin shook his head.

"I did not," Gurmund replied. He, too, was displeased by the sudden appearance of these strangers. They had important things to discuss today that were not for the ears of others.

Adrian glanced around before speaking. "I also agree, but perhaps we can give Volka a moment of our time and see why he thought breaking practice was so important."

Frieda's nostrils flared, and Gurmund half expected her to burst from her chair and physically remove the trespassers. He would even join her except . . . his shoulders dropped, he was trying to let Adrian lead. For hundreds of years the Eagle Clan led the rest of them. If Adrian was going to grow in his position as both leader of his clan and all of Nordica, the others needed to let him lead.

Even if they didn't fully agree.

"Thank you, Adrian." Volka moved around the chairs toward his own on the right side. The other figures followed. They were not Nordic, that was clear by their appearance and attire. All three wore long, dark cloaks with the hoods pulled over their heads. Two men and one woman. Their skin was smooth and clear with perfect lines and jaws, high cheekbones, and defined lips. Beautiful and exquisite in an exotic sort of way. Gurmund frowned. Where did they hail from? And how did Volka know them?

Volka sat and crossed one leg, appearing relaxed in his clan's ancestral chair. The three strangers gathered around him like sentinels.

"First, introductions. These three hail from over the Ari Mountain range on the west side. A company of my clan ran into them a few months ago, and they have sat at my fire since."

It wasn't uncommon to let strangers sit at one's fire. Years ago Gurmund hosted a group of Ryland officers when a blizzard sent them off course and into Nordic lands. But this seemed to be more than providing hospitality.

"You said they could prove useful in our conflict with the south," Bodin's smooth voice carried across the hall as he spoke for the first time. His owl blinked.

"Yes," Volka said.

"And what conflict would that be?"

Gurmund leaned forward, curious to see how Volka answered. The Owl Clan lived to the far north in the Kenshim Mountains and away from the border. Perhaps they were unaware of the border crossings by the Rylanders and Avonai. Then again, their specialty was secret knowledge. They had to know.

Volka uncrossed his legs and sat up. "I don't know how it is for your clan—or anyone else's here beside the Bear Clan—but there is no respect for boundaries by the south. For the last few years, Rylanders have been crossing our borders, stealing from my people, and they are now beginning to encroach on our land."

"Are you saying they're settling in your land?" Gurmund asked.

Volka looked at him. "Yes. Our land is more desirable than the wastelands your clan rules."

Gurmund bristled. Volka wasn't wrong. The Bear Clan oversaw the large swath of land from the Keshmin Mountains to the Ari range. Most of it was empty and frozen, earning the name the Wastelands. But why would Rylanders risk conflict with the Wolf Clan by expanding up along the Ari Mountain range? He wasn't convinced.

"I've heard that you have not been honoring the treaties in place between our countries."

Volka bared his teeth. "They drew first blood. We retaliated."

"Even so, that is not how conflicts should be handled."

"When did the Bear Clan become so cowardly?"

Gurmund snorted. He would not be baited. "There is nothing cowardly about honoring agreements made between our countries."

"Even if they do not honor those same agreements? I know they've been crossing into your lands as well. But you just keep sending your son to quell the fighting. It makes you appear weak. That is why they keep pressing in."

Gurmund hated that there was some truth to Volka's words. In his younger days, he might have even taken the fight to the Rylanders, as Volka was doing now. But did they really want war? Their people were starving and barely clothed. How could they go to war in such conditions?

"Volka's right," Frieda said.

Gurmund glanced at her. "You agree that we should use force along the border?"

"We have tried to honor the treaties between our countries, but even along our own lands the Avonains have joined the Rylanders in their push for the north."

"Avonai as well?" Adrian asked, surprised.

"Yes, all of this recently. This is one of the items I wanted to bring up during this meeting."

Gurmund narrowed his eyes. It was one thing to have a few cross the border. But this sounded more like a coordinated push. Was that what Lord Rayner and King Erhard were aiming for? Did they truly think Nordica was weak?

"And I bring news from the trade guild," Adrian said. "Ryland Plains and Avonai still refuse to trade with us. Our envoy arrived three days ago with this news."

"This person actually talked with Lord Rayner and King Erhard?" Gurmund asked.

"Yes."

Volka sneered. "As you can see, Gurmund, it's not a simple matter of scuffles along the border. The south is coming. What better way to take over a country than by watching it starve and slowly encroach on its land? The moment we are finally weak, they will march on us. Already the pyres are burning night and day with the young and strong who have succumbed to starvation. If we don't do something soon, it will be too late."

"What are you proposing?" Gurmund asked.

"We fight back."

"You mean war?"

Volka shrugged. "If it comes to that, yes. First, we have a show of power. That is what my friends are here for."

All eyes turned to the three figures. What could these strangers possibly possess that the northern people did not?

"Do you recall the stories of beings who once dwelt in the lands, beings with powers beyond humankind?" Volka asked.

Gurmund froze. His grandmother once talked about them. It was thought maybe the fighting spirit of the Vilrik came from a distant ancestor related to them. But there had never been such people in Nordica. A shiver rippled down his spine. Was it possible those robed figures were such beings?

"I do," Bodin said. "But very few exist if they still exist at all."

"They exist." Volka smiled. "And they are willing to help us."

"Why?" Frieda asked.

The tallest man stepped forward and pulled back the hood of his cloak. Black hair fell along his shoulders, and his heavily lidded eyes were light blue, bordering on white. "I am Armand. These are my companions, Viessa and Peder."

Viessa removed her hood. A white streak followed the curve of her hair along the right side of her face, a contrast with her silky black strands. Bright-green eyes peered out from black sockets, as if she had smeared kohl around her eyes, and a smirk played across her full dark lips.

The other figure grinned as he removed his hood. His copper hair hung in thick strands around his head and matched his amber-colored eyes. There was a lean strength to his figure that hinted at hidden power.

"You asked us why we want to help?" Armand said, addressing Frieda.

"Yes." Frieda sat with her arms folded and a stern look on her face.

"It is simple. We were shown hospitality by your people, specifically the Wolf Clan. When we crossed the mountains, we were on the verge of death from the cold and starvation. Volka and his people nursed us back to health. In return, we would like to use our power to aid the Nordic people."

"Power?" Frieda asked.

"Yes." Armand extended his hand and held it palm up. A black mark encompassed his palm as if his hand had been pierced and all that remained was an inky emptiness. "I am an Oathmaker. I can bind people to their words, giving them strength and power. Viessa can command the unseen. And Peder is an exceptional fighter."

"What brought you across the mountains?" Gurmund asked. "Are you from Kerre?"

"Kerre? No. We are from the northwest, near Everin."

"Everin? There is nothing there except for vast forests and remnants of the land bridge from the beyond."

"Yes. That is why little is known of our existence. It has been a secret all these years. However lean winters and dry summers have led some of us to seek a home elsewhere."

Gurmund sat back and crossed his arms. "So why did you cross the mountains and come here? The land of Kerre would have been closer and provided you with more than we can."

Armand's face grew hard. "That we cannot say."

Gurmund stared intently at the man but could read nothing on his face. If he knew any better, he would say these three were running from something.

"We feel for your people," Armand continued. "On our own, my companions and I could do nothing for ourselves except leave our land behind. But if our people had possessed a population like your country, we might have been able to stay in our homeland and found a way to thrive."

"So you three are the only ones left of your kind?"

"No. We are scattered across the Lands, but there are few of us. Hardly enough to fill a city. Certainly not enough to provide for ourselves. We came here hoping to become part of your people. And we offer what we have: our power."

"Explain how your power would help us," Adrian said.

Armand turned toward the young leader and smiled. "We would make your people powerful. The oathbinding I provide not only binds people to their vows, but also gives them superior strength to fulfill their vows. Under the binding, your warriors would be twice the fighters they are now. And my companions can help subdue your enemies."

"And you would lend us your power because you want to help us?"

"Yes. By helping you, we would be helping ourselves. We would be paying back the debt we owe to the Wolf Clan and securing new allies. Perhaps even our new people, if you would accept us."

The room grew quiet as those gathered sat silently around the fire. Bodin finally spoke up. "Your power is most impressive, *if* what you are saying is true."

"Then let us show you. Gather a group of your best warriors. I will bind them with my power, then let them fight. You will see that what we offer will guarantee you victory over the south."

"What do you think?" Adrian glanced around at the clan leaders.

"I think we should at least see what this power does," Bodin said.

"I agree," Frieda responded.

"You know my answer," Volka said. "I've known about their abilities for months. With these three, we would be unstoppable."

"Gurmund?" Adrian asked.

Everything inside Gurmund was shouting for them to run from these beings. Something was there, something he could not see but could feel from his many years of living, that told him not to put their lives into the hands of these strangers. But as he studied those around him, the others appeared to be watching Armand attentively. Almost hungrily. Without proof, he was only one voice.

Gurmund let out a long breath. "I have lived through many winters, more than anyone else here. And in that time I've seen and heard many things. I believe the Nordic people should fight under their own power, and only if it comes to that."

Adrian folded his arms. "Then it is four to one. Let us see this demonstration of power in the arena. Each clan will provide four warriors. Then we can decide if there is an alliance to be made."

The others agreed, even Bodin, which surprised Gurmund. He finally nodded as well.

As the meeting finished, Gurmund headed for the door. He needed time to think, away from the other clan leaders and these strange visitors. Maybe the upcoming display would not be convincing and he had nothing to fear, but he doubted it. His grandmother's tales were full of the eerie power these beings possessed. Power that could end wars, bring peace, and heal nations. But that same power could start wars and annihilate entire civilizations. And he wasn't convinced Armand was interested in peace. In fact—he glanced back at the council hall—it almost felt like Armand had been controlling the room like heady incense.

That thought sent another shiver down his back, and Gurmund hurried away.

If he really wanted to stop them, he would need to speak to the other leaders privately, away from Armand. Power or no power, the Nordic people should stand on their own. He let out a long breath. *Why do I feel like we are making a pact with Morrud himself?*

12

Brighid entered the house with the black door.

Located at the end of the street near the walls of Ragnbork, it appeared like any other hovel in the clanless district: small, dirty, and unkempt. The inside was no different. Furs covered a bed in the corner, a firepit filled the middle of the room, and a cupboard held a handful of cracked mugs and wooden plates. The first time she arrived three months ago, she had been initially unimpressed with the place. How could an eljun of this size exist here? That was before she learned of the false door beside the cupboard.

She found the indent in the wood, placed her fingers inside, and pushed the door to the side, exposing a tiny second room. There were no windows in this room. Instead, fre stones, mined from the Ari Mountains, cast their unending blue light from where they hung on the walls, illuminating the area. A narrow staircase stood to her right, leading down into caverns below.

As she descended the stairs, voices echoed along the stone walls. Over thousands of years, layers of Ragnbork were buried as the city grew, leaving behind ancient dens and alcoves beneath the streets. This was where the eljun of Roldar resided. They were about 50 now in number, and twice the size of any other eljun. All were young, restless, and clanless.

At the bottom, a muscular Nordic greeted her.

"Brighid," he said in a deep voice.

"Johan," she replied. She passed him and followed the narrow corridor. At first, the cramped spaces of this underground dwelling made her uncomfortable, and she wasn't sure how the larger members could stand the tight enclosures. If it wasn't for the thin shafts that let in fresh air, she would have left that first day.

She passed by one and took in a deep breath, then continued. There were a dozen small rooms used for sleeping, a storage room, training room, and meeting room, all jutting out from the main chamber.

As she entered the main chamber, one of the eljuns motioned to Brighid. "Roldar's been asking for you." She pointed toward the one sleeping room set aside for the leader. Metal clanks and a yell came from the training room, and a savory scent drifted from the firepit nearby. Three eljuns sat around the firepit, speaking in low voices.

Brighid's heart sank. She hated meeting with Roldar alone.

She crossed the room and moved back the deerskin door.

Roldar's room was like everyone else's with a pile of furs and worn blankets in the corner. The only difference was he didn't have to share his space. That, and a small private firepit for warmth, a thick table and chairs and candles for light instead of the blue fre stones. He looked up from the table, where various mugs held down a map, and frowned.

"Where have you been?"

"Personal business."

"There is no personal business in my eljun."

Brighid stiffened. "Visiting my mother."

He huffed. "Your mother is dead."

She clenched her hands. Yes, Elphsaba had been dead for almost a year, but she still felt her absence as keenly as she had that first day. "It is the Nordic way to remember the dead." Today had been especially painful, so she had left the city early that morning to visit the hills where she had let Elphsaba's ashes go.

"You never asked."

Brighid glared back. "I didn't realize I needed to ask."

"Every eljun of mine comes under my protection. How can I take care of you if I don't know where you go?"

She stared back. She didn't care about how Roldar felt. She was here for one reason: survival. He provided protection and food. She'd joined because he said he wanted her skills as a fighter. But lately he had been hinting at more . . .

He came around the table. "It worries me when you disappear." He spoke softly and reached for one of the braids that hung over her shoulder.

She stepped back and out of reach. "Tell me why you wanted to see me."

His face darkened. She shivered inside but didn't show any external fear. He was becoming more daring.

He relaxed a moment later and rested against the edge of the table. She wasn't fooled. He was still simmering inside. "We have our first big job. And it's a well-paying job, one that will set us ahead. The mining guild has secretly asked us to visit the blacksmith Havard in the Stag District. Apparently the man has not been going through the guild for his supplies. They already sent him a notice, but he's chosen not to listen."

"Stag District? We are expanding beyond the clanless district?"

"Yes. There are those who are starting to realize we have power, and unlike the clans, we can do things they cannot. We will head there tonight and deliver their message. Nothing too rough, just enough to bring him back to his senses."

Bile filled her throat. It was one thing to fight other eljuns over what meager provisions there were in Ragnbork, and another to hurt a hard-working Nordic. When had she slipped into the role of a thug? What would Elphsaba think of her?

She mentally shook her head. She couldn't go there. Things had changed. "Who's going?"

"Me, Johan, Durant, and you."

Brighid ticked off the names in her head. Roldar as the leader and mouthpiece, Johan and Durant as a show of strength, and her.

"What time?"

"Two hours after dusk. Meet at the foot of the stairs."

She acknowledged the time and left.

Night came and the four of them left under the cover of darkness. Under the tutelage of Roldar, she had learned how to blend in with the shadows, move silently along the streets, and take what she needed.

The moonlight lit their way. As they approached the smithy, she sensed the presence of others. Did Havard know they were coming, and had he prepared for a fight?

Roldar reached the door and pressed down on the latch. The door opened without a sound.

"I was wondering if someone would come." A gruff voice spoke from within the doorway.

That answered her question. Roldar didn't reply. Instead, he led them through the opening. The coals glowed red from the forge, the only light inside the large room. The anvil stood near the forge, and various hammers and tools hung above a workbench near a trench of water.

Havard waited next to the anvil with his arms crossed. His thick rye-colored beard hung down to his chest, and firelight reflected across his eyes. Barely visible, two other men stood against the wall behind him.

Roldar stepped into the light. "If you know why we are here, then let's do this the easy way. You agree to go back to using the mining guild's resources, and we leave."

Havard glared back. "I never agreed to be supplied by the guild. A man should have the ability to choose for himself and his business where he gets his materials, not be coerced by the guilds. It is dishonorable that the mining guild would stoop to hiring a bunch of clanless thugs to get their way."

Brighid bristled at his words. She might have felt sympathy for him earlier, but now that was gone. They were clanless thugs because of people like him who withheld support and necessities from those beneath them.

Roldar didn't react. "I'm just here on their behalf. Either you agree or we find a way to make you agree."

The two shadowed figures stepped forward. Johan and Durant flanked Roldar.

Havard crossed his arms. "You'll have to make me."

"So be it."

The two sides clashed.

Brighid joined on Durant's side. She grabbed his opponent's arm and twisted it while waiting for the red haze to take over, but it never came, and she barely held the man.

He swung back and sent her flying into the workbench. Her hip slammed into the edge, and pain blossomed across her side. That would leave a bruise.

She went into the fray again but was thrown seconds later. A trickle of fear entered the back of her mind. Where was the red haze? That fighting spirit that usually guided her movements and filled her with intense energy and strength. Tonight she felt empty.

Durant subdued his man, and Johan was locked in a hand-to-hand grapple.

Roldar peered over his shoulder. "Brighid, help me!" Then he drove a fist toward Havard's face. The man lifted his arms to block, and Brighid followed with a kick to his side. Her foot smacked his middle. It felt like she had kicked a stone wall.

Fear turned into a torrent. What was wrong with her? She should have been able to crush his side. She went for another kick. This time, her foot crumpled against his solid body, causing her to cry out.

Roldar cursed and pummeled the man as hard as he could. Brighid took a step back, staring at her palms. Was her power gone?

Johan's opponent fell in a dead heap. "Johan, help me," Roldar said through gritted teeth. Johan gripped one of Havard's arms. Durant went for the other. Now secured, Roldar stepped back, panting. He wiped his face and stared at Havard.

"Now, will you agree to work with the mining guild, or do we need to take a life?"

Havard stared back with a stony face.

"Brighid, take out your dagger."

Blood pounded in her head. *What?*

"Now."

Without thinking, she reached for the dagger she carried at her side. She undid the leather loop and pulled it out.

"Kill the man on my left."

Ringing filled her ears as she glimpsed the prone figure on the ground. She took a step forward. Her body felt like she had plunged into an ice-covered river. The ringing grew louder. She knelt down, dagger in hand. Her heart thudded madly.

"Do it."

She gripped the man's hair and hauled his head up. He was out cold. She couldn't breathe, couldn't see. Was she really going to do what Roldar ordered her to do? It was one thing to fight, and another to take a man's life—something she had never done before. She brought the dagger toward the right side of his Adam's apple. Just as the tip touched his skin, Havard yelled, "Stop!"

Brighid paused. A tiny prick of blood appeared at the point of her dagger.

"Don't kill him!"

"Will you comply?" Roldar asked.

"I . . . I . . ." Havard's head dropped in defeat. "Yes. I will do what the mining guild asked."

"Good." Roldar stepped back. "I will let them know. But we will be watching. And the moment you break your word, a life will be taken. Do you understand?"

"I do. I vow on my life! Just have her back away from him."

Roldar jerked his head. "Go ahead, Brighid."

Brighid stepped back and stood, her eyes still pinned on the unconscious man.

"Johan, Durant, our work here is done."

The two Nordics stepped away cautiously, ready to pounce if Havard did anything. He massaged his arm as he watched them go.

Roldar cast one last glance at Havard. "We're done here. Make sure you fulfill your vow."

Havard didn't answer.

Roldar turned and headed for the door. Brighid caught up with Durant and Johan, and the three of them followed him outside the smithy.

The walk back to their base was silent. Brighid felt numb. She hadn't been able to fight. And then Roldar told her to—

She clenched her hands against the shudder that rippled through her body. Would she have done it? She could see the man's neck in her mind, red in the forge's light. And the even darker spot of blood when her dagger pricked his skin.

If Elphsaba had seen her tonight . . .

She shook her head vigorously and willed the hot tears forming to remain unshed. Elphsaba never knew the world Brighid lived in now. A world on the edge of life or death. But—

Her head shot up. One thing hadn't happened tonight. She hadn't felt death. She never felt its cold presence or its long, reaching claws. But if that man was going to die, she should have felt it, right? Or was it because the man was never really in any danger from her?

She wasn't sure about that. Deep down, she wasn't sure what she would have done. A numbness had stolen over her, and she replayed the feeling of the dagger, its edge along his jugular.

Was it possible death didn't make its presence known . . . when death was delivered by her own hand?

Roldar rounded on Brighid once they were back at the base and inside his room. "What was that about?"

"What do you mean?"

"You could barely land a kick or move a man. That's not the fighter I know. You are savage; you are brutal. Tonight? You were pathetic."

"I don't know!" She crossed her arms and gripped her elbows. "I don't know why I wasn't able to fight."

He stepped toward her and pointed a finger at her chest. "Then you better figure out why. I didn't bring you into my eljun out of pity. Everybody here serves a purpose. If you can't fight"—his eyes took on smoldering darkness—"then you can serve in another way."

A fire erupted inside her soul. The same one that overtook her before she fought. The red haze. She barely realized she was reaching for her dagger when her senses came to. Luckily Roldar had turned toward the table and never saw her movement. She blinked. Why now? Why did this intense feeling flood her now, sending adrenaline buzzing across her limbs? Her fingers trembled as she placed her arms down at her sides. Her heart still pumped with heavy beats, each one urging her to leap upon the man and rip him apart.

Roldar didn't seem to notice as he looked up from his desk. "Figure it out. You're dismissed."

Brighid spun around and placed a trembling fist to her heart, willing the bloodlust to settle. She stumbled into the main chamber and turned right toward one of the smaller rooms where her bed and small chest were located.

What was this thing inside of her? This . . . fight? What made it rise? What made it ignite?

The blue light from the fre stones illuminated the enclosure. Three other women were already asleep on their piles of fur and blankets. Brighid passed them, then fell across her own makeshift bed next to the cave wall. She curled into a ball on her side. The heat in her heart turned to an aching pain. "Elphsaba," she whispered. "What am I? What is wrong with me?"

She buried her head inside the ragged blanket to muffle her sobs. Truth be told, Elphsaba would be displeased she had joined an eljun. "But what was I supposed to do? Die of hunger?"

And what if Roldar asks more of you? Will you give everything to him?

Brighid swallowed hard. How far would she compromise to live?

13

"Did you see the news?" one of the newer eljun recruits, a spritely boy no older than fifteen, asked. A handful of people sat near the firepit in the main chamber, quietly downing the grey gruel that passed as food. Brighid found a small chewy piece in hers and grimaced as she swallowed it quickly. She didn't want to think about what it was.

"No." Johan looked up from his bowl.

"I was out early this morning, and there are notices posted everywhere."

"What did they say?" one of the women asked.

The boy hesitated. Brighid watched, her gruel growing cold in her bowl. "They said there is to be a competition in the arena. In three days."

"You can read?" Johan asked.

"Yes," he replied timidly. Almost everyone here was uneducated. Reading, writing, those were foreign skills. "There were illustrations too. With the runes for *fight* and *strength* and *victory.*"

"So what?" another person asked nearby. "There are always competitions between the clans in the arena. Why would this one be special?"

"Because the clanless are invited!"

A few more heads came up. Brighid found herself leaning in to listen.

"Why would the clanless be invited?" someone murmured.

"The notice said the clans are forming a vast company, and the winners of the competition will be allowed admittance, no matter status, clan, or family. All are invited."

"You mean it wouldn't matter if we are clanless?"

The boy shrugged. "That's what the notice says."

The man next to Brighid frowned. "Why are the clans forming a company?"

"War," Johan said, then took another sip of his gruel.

"War?" the man asked, echoing the same thought in Brighid's mind.

"It was inevitable. The south has been pushing against our boundaries for years, stealing our food, our homes, and leaving us to starve. I'm sure I'm not the only one here who came to Ragnbork because of that."

A few heads bobbed up and down. Brighid continued to watch the conversation without engaging.

"But this is new." Johan glanced up. "The clans have never invited the clanless to join."

"Humph." An older man in the back stood with his bowl in hand. "They just want to use us."

"I don't know." The boy scratched the back of his head. "I think they are looking for warriors, people who can fight."

"And there are more clanless now than ever," Johan said. "Which means potential gifted fighters they know nothing about. Our eljun can attest to that. Almost everyone here can fight." The others murmured in agreement. "The clans would be foolish not to search the clanless and find what warriors are hidden. This competition is probably their way of finding those fighters."

"But is it worth it?" the man next to Brighid asked.

"If it means elevating my status and being considered equal with a clan member, then I would be willing," Johan said.

Something burgeoned inside of her. Was there a way to escape the eljun and live? Even more, be considered equal with a clan member?

"You would go to war?" one of the women asked.

"Yes."

The woman continued, "And what happens if you lose in the arena? Is it a fight to the death?"

Johan shrugged. "I don't know."

The boy shook his head. "I don't know either."

Brighid finally spoke up. "Can women participate?"

The boy turned her way. "As far as I could tell, everyone is invited."

Excited murmurs broke out around the firepit. Brighid sat back, her mind turning over this new information. An opportunity to leave this life behind. Become something more. But did she have what it would take to win in the arena? She looked at her hand. Could she summon the red haze and fight?

Johan walked past her as he headed toward the back to drop off his bowl. He was a muscular man. He had the strength and body of a fighter. Of course the clans would want someone like him. But what about her?

She made a fist. If she could fight with the red haze, she had a chance. But that meant figuring out why and how it worked.

The news about the upcoming competition spread across the clanless district. A light that had been absent from people's eyes for so long now shone brightly in every gaze. Along the streets and in doorways, people chattered about the chance to fight and prove themselves. Men. Women. Young. Even the elderly. No more living in squalor, no more hunger.

Hope burned in the hearts of these Nordic people.

Brighid arrived at the black door with purpose that evening. Her own spirit was ablaze with a fire she realized had been quenched when she first arrived in Ragnbork with Elphsaba. Scrapping by with barely any food or shelter had dimmed her life. And the eljun, although providing a means to survive, was also a trap with Roldar slowly placing a noose around her neck, ensnaring her until she finally laid down everything and became his.

Not anymore.

She was a true Nordic daughter, and now she would prove it with the fighting spirit of her ancestors.

"I'm leaving, Elphsaba," she whispered as she opened the door.

"I'm going to forge my own way in life. You'll see." She paused and brushed the sun tattoo around her eye. "I'll make you proud."

As she descended the stairs, an unease fell over her. Something felt off. The excitement from moments ago dissipated. With her senses heightened, she entered the main chamber.

The area was empty.

That wasn't uncommon at this time of day. The den served more as a safe place to sleep at night or a fire to warm oneself. And today, everyone was out on the streets.

Brighid crossed the room toward the corridor on the other side. Usually she liked it when the underground was empty and silence filled the place, but tonight it felt heavy, and the blue fre lights that lined the hall were cold and harsh.

At the end of the corridor, she pushed the deerskin door aside and entered the sleeping area. As she approached her own bedding across the room, a voice came from the shadows.

"I've been waiting for you."

Brighid spun around, her heart suddenly thudding inside her chest. "Roldar, you scared me."

He stepped near the fre stone imbedded in the wall. The blue light made his otherwise handsome face appear severe. "Where were you today?"

She let out her breath. She didn't want to argue with him again. "I spent the day outside. I needed to clear my head." Why was he here? He usually spoke to her in his own room.

"I took all of you in. I built a place for those who had no clan. I gave this eljun purpose. So why in *Morrud's* name is everyone leaving me?" He slammed the side of the doorway with his fist, then lifted a wooden tankard to his mouth and took a long drink. "At least you came back."

A scattering of thoughts clicked into place. Roldar believed the eljun was falling apart. People were already leaving for the competition. Roldar was drunk. And he was blocking the only way out. She would need to tread lightly if she wanted to escape.

"Yes, I'm here." She had come to collect her belongings, but he didn't need to know that. She made a show of shuffling her blanket across the furs.

"So where were you today?"

She watched him take another swig of whatever was in the tankard. Was this why the main chamber was empty? Did the others know Roldar was in a foul mood and were avoiding him?

"Like I said, walking around the city," she replied.

"Walking around, eh? You always did come and go as you pleased." He laughed, but it wasn't a pleasant sound. Brighid lifted the lid of the small box at the foot of her bed. She withdrew a few silver coins she had hidden in the corner while her mind worked for a way out. After stuffing them into a small pouch around her neck, she turned. She would leave the rest of her belongings, along with furs and blankets behind. What was more important now was getting away.

Roldar watched as she walked toward him. She kept her back straight and exuded a boldness she didn't currently feel.

"Where do you think you're going?" As she drew closer, the strong scent of honey mead rolled off him. Her heart beat faster. She'd seen him drunk once before, and it wasn't a pretty sight.

"To find food. I haven't eaten all day." It wasn't a lie, nor was it the full truth.

"Didn't I tell you before not to leave without my permission?"

She didn't answer. Instead, she started around him. As she stepped beside him, he turned and gripped her arm. "Don't go."

"I said I was going to find food."

"Food can wait."

She felt like invisible fingers were squeezing her throat shut. *Breathe, Brighid. Breathe.* She took in a deep breath and looked at him. "What do you want, Roldar?" She was thankful her voice didn't quiver.

"Want?" He gave her a lopsided grin but never let go of her arm. "That's an interesting word. *Want.* Let me tell you something. Yes, I wanted your fighting skills the moment I saw them that first time. You were a sight to see, the way you moved, the way you overpowered those around you. Almost like a berserker in a female body. But even more"—he yanked her to his chest—"I've always wanted you."

Before she could scream, he crushed his mouth over hers. She tried to jerk away, but he held her arm with a viselike grip. She gasped for air, and her heartbeat thrashed inside her ears.

This wasn't happening. *This wasn't happening.*

You won't take me!

Her mind snapped, and her vision went red. In that moment, she felt death enter the room, eager, hungry. And for the first time, it didn't scare her. Nothing did. She twisted her arm out of his grip and heard his wrist crack. She kneed his groin while reaching for her dagger.

He dropped to his knees with a loud groan, and the tankard crashed, then rolled away. In one movement, she jerked his head back and held her dagger poised along the base of his neck.

"You will never, ever touch me." Her body fluctuated between the heat of the fight and the chill of death that clung to her, urging her to finish him. She tightened the grip on her dagger as he stared up at her with wide, sober eyes.

Do it, death whispered.

She paused. No. She would not give into death. "I am going to walk out, and you will not follow me."

She slowly drew her dagger away but kept her fingers threaded through his hair, twisting his head as she walked around him. Once she reached the doorway, she spoke to him one more time. "I'm leaving now."

She let go of his head and kept her dagger pointed at him as she backed out into the corridor. He never turned around. She continued along the passage, her entire being focused on Roldar kneeling in the doorway. When she reached the main chamber, she spun around and ran across the room, up the stairs, and out into the cold night air.

She put her dagger away, drew her cloak closed around her body, and headed for the city wall. She would sleep there tonight, then make her way to the Elding Citadel, where the competition would be held. She would fight. After all, that was the sum of her entire being. Fighting. Fighting for food. Fighting others.

Fighting to live.

14

Brighid stood along the outer edges of the crowd gathered along the bottom steps of the Elding Citadel two days later. Dark clouds hung over Ragnbork, threatening to cover the city in a spring snow.

To the right of the citadel was a two-story round structure, double the size of the citadel and the largest building in Ragnbork. This was the arena, the place where the clans proved their strength and valor. And today it would decide who was worthy among the clanless.

The symbols of the five clans were etched along the thick wooden beams that reinforced both buildings: the eagle, the wolf, the bear, the stag, and the owl. The pillars that supported Nordica and led her people. Brighid knew very little of the clans and what they provided for her country. In her eyes, and the eyes of those gathered, their symbols meant status and acceptance, and a chance to rise above the low station of clanless.

She spotted a few others from Roldar's eljun among the crowd. Johan stood near the double doors to the arena. Durant was with him. Both were tall, burly men. No doubt they would pass. There were even a few other women in the crowd. One in particular caught her attention, a woman no bigger than herself with fiery red hair swept up in a dozen braids and the rune for strength tattooed across her upper arm. For a brief moment, Brighid wondered who the mark was for. A fallen father? Brother? Perhaps a lover?

She snorted at that last thought. She couldn't imagine having a lover. Roldar's face flashed across her mind, and her jaw tightened. Never.

A few flakes fell and the crowd grew restless. Brighid gazed at the massive doors ahead. How would the competition be handled? Would it be an all-out fight? One-on-one battle? Would there be weapons? Or would it be by hand?

And how would she get the red haze to trigger?

That's all I need to do, she thought, taking in a deep cleansing breath. *Embrace the red haze and let my body fight.* In that state, she might even be able to take on Johan himself. She had yet to find out the limits to her unique fighting ability.

Snowflakes appeared. Brighid pulled her hood up over her head. Just as her fingers grew cold, a horn blew above the crowd from the citadel balcony.

Brighid glanced up. A handful of Nordics stood along the balcony, dressed in fur-lined cloaks and finery. She'd never seen them before, but she knew immediately they were the hjars of the Nordic clans.

After the horn finished, the youngest-looking hjar—a brawny man with shoulder-length golden hair and matching beard—approached the railing and raised his hand. A hush spread across the crowd.

"Hail, sons and daughters of the north. I am Hjar Adrian of the Eagle Clan, and I greet you. Today is your chance to prove yourself. If you succeed, you will be granted a rank among the clans and will join our company. May the strength of mountains be with you."

Adrian stepped back, and another man appeared in his place. He appeared slightly older, with long dark hair and a Mark of Remembrance across one eye. His face held a rugged appearance, and the black fur and leather attire accented this. A timber wolf stood on either side of him like twin sentries.

"I am Volka of the Wolf Clan, and I will explain today's trials."

The competition would be held in the three rings inside the arena. Weapons were available from the racks inside, blunted so as not to kill. Five minutes to fight. The hjars and their skals would watch and judge.

Brighid let her breath out with a slow whoosh after Volka finished. "I can do this," she whispered as the crowd shifted toward the arena doors. Her fingers tingled, and her heart pulsed rapidly.

The doors slowly opened, and the crowd surged forward. "Stand along the perimeter," shouted one of the guards near the doorway.

"Wait to be called to the ring," shouted another.

As she drew near, another guard raised his halberd. "If you are caught fighting before you are called, you will be cast out. No exceptions."

Brighid bypassed him and entered. An array of windows lined the upper half of the walls. A balcony stood to the left where the arena connected with the citadel. Lit torches lined the stone walls. A wooden walkway about ten feet wide encircled the area with gaps that allowed entry into the fighting space below.

The crowd parted, one half lining the right side, the other the left. Brighid went right. She spotted the fiery redhead nearby, a fierce grin on the woman's face. She felt that same passionate spirit rising in her own soul.

Halfway around the circle, she stopped. From here, she could see both the balcony where the hjars were gathering and the five white circles painted across the bare ground in the middle of the massive room. She spotted the racks of weapons farther to her right. Swords, axes, halberds, and a couple small round shields.

A cacophony of voices began to fill the arena until a mighty roar echoed throughout the room. Then a chant started. "Til Val! Til Val! Til Val!"

Brighid joined in. They stomped and clapped after each word until it felt like the entire building was shaking. Yes, they were clanless, but at this moment, it didn't matter. They were also Nordics. And the blood of their fighting ancestors flowed through their veins, that same spirit that allowed them to conquer the north over a thousand years ago, to live in a savage land, to fight the deep winters and survive when no others could.

Hjar Adrian came to the front of the balcony inside the arena and raised his hand. It took a couple minutes for the crowd to quiet down. "Our warriors are spread across the room. They will direct you to a circle when it is time. You have one minute to choose between the weapons available, or you may fight barehanded. When the horn blows, the fight will begin in each circle. Fight with honor, fight like a Nordic. If you step out of your ring, you lose. When the horn blows again, your time is done. Exit the ring. If you fail to exit, you will forfeit and be expelled from the arena. Winning does not mean a place in the new company, losing does not mean all is lost."

He peered across the crowd, his face serious. "We are looking for warriors who will fight for Nordica. This is your chance to rise above and honor your ancestors. So fight as such. And we will be watching." He raised his hand again, then brought it down in a sudden slash. "Let the trials begin!"

The arena boomed with shouts as designated clan warriors named the first to compete. Brighid watched from her position as the first fighters chose weapons and entered the ring. The horns blew and the fights started.

The first set of combatants didn't have much to show. There was a lot of clashing of swords and shields, and one used a halberd but didn't have much control. The contenders around the arena yelled and jeered at the fighters. One received a blow to the face, and blood spurted from his nose. The horns sounded five minutes later, and the first ten walked away from the rings.

Brighid shook her head. In her opinion, there wasn't a warrior among the first batch.

The clan warriors chose ten more, and another round began.

Brighid peered up at the balcony again. Adrian stood by an older man with silver hair that brushed along his ears and a matching beard. The two seemed to be speaking quietly to each other, like a mentor and his apprentice.

Next to them was the only woman on the balcony, a stout woman with a piercing gaze and arms folded across her chest as she watched the fights below. Her entire being exuded strength and endurance.

Alone in the shadows stood a tall thin man with dark circles around his eyes and long auburn hair and beard. An owl perched on his shoulder. He watched the fight with the same intensity as the woman.

On the other side was the Wolf Clan hjar, Volka, with three strangers, all covered in dark cloaks with their hoods pulled over their heads. Only the lower parts of their faces were exposed. Brighid frowned. If there were five clans, who were the three strangers? Before she could think more on that, a shout came from the rings.

She turned her attention back to the fights. One fighter had his opponent pinned from behind and held a dagger to his throat as he yelled something she couldn't hear. Probably for his opponent to yield. The man hesitated. Everyone could see he didn't want to surrender. The victor yelled again, and the man finally raised his hand indicating defeat. Their fight ended before the horn sounded.

Minutes later, the horns ended the other fights. Ten more were chosen from the crowd. Brighid perked up. Both the fiery redhead and Johan were chosen for two different fights. This would be interesting.

The woman chose a sword, and Johan indicated he would fight barehanded. His opponent indicated he would do so as well. The horn blew.

Brighid watched Johan first. Even though he was a big man, he was fast. He and his challenger clashed like two bucks and locked forearms. They stood there for a moment, staring at each other while their bodies strained against the strength of the other, then Johan let out a shout and with a great heave sent his opponent backward.

Before Johan could take advantage of the man's broken stance, his opponent caught himself, then lunged forward, and they locked arms again.

Brighid glanced over to the ring where the redhead fought with a sword and shield. She held her own against a lanky young man. His range was longer, but she was faster and darted in and out of his reach until she landed a jab to his middle. He stumbled back and pressed a palm to the area. If the sword had been real, he'd have a gaping wound. Instead, the blunted wooden edge would leave only a bad bruise.

Brighid continued to watch the woman's fight with interest, her gaze switching to the rack of weapons for a moment. What weapon would she choose? She had never used one before, but as her eyes lingered over the options, the small round shield called to her. She could picture herself gripping it with her left hand and wielding a sword with her right. Almost like a ghost memory.

The horn rang a couple minutes later. Johan had his opponent pinned in his ring, and the redhead was the clear winner in the other, with her sword raised in the air and her grin pointed at the crowd as she slowly turned.

"You're up," a man said to Brighid. She glanced over to find one of the clan warriors pointing at her. "Third ring."

Her heart jolted at his words. This was it.

With adrenaline racing through her limbs, Brighid made her way to the weapons rack. She grabbed the small round shield and sword beside it. The moment she touched the two, she knew they were the right weapons for her. They molded into her grip as if an extension of her body. She let out a long breath and turned.

Excitement and fear waged war across her mind and body. Like fire and ice. She moved through the crowd toward the gap where she could step down into the arena. As she descended the couple of stairs to the packed ground, she spotted a figure approaching her from the other side. Both headed for the same ring.

She reached the painted circle, paused, and looked up. Her heart stopped and her entire body froze as if she had plunged into an icy lake.

There, on the other side of the circle, stood Roldar.

15

What was he doing here? Was he here to fight? But why? Had everyone left the eljun?

Roldar stared at her from across the ring, then his lips stretched into a wicked grin. He had chosen a sword, which he held with both hands. "So it has come to this." He entered the circle. "We will fight each other. Seems fitting, considering how you left me."

Brighid clutched the shield to her chest and stepped forward. "A better opportunity came. So I took it. Isn't that how life works?"

He scowled. "But what of loyalty? Of devotion?"

"What of honor? Of respect? You showed your true colors the other night. I joined you as a fighter, but you wanted more."

He began to move around the ring. "I gave you purpose. A family, a home. And you crushed my goodwill beneath your feet."

Goodwill? He'd used her. And she'd let herself be used. She wouldn't deny that. It was that or die in the bitter cold. Brighid pressed her lips tight and countered his steps. Now she had a choice. She tightened the grip on her sword. She would win this fight.

A horn blew across the arena.

Roldar moved first.

Brighid countered him with the shield, then followed with a swing from her sword. How strange. She had never used either weapon, and yet they felt familiar and natural.

Roldar bounced back and circled her again.

Brighid held her sword and shield before her body.

He moved in again with the blade. She countered.

"You think you can beat me?" he taunted as he moved around her. "Your fighting skills might be impressive, but I'm still stronger."

Before she could respond, he slashed forward and hit her shield. And hit it again and again.

Each blow ricocheted through her arm. In past encounters, she hardly remembered fighting, only the red haze and her opponents on the ground afterward. But there was no red haze at this moment. Just Roldar beating her shield until she fell to one knee.

She slashed out with her own sword, sending him bounding back.

Brighid jumped to her feet. A trickle of fear appeared in the back of her mind. Right now, Roldar had the upper hand. It didn't matter if she could use the weapons if she couldn't overpower him. She needed the red haze for that. But nothing came. Just like that night with the blacksmith.

No.

She planted her feet and raised her shield.

I will not go down.

She steadied her blade.

I will fight. I will not go back.

She drove forward. Roldar swung, but she caught his sword on her shield and sent it sliding while she thrust forward. This time she caught him in the chest. If the blade had been sharp, it would have slashed through his tunic. Instead, it struck his chest, and she heard the whoosh of his breath as he staggered back. It wasn't her red-haze strength, but there was power behind it this time. Her power.

He wheezed out a breath and glared. "Is that all you can do?" He spat on the dirt. "Pathetic. Just like that night." He raised his sword, then rushed forward.

Brighid tried to sidestep, but there wasn't time. She barely placed the shield between them when his sword smashed into her, shoving her across the ring. He kept after her, delivering blow after blow until her entire arm felt numb. Somewhere in the back of her head, she was surprised he hadn't broken her wrist.

From the corner of her eye, she realized she was almost at the edge of the ring. Was that his plan? To disqualify her?

Sweat trickled down her face and stung her eyes.

She took another step back. One more and she would be out of the ring.

Roldar pressed his sword down across her shield and leaned over her. "You are nothing," he whispered as he gazed at her with ferocity. "Nothing. And I will crush you in front of this crowd, and you will never rise again."

His mass and sword bore down until her knees shuddered under the weight. Willpower alone was holding her in place. But it was cracking and then she would fall.

Her vision narrowed until all she could see was Roldar's face. Adrenaline raced through her body like the rapids of a river. No longer was she in the fighting ring. She was standing on a ledge. One step back, one false move, and she would plummet to her death.

That . . . that couldn't happen. This was all she had left.

She gritted her teeth and breathed in through her nose. *I won't. Go. Down!*

Her body exploded into action as her vision went red. Overwhelming strength filled her, guiding her, moving her. She barely saw Roldar now. She barely saw anyone. There was only one sound, the sound of a mighty wind in her ears as she struck his sword with her shield and thrust with her own blade.

Every time he lifted his sword, she hit it away or met it with her own. She pushed him back, her movements a whirlwind of arms and weapons.

At one point, she caught him in the face, leaving a scarlet welt along his cheek. But it still wasn't enough. There was no stopping the red haze now. It wouldn't end until Roldar was on the ground.

She heard him swear and pant with heavy breaths. Over and over she brought her sword down, just as he had done to her seconds ago. The arena filled with the sound of roaring, and she couldn't tell if it was the blood pounding in her head or the crowd around her.

Then Roldar trapped her sword with his own, leaving only her shield free. Without thinking, Brighid planted her feet and drove her shield up beneath his chin.

His face snapped back with a loud crack. He staggered for a couple of steps, then collapsed to the ground.

In that moment, she felt it. The chilling rush of death.

Brighid whipped her head around. Where? Where was it? Who was dying?

She heard Roldar gurgling. With horror, she turned her gaze back to his prone form. He wheezed and coughed. Blood shot out across the dirt. He clawed at his throat, then the ground. Each breath was a high-pitched whistle, rapid, then it slowed.

Invisible, death flew past her and embraced Roldar. As she watched, his eyes grew dim until the light went out. The crowd, boisterous at first, quieted as if sensing the dark presence in the ring.

A horn sounded and the other fights ceased.

Brighid stood within the circle, Roldar dead at her feet. The sword and shield grew slack in her hands as numbness encompassed her body. A couple of guards entered the ring, and one knelt down by Roldar.

"Dead." He stood, first glancing at Brighid, then at the balcony where the clan leaders stood. "The contestant is dead," he shouted. "By blunt blow. Ruling is accidental."

The crowd started to speak while Brighid stared at Roldar. It wasn't possible. She couldn't have done that. It was just a fight. To show her strength. To be worthy of something more than her clanless status.

She'd never . . . She couldn't have . . .

"How could a mere woman kill a man with a shield?" someone said nearby.

"Did you see her fight? Like she was possessed!"

"I thought she was clanless. How was she fighting like a Bear Clan berserker?"

The crowd's words wove in and out of the fog that filled her ears and mind.

The guard who had pronounced Roldar dead approached her. "Time to leave the ring. Your fight is over."

Brighid stared at him with dull eyes. Two other guards were already grabbing Roldar under the arms and pulling his body away. She wanted to shout at them and tell them to stop, that he wasn't dead, just unconscious. She wanted him to be unconscious. Because he couldn't be . . .

She twisted around and moved away from the ring.

"Look at her. No emotion," someone said as she walked up the stairs. "A fighter through and through."

"Pity her opponent died, but that's the risk of the ring."

"I can't believe she killed a man with a blunt weapon." Those words were said in awe rather than disgust.

Brighid paused near the back wall, her face furrowed. Wasn't anyone horrified that someone had just died? Her hands began to shake, so she gripped them tight around the sword and shield. Death had visited their presence, and they were in admiration of it. No, they were admiring her. Her! The one who had delivered the deadly blow.

I can't stand this! I need to get out of here, now!

Brighid left her weapons on the rack, then made her way around the arena, staying near the outer wall until she reached the wide doors that led outside. Dozens of eyes followed her, but no one stopped her. The horns sounded behind her as another round of fights started.

"Leaving already?" the guard next to the door asked. He must not have recognized her or known what happened.

"I need some fresh air."

"If you leave, you will miss out on your turn to fight."

"I already fought. I need air."

He paused and must have seen something in her face because a moment later he opened one of the massive doors. Thick white flakes fell fast, and snow was already accumulating across the street. "Knock if you want back in."

Brighid nodded and stumbled out into the cold air. Bile surged up her throat. She fell forward and caught herself on one of the thick wooden pillars that supported the arena, hardly able to stand anymore. She barely felt the cold across her body. At the very edge of her consciousness, death was already fading away, having claimed its victim.

She pressed a hand to her mouth and dropped to her knees. She didn't feel sad. She didn't feel guilt. She didn't feel anything but sick at the thought that by her own hand she had brought forth death.

"I didn't mean to," she whispered. The red haze had never taken a life before. And Roldar . . . "He didn't deserve that," she whispered.

A hand came down across her shoulder.

She started at the touch and jumped to her feet, fists up and ready to fight.

"I came to see how you were doing," Johan said.

"Johan."

"I wanted to ask if you meant to do it, but it's written all over your face."

She shook her head. "No, I didn't. I . . . I lost control." Not that she ever had control when the red haze took over, but she never thought she would kill someone with it. She stared at her palms, imagining them red with blood.

Johan reached over and placed a hand on top of hers. "It's done now. And by all accounts, it was an accident. A powerful blow at just the right angle."

She replayed the last few moments of the fight, how her blood pounded with strength and power, how she slammed the shield upward—

She swallowed and dropped her head. "We had a fight just before I left. He . . . he said and did things that angered me. But I never would have killed him over that."

"I don't think you're that kind of person."

She looked up.

He raised an eyebrow. "However, this won't be the only time you deal death, not if you wish to continue on this path, past the arena and the competition. War is coming, and if you are chosen, you will be a warrior. That means bringing death to our enemies so our people might live."

Brighid nodded. Only now did she start to understand what that meant.

"If this is not the path for you, leave now. Walk away. No one who saw you fight today will think you are a coward."

She swallowed hard. But there was nowhere else to go. The eljun was gone, now that Roldar was dead. And surviving in the clanless district was waiting for death to come in the form of exposure, hunger, or disease. Wherever she looked, death was there, with fangs gleaming and eyes as black as the Abyss. At least in the ring and on the battlefield, she could fight back.

Deep inside, a child version of her was crying. She didn't want to die. She didn't want to cause others to die. But there didn't seem to be a choice. Life was just hard. From the moment of birth until the bitterness of the end. It wasn't fair. What purpose was there in living?

Brighid turned away from Johan and finally cried. She let the nauseating feelings flow from her. But this would be the last time. Once she walked back into the arena, there would be no tears. Not for anyone. Even herself.

16

Gurmund stood with the other hjars, watching the fights below inside the arena. The fighting today was different from the fights that took place over a month ago between the clans' warriors. Those had been a demonstration of Armand's oathmaking power. After a few words, the warriors were indeed more powerful. Perhaps even more than a Bear Clan warrior under the Vilrik.

It had both amazed and terrified him. That kind of power did not belong in the realm of man. But the other clan leaders could see only the possibilities of having an army with the ability to overwhelm the south.

The horn rang across the arena, and another round of fights started in the five rings below.

He crossed his arms and let out a long breath. A few had shown skill, but most of the clanless fighters were average. A particular battle in the farthest ring caught his attention. A woman with a sword and shield was up against a man with a sword. It started out in normal fashion with one opponent stronger than the other. Just as he started to turn away, the crowd began to shout, and he glanced back.

He frowned. The woman fighting now was not the same woman from a minute earlier. Her style was different. No. More than that. Her very essence seemed to have changed. Instead of meeting the man's attacks, she overwhelmed him.

The crowd grew louder.

He leaned forward, narrowing his gaze on the woman, watching her savage moves. If he didn't know better . . .

She planted herself, then slammed her buckler into the man's jaw. In that moment, he knew the outcome. He'd performed the same move many years ago during a fight on the border, leaving a Rylander dead.

Sure enough, the growing silence of the crowd, then the announcement from the guard confirmed it. She had killed her opponent with her shield.

Guards retrieved the body while she stood alone in the ring. Her fight had drawn the attention of all the clan leaders and their guests, Volka in particular. He watched her with the same intensity as his wolf companions, who stood on either side of him.

As she left the ring to return her weapons, Adrian came up to Gurmund and slapped him across the back. "What a fight! Are you sure she isn't one of yours, Gurmund? She fought like a bear."

"No," he said slowly, his gaze still on the woman. "No, she's not."

"Well, she sure was one unbelievable fighter. Wonder where she came from?"

Gurmund wondered that too.

As the horn sounded and a new set of fights commenced, Gurmund made his way to the back and down the stairs. Turning a corner, he approached the doorway to the arena where Tor stood, the captain of the city guards and overseer of this event.

"Captain Tor."

The man turned, then clapped a fist to his chest and bowed his head. "Hjar Gurmund."

"Do you know where that woman was from?"

"Woman?"

"The one who killed her opponent."

"She's clanless, from the clanless district."

"Of course." Gurmund frowned. "But do you know anything more? Have you seen her fight before?"

"No. But I heard she ran with an eljun. And I believe the man she killed was the leader. Given how she responded, I don't think she meant to take his life."

"Is it possible she was under the Vilrik?" Gurmund murmured.

He'd seen enough of his men fight and experienced it himself. But how could a young, clanless woman possess the red haze? Who was she really? A distant relation that departed from the clan generations ago? "Make sure she is placed on the list and summoned back."

"Yes, Hjar Gurmund."

Gurmund turned and headed back up the stairs. He would keep an eye on her. Once he was next to the railing, he looked for the young woman. She was gone. He searched the crowd once more, but she was nowhere to be found. The crowd shouted as another clanless Nordic proved his worth in the rings.

Gurmund leaned against the wood as the horn sounded and a new set of potential warriors entered the arena. Given the crowd from this morning and more gathering outside, the competition would go on for a couple of days. He would have Bard stand in for him tomorrow. If the current talent was any indication, there would be enough clanless to form a good-sized company. And under the power of their new comrades, every warrior would have the fighting capability of three to four normal soldiers.

But was it right?

He studied Peder and Viessa standing in a dark corner with their leader, Armand. They spoke among themselves, hardly paying attention to the fighting below. A shadow passed over his heart. This didn't feel right. *They* didn't feel right.

Armand lifted his head, and his gaze caught Gurmund's across the balcony. The two men regarded each other for a moment, then Armand turned away with a veiled look on his face.

Once again Gurmund thought of the god of the Abyss and death, Morrud. If he believed in the old tales, he would think Armand and his companions were that god incarnate. And that was not a pleasant thought.

Five days later, that impression grew even stronger inside of Gurmund. The clanless competition had ended the day before, and now the hjars were sifting through the names of those who had fought. As they finished the names, the three strangers entered the room.

Gurmund scowled. More and more, these beings were allowed anywhere they wanted. He had taken Adrian aside weeks ago and spoken caution to the young man, but Adrian was enamored by their power, along with the other hjars.

They had already seen Armand's ability when he bound the clan warriors to his words for last month's demonstration. Even Gurmund had been grudgingly impressed—and secretly terrified.

If that was what Armand could do, what about the young woman and the copper-haired man?

Volka stood and motioned to the chairs on the other side of the empty firepit. Gurmund's scowl darkened. As leader of Nordica, Adrian should be the one inviting them in, not Volka. He cast a quick glance at Adrian. Did the young leader realize he was silently being supplanted by Volka?

I wish Ana were here. I need her counsel. Gurmund rubbed the bottom of his right eye as the three moved around the room to the chairs. His wife was one of the wisest women he knew. Which was why he sometimes wondered why their daughter . . .

He sighed and dropped his hand. No, he wouldn't think about her now. She had been gone for almost eighteen years. Disappeared. He had to let her go. And for the last few years, he had. So why was he suddenly thinking of her now?

Bolva! He shook his head. *Get your head in the battle!*

Volka remained standing. "We've seen what Armand can do for us a couple weeks ago. Today Viessa has volunteered to show us her power."

"Good timing," Adrian said as the scribe beside him finished the list they would announce tomorrow. "Jaro, please see to it that Captain Tor and his men receive this list. You are dismissed."

The man bowed his head. "Yes, my liege."

As the scribe left, Viessa approached the firepit. Her black hair hung over her shoulder, with one silver stripe following her hairline. She wore dark robes in a fashion similar to those who hailed from the country of Kerre. Her sleeves fell back as she lifted her hands.

Gurmund caught a glimpse of a black mark across her palm before a flash of light obscured his vision. A strange rupture appeared above the firepit as if the air had been sliced with a knife, revealing a shadowed world beyond.

"What the—" Frieda went for the dagger at her side. Bodin leaned forward, his ash-rimmed eyes wide and bright. Aisling, his owl, gave a startled hoot. Gurmund stared at the tear while clutching the arms of his chair. There was something inside, something dark, darker than the shadows in the room.

"I mentioned before that Viessa has the power to command the unseen," Volka said, motioning to the tear. "She has torn the veil between our world and the hidden world. As you can see, there are creatures who live inside. Viessa has the power to control them."

Gurmund noted the strain on Viessa's face, despite the satisfied smile she wore. She might be able to control them, but it appeared to take a toll on her.

Long, inky-black fingers emerged from the tear. Viessa twisted her right hand at the wrist. The tear sealed and the fingers—cut off from whatever body they had moments ago been attached to—went up like smoke, disappearing into the ceiling above.

Adrian shot to his feet. "What in the Abyss was that?"

A cold sweat collected along Gurmund's back and neck. Frieda also appeared shaken.

Volka laughed. "Mordra. Shadow-like beings who existed here in the Lands during the Great Battle, then were sealed behind the veil at the end of the war. Viessa can access and control them."

"Why do we need such creatures?" Adrian asked, his gaze still pinned to where the tear had been moments ago.

"They can serve as a vanguard. As we march south, we will need supplies. We can attain those supplies from villages along the way. And instead of using our own soldiers to take over small villages, we can use these shadows. After a village has been wiped out, we walk in and take what we need to keep advancing."

Inside, Gurmund shook his head. No, no. This wasn't right. They were crossing a line. Inviting into this world beings sealed away—perhaps in the Abyss itself—after the Great Battle? There was probably a very good reason the creatures were banished from the Lands. Why were they even contemplating bringing them back?

I can't be a part of this.

His thoughts startled him, yet he felt the iron-clad conviction of those thoughts. He couldn't pull his clan out. Not at this point. War was coming. Indeed, it was already here. But he could hold back his son and a few of his best men and find a way in secret to save his people.

Because if he didn't, Morrud would rule Nordica.

17

Brighid stood at the bottom of the road that led to Ragnbork. The valley below the city was filled with thousands of tents, fires with smoke spiraling into the air, herds of horses grazing in meadows of green, and crowds of Nordic warriors gathered across the vast encampment. Different colored banners waved in the early morning breeze, each heralding its clan. Blue, green, red, black, and yellow, with an image of the animal that represented the clan.

One more banner waved at the southern end of the camp, near the tree line. White with a hammer painted in grey. Brighid's chest tightened, and she gripped the strap of her pack. Of course it was a hammer. The clanless were not even accorded a guiding animal. Instead, a tool was used. Just like they were a tool.

She let out her breath and straightened her back. No matter. They were fighters, too, as the arena had shown. And they would prove to the rest that Nordic blood ran through their veins, just like it did through their brothers and sisters.

Brighid walked along the road toward the southern end of the encampment. A large group gathered below the white banner. Near the edge she spotted Johan along with two others from Roldar's eljun. She approached with her pack slung over her shoulder—retrieved from her eljun room after the arena fight. The air had noticeably grown warmer since the competition from a week ago, and small shoots of green were popping up everywhere. Only along the mountaintops did snow still cover the ground.

The crowd was noisy as hundreds of chosen clanless waited for instruction. More joined every minute as they came from the city above or the roads that led to Ragnbork, while others skirted the group, heading to their own clans.

As she drew near, a cool wind blew across her face and pulled at the small braids she had woven through her hair that morning. A weight lifted from her shoulders, and her stomach slowly unclenched. For the first time in a long time, maybe ever, she felt a sense of belonging. These were her people. The ones living on the edge, finding a way to survive where not even the clans could. The outcasts, the unwanted. But not anymore.

A shadow fell over her. The price it cost her to be here today . . .

She gripped the strap of her pack. Every night Roldar haunted her dreams like a vengeful apparition who wouldn't depart to the lands beyond. Every night she watched him die. Every night he stared at her with dead eyes—

"Brighid."

Brighid looked up. She had reached the edge of the crowd.

"Brighid," the voice said again.

She located Johan a few feet away.

"Johan." She went to stand beside the large man and felt a small measure of comfort in his presence. Ever since the day she'd fought and taken Roldar's life, Johan had stuck by her like a silent guard. He never asked her any questions, and he never spoke of that day. She appreciated that. Even now, he simply stood beside her, his arms crossed and his shadow falling over her. She wasn't ready to speak again of Roldar. She wasn't sure if she ever would be.

As the gathering crowd grew, Brighid spotted the fiery-haired woman from the competition standing thirty feet away. She was grinning and talking excitedly with those around her. Was she really a clanless one? Brighid couldn't recall seeing her in the clanless district. Maybe she had traveled here like some of the others clanless who fought in the arena.

Voices rose. Some boasted of their fights, their future, and the possibility of war. Brighid relaxed her shoulders and listened. One man gestured wildly as he spoke, then he spotted Brighid and twisted around. "There she is!" He pointed. "The woman who killed her opponent."

Brighid froze as people turned in her direction.

"I saw your fight," a young man said. "How did you learn to fight like that?"

"Maybe she's not clanless," the first man said. "I've seen the Bear Clan berserkers fight, and the way she changed during the fight reminded me of them."

Brighid raised her chin. "I'm clanless, just like the rest of you."

"Are you sure?" another man asked as a small crowd gathered tightly around her.

Johan, seeming to sense her discomfort, took a half step forward. "She's clanless," he said. "I've known her for months now. She survived in the clanless district, like the rest of you."

"But maybe—"

"There you are!" The crowd parted, and the fiery-haired woman stepped forward. "I was hoping to see you. Always good to meet another woman warrior. My name is Marta. What's yours?"

"Brighid," she replied.

Marta stuck out her arm. Brighid stepped forward and clasped it. "We'll show these dogs what warriors really look like." Marta laughed, a full throaty sound. Brighid smiled back. "Oh, come on," Marta said as she noted the frowns on some of the faces around them. "Laugh a little. None of you would be here if you couldn't fight. It is time to celebrate, before they whip us into fighters."

"She's right," the first man said. The others slowly agreed, and the air brightened again as the small crowd dispersed, and everyone resumed talking among themselves.

Marta moved to stand on the other side of Brighid. "Let's stick together. Who's your bodyguard?" she asked, glancing Johan.

"Johan."

He bowed his head toward Marta.

"The strong and silent kind. I like him already."

A horn blew and Brighid looked up. She couldn't see past the multitude. "What's going on?" she asked Johan.

As if in answer, the hjars gathered along the top of the nearest hill as a horn blew again. It took a few seconds for the crowd to quiet. Some of the clanless snickered while others crossed their arms and frowned. A general unrest settled over the crowd, but those on the hill didn't seem to notice.

The bulky blond man—Adrian, Hjar of the Eagle Clan—stepped forward to address them.

Brighid was surprised she could hear him despite the distance. He spoke of their ancestors and the honor of fighting for their country. A couple fighters around her frowned and looked away. She silently agreed with them. Only a few weeks ago they were clanless, not fit to live anywhere but the rundown district given to their kind. But a handful were listening attentively. She could almost see the hope blossoming across their faces. A chance to become a warrior, perhaps even a chance to be grafted into one of the clans.

She wasn't sure what she thought about that. She was here because it was her chance to rise above her current station. She would fight for that.

Adrian finished his honeyed words and stepped back, replaced by a taller man with long black hair and vivid blue eyes. His face was hard and angular with full lips and a Mark of Remembrance across his left eye. Two timber wolves flanked him, coming up to his waist, with thick grey fur and yellow eyes.

"Volka," the crowd whispered. Volka, Hjar of the Wolf Clan.

He stopped at the edge of the hill, and his gaze roved across the gathered clanless. For a moment, it felt like he paused on Brighid. A chill swept over her before he moved on. She sensed something predatory about him, something dangerous. A man to avoid.

Volka's deep voice echoed across the arena. Every eye turned toward him, every face in full attention. He spoke of the ills suffered by the Nordic people and slowly wove in the need for a fight until, minutes later, they were speaking of war.

"The south breaks our treaties, trespasses onto our land, and takes what is ours. Not what belongs to just the clans, but to all of us. This land is for every Nordic!"

The crowd burst into shouts of accord. Even those who earlier showed contempt for the clans were swept up in Volka's words.

"We will fight. We will fight together. There are no clans, only one people. What we take will be given to everyone equally, no matter status. The spoils will belong to everyone. Earn your own honor."

Volka continued, elevating the crowd until the entire area roared with enthusiasm and shouts of "Til Val!" Brighid had a feeling if any

Rylanders or Avonains stood nearby, they would have been consumed by the passion burning within the clanless gathered. What would it be like when every clan and Nordic stood shoulder to shoulder and marched on the southern lands? Volka had stirred those gathered into wild frothy waves, ready to crush the south. Bloodlust rose in her own chest despite her reservations of the man.

He ended with instructions for the next couple of days, then let the group disperse. Those gathered surged for the camp that had been designated for them. Someone started chanting an old Nordic chorus, and the rest joined in. The sound carried across the valley, and even those within the clan camps glanced over.

For the first time, Brighid felt a burgeoning of pride. No matter their status, these men and women gathered were strong, full of courage, and they would fight. Let the clans see that even the clanless were warriors. They would be the ones to bring back honor to Nordica, free their lands, and thrive in the harsh country of their ancestors. After all, they were one people.

※◇※

Sweat poured down Brighid's face and stung her eyes the next day. Her arms and thighs screamed from running since the sun first appeared that morning.

"Again!" Borre shouted, one of the skals from the Eagle Clan who had been appointed to oversee the training of the clanless. He was a stern, short man with a long, peppered beard and thick muscles.

Brighid lifted her shield and sword and dashed through the woods toward the meadow ahead. Skal Borre said they were building stamina. Part of her wondered if he wasn't just trying to kill them. Johan ran ahead of everyone, bounding over logs and dodging bushes gracefully despite his large body. Marta kept close behind him like a red fox.

Brighid leaped onto a log and launched herself over the brambles. She came down on a clear patch and ran. She was in the middle of the pack, neither fast nor slow. After two more runs through the same forest, Skal Borre halted the exercise and sent them off to eat and drink.

Her arms hung limply at her sides, her fingers barely holding the sword and shield above the ground. Luckily she had filled her waterskin last night and still had grain left from the provisions that were passed out the first day.

She stumbled into the clanless camp and toward the circular firepits until she found the spot she had claimed as her own. Her pack and blanket lay untouched where she had left them at the break of dawn. There was no worry of theft; anyone caught stealing was hung from the old oak tree in the midst of camp for all to see, as evidenced by the still swinging body of a gangly youth who learned the hard way. Thankfully she had been far enough away to feel only the brief passing of death as it took the boy. She still avoided looking in that direction when she could.

Brighid set down her gear, then dropped to her knees as she grabbed her waterskin and drank deeply. The sweat across her skin began to disperse in the cool wind blowing across the valley. The sun reached its zenith and provided warmth that felt good on her muscles.

Marta sat down beside her. "Skal Borre is ruthless." She reached for her own supplies.

"You didn't seem to be having too much of a problem running," Brighid pointed out.

Marta grinned before taking a large gulp of water. She wiped her mouth. "Grew up in the Ari Mountains in Wolf Clan territory and used to be a runner for the villages. I've been running through the forest my whole life."

Brighid tossed a handful of dried fruits, grain, and nuts into her mouth as others gathered around them. There were no tents for them, just a tiny plot of land staked out by one's pack, blanket, and supplies.

"How about you?" Marta asked.

"What about me?" Brighid asked after she chewed and swallowed.

"Where are you from?"

"Folkvar." It was the last village she and Elphsaba had lived in, so she claimed it as her home.

"Bear Clan territory. Any family?"

Brighid shook her head. Johan joined them with his pack in hand.

"What about the sun mark you wear on your face?"

Brighid touched the area around her left eye. "It's for the woman who raised me."

Marta studied the mark. "She must have been someone special to earn a mark on your face."

Brighid paused as her heart constricted with a sudden pang of grief. She swallowed the lump in her throat and reached for another handful of grain. "She was very special." Marta didn't seem to notice Brighid's stillness, but Johan did. Brighid caught him watching her as she tossed back the mouthful of grain and chewed silently.

Marta reached into her pack and brought out a travel biscuit. "I didn't have much family. And certainly not anyone I would wear a mark for." She bit into the biscuit. "Had to fend for myself when I turned twelve winters. Learned to run, to fight, to survive. Like most clanless." She glanced at Johan. "What about you? What's your story?"

Johan finished his waterskin. Brighid was also curious. She only knew Johan from their eljun.

"Not much to tell," he finally said. "Grew up in Udenhalla and worked the fields with my parents and sisters until the bitter winters came. Hardly anything grew after that, and whatever did grow the Rylanders would steal. My family all died that first winter. I held on as long as I could until I finally left for Ragnbork three winters ago, hoping to find work. Now here I am."

"Stag Clan country," Marta said. "Is it as pretty as others say it is?"

Johan studied the biscuit he had pulled from this pack. "Yes. Hills of gold in the autumn when the wheat turns. Rivers of the deepest blue full of fish the length of my arm. Herds of deer that could feed a village for an entire winter. At least, until the bitter winters came. Then everything disappeared. Still pretty. Just empty."

The three grew quiet and finished their meal. Conversation carried from the other firepits across the camp. Brighid finished the rest of her water, then stood. "I'm going to fill my waterskin. Anyone else need theirs refilled?"

Johan and Marta held theirs up, and Brighid gathered them. "Thank you," both said.

Brighid nodded and left the firepit, her mind mulling over her companions' stories. It seemed more than their clanless status bound them together. They were also without family.

The Varen River ran south of the camp and supplied the warriors with water. Brighid made her way through the trees, using a worn path that might have once been a game trail to the river ahead. Sunlight glinted through the evergreens and dry needles crunched beneath her boots. Far away, she could hear the din from the camp: a combination of voices, boots, and weapons.

She took in a deep breath, feeling that first wave of peace from being away from everything. A bird tweeted softly from the trees, and as she drew closer to the river, she could hear the rushing of water, a pleasant and soothing sound.

She reached the water's edge. Most of the bank was made up of boulders and logs, but a couple places were clear of debris. She stood on the edge of the rushing river and closed her eyes.

Breathe in. Breathe out.

The moment reminded her of the times when Elphsaba would be delivering a baby and she would be outside, drawing on nature to clear away the chilling presence of death. Sometimes she almost felt like she could hear words in the wind, like a gentle whisper. Or in the song of a bird. The rustle of the wildflowers in wide-open fields. The rivers and streams.

Like now.

Inaudible words, but words just the same. As if someone was continuing to speak in a calm, low tone.

Deep male voices broke her reverie, vastly different from the soft voice in the wind.

Brighid opened her eyes. Others approached the river. She pulled out the waterskins and knelt to finish her job. The water felt icy on her fingers as she filled one, then two of the waterskins. As she started on the third, the voices stopped, and she felt a pair of eyes on her. The river was always busy with those camped nearby retrieving water for their daily needs, but this gaze felt different. Heavy. Penetrating.

She peered to her left and found Volka twenty feet away on the other edge of the pebbled bank along with his wolves. Two warriors flanked him. They talked to each other while Volka and his wolf companions stared at her with that same predatory gaze she'd experienced on her first day here. His vivid blue eyes were like shards of ice and chilled her to the bone. Brighid turned away and dunked the last waterskin into the river. *Don't come here,* she chanted inside her head. *Just leave me be.*

"You," Volka called out. She watched him walk toward her from the corner of her eye. One wolf eyed her from his master's side while the other began to circle her. Volka wasn't tall, but he was very muscular. Thick bands of muscle stuck out from beneath his black wolf-skin cloak, and his face was hard and rigid. The aura he exuded was one of power and aggression.

She wanted to ignore him but had a feeling that doing so would provoke him—not a mood she wanted to meet him in. So she turned his direction and bowed her head.

"Yes, Hjar Volka?" She could feel the presence of the circling wolf.

He stopped five feet away. "I saw you fight during the clanless competition. Where do you hail from?"

"Folkvar."

"Folkvar," he murmured as he studied her. She felt his eyes trace her body again and shivered inside. "I will be watching you in the upcoming battles. If you prove yourself, you might be worthy of the Wolf Clan."

Brighid kept her head bowed. "Yes, hjar." *Never.* If there was one clan she had no desire to join, it was the wolf. A darkness tainted that clan. She could feel it, almost as strongly as she could feel death.

His gaze lingered on her a moment more, then he turned away. The wolf completed its circle and returned to Volka's side. She let out the breath she'd been holding, finished filling the waterskin, then ran.

Twice she stumbled over a log or a jutting root, her mind reeling from the brief encounter with Volka. She would need to be careful not to attract more of his attention. She was sure he was a man one could not say no to, despite the honor his clan would bring her. There was a raw savageness in his face, and she had a feeling it reflected his soul.

18

The days grew longer, and spring took hold of Nordica as the clans and clanless prepared for war in the valley below Ragnbork. By the time the skals announced the first march would begin, Brighid's muscles had grown long and lean. She could run miles without stopping. The sword and shield were now as much a part of her body as her own arms and legs. Wide leather belts were given to the clanless warriors for protection of their midsections and carrying their tools and weapons. Packs were reinforced, waterskins checked for cracks or leaks, and cloaks were rolled away to be used for bedding.

Then the day arrived for the oathbinding.

Brighid stood alongside the other clanless in long rows below the hill where Hjars Adrian and Volka greeted them the day they first arrived. Eight weeks later and they were warriors ready to fight for Nordica.

The sun beat down on the group, and Brighid fingered the blade at her side. Her shield hung on her back, and she had carefully braided her hair that morning, leaving the back to hang loose in long, golden strands.

Minutes later, three figures dressed in dark robes approached the hill. Brighid frowned. The foreigners she'd seen during the clanless competition. What were they doing here?

Volka and the other hjars followed them until the five leaders and three foreigners stood before the clanless. There was still no love between the clanless and the hjars, but there was a measure of respect now. Adrian stepped forward as the hjar of the Eagle Clan and leader of all of Nordica.

"Fellow Nordics, you are gathered here today to take the oath. You will be bound by your words to our nation and country, and by fighting you will gain honor and a place within our clans. We also have allies who will join us in our fight with the south." He motioned toward the three strangers. "They are blessed with power beyond the physical realm, power they have agreed to use to aid us. One of them is an Oathmaker, and he will be binding each of you to your oath today."

Murmurs broke out among the clanless. What did that mean? Was one's word not enough?

Brighid studied the foreigners anew. Power beyond the physical? Like the gods? Were they gods here in the flesh? And what did Hjar Adrian mean by *binding*?

"I don't like it," Johan muttered near Brighid. "I've heard stories about beings with power."

"I have as well," Marta said on her other side. "They live on the western side of the Ari Mountains, a group of beings who fought in the Great Battle. They are able to twist people's minds, summon spirits, or even endow people with strength."

Brighid glanced ahead again as the three foreigners stepped forward. They drew back their hoods. They appeared human . . . and yet so much more. The first one had hair like copper that shone in the sun in thick, jagged strands around his head. His face was angular and handsome, and his smile seemed to hold a secret.

The middle stranger was a woman, shorter than her counterparts. Her dark hair fell below her shoulders and moved like silk when she turned her head. A silver stripe flowed through the black strands and followed the curve of her face. There were shadows around her eyes, and her lips appeared almost black. Her body was small and lithe, and there was a dark playfulness to her face.

The third one was tall and lean. Something about him made Brighid believe he was the strongest of the three. His skin appeared as if he had never been in the sun, which contrasted with his black hair—hair even darker than the woman's. His face appeared angular, solemn, and more beautiful than any other man's face Brighid had ever seen.

Her eyes moved from one foreigner to the next. What powers did they possess? Could they really do what Marta said?

Volka stepped forward. "Armand will be binding you to your oaths today. With his binding, you will receive strength and courage. The binding will hold you to your oath. If you break your oath, desert your fellow warriors in the fight, or do not have your oath renewed after the battle, you will not only lose the strength and courage conferred to you but you will undergo great agony. Do not shame our people. Fulfill your oath and you will be rewarded."

The beautiful dark-haired man stepped forward as his companions moved away with visible deference. She was right; there was something about this man-being . . . an aura of power. He peered over the crowd.

"I am your Oathmaker."

Her eyes widened as his words washed over her. She could hear him as clearly as if he was standing in front of her. And his voice . . . . She breathed in deeply. It was like a cool wind brushing her face, blowing through her hair, bringing a pleasant sensation to every part of her body.

"I don't like this," Johan said again. "I know a little about the Oathmakers, and this doesn't sit well with my soul."

"Why?" Brighid asked. How could someone so beautiful with a voice like that be anything but good? She watched as Armand made his way down the hill, flanked by two warriors from the Wolf Clan.

"I only know from stories told by traveling bards," Johan whispered. "It is said the Oathmaker binds a person to their oath and that the binding is one of the mind and body. But I don't recall anything about pain."

"Who cares as long as the oath gives us power?" Marta said as Armand made his way along the first row of clanless warriors. They could no longer hear his voice, only watch as he raised his hand as if in blessing. "Hjar Volka said it will give us strength and bravery."

"But at what cost?" Johan said quietly. "Our people have always valued freedom. We should be fighting as free men, not bound by some oath, especially not a mystical one."

Marta laughed. "Do you really think we can take on the south as we are? They have trained armies, healers, fortified cities, weapons. We are strong, but we fight according to the old ways."

"Never underestimate the power of fighting for freedom," Johan said. "I'm fighting for our land and for our future. But what if those above us decide they want more? Power can be a heady thing. Conquer one land and suddenly you need to conquer another. What if we don't stop at our border? What if our leaders decide they want the Ryland Plains and Avonai for themselves? Will you fight for them then?"

Marta didn't answer. Brighid also didn't have an answer. She was here so she could leave the clanless district and the life of an eljun behind. She had no desire to take over other lands. *I just want to be free.*

A shout went up near the end of the first row of warriors where Armand was finishing the oathbinding. Then more shouting. Brighid caught a few of the words, and it seemed one of the clanless didn't want to take the vow. The young man turned and ran.

Volka lifted his hand into the air and shouted a command. Three arrows were let loose from the forest, and the young man fell with two lodged into his back.

"There will be no deserters," Volka roared from the hilltop. "Such dishonorable actions will be dealt with swiftly and harshly."

Murmurs broke out among the rows of clanless. It was one thing to refuse the oath and another to run away. Cowardice was worse than being clanless. There was no sympathy for the runner as two warriors came to take away the body.

Johan's face grew dark. "It seems we have no choice but to be bound. I hope our leaders know what they are doing allying with these beings."

Armand started down their row. As he drew closer, Brighid noted his pale lips and the sheen of sweat across his face. The binding seemed to be taking a toll on him.

Then it hit her, and she had to do everything not to stagger back.

Death. It was here.

She could feel it. She glanced around. Was it from the young man who was just shot? No, this presence was much too strong. A swift death left only a small trace. The chill expanded around her until the warmth from the sun faded from her skin. Her heart beat rapidly. Why could she feel death here? Was someone sick? But then they would have been cast out.

It was coming. Closer. Closer.

Armand stopped before her. She could see his eyes now. Light, a clear summer day. And stunning. His face, too, despite the paleness of it. He raised his hand and said something, but she didn't hear his voice this time. All she could see was the horrid, blackened spot across his palm.

Her breath stopped. The feeling of death. It was coming from him. "You," she whispered. "You are death."

His hand paused midair and he stared at her. No longer beautiful, his eyes reminded her of a vulture's. Then he spoke, and his words were a rush of wind, weaving around her, gripping her in a cool embrace. As the coolness stole over her, her mind went blank.

Brighid blinked. What was she thinking about a moment ago? She couldn't remember. All she could feel now was . . . nothing.

Armand moved on to Marta.

Brighid breathed in. Something was wrong inside of her. She raised her hand as if expecting to see a difference, but her body looked the same, felt the same.

She watched Armand as he continued down the row of warriors. The memory was there, just on the cusp of her mind. But no matter how hard she tried, she could not recall anything from the last minute, only a hint of fear. And something about his eyes.

Did it matter?

"So this is what the binding is like," Johan murmured next to her. None of the hesitation from their previous conversation remained, and his eyes held a far-off look.

"I feel like I could take on twenty men," Marta said with a grin.

Brighid glanced between her companions. She felt neither strong nor somber. Just empty. Like her heart had been carved out, leaving a hole inside. Only a flicker of an ember remained deep within. And it was whispering to her: *this isn't right*. But even as the words echoed in her mind, they disappeared, and she remembered no more.

19

A fortnight before the Summer Solstice, the Nordic forces started their march toward the border between Nordica and the southern lands. Many came out of the city of Ragnbork to cheer them on, lining the road below the city with cries and shouts. The warriors walked by, heads held high and proud. Even the clanless were cheered on.

Brighid glanced at the people who had come down and felt nothing. No eagerness for the upcoming battles, no motivation from those gathered, no fear or anxiety. Whatever happened that day when she was bound to her oath had left her a shell. The only thing she knew to do was fight, and the red haze came readily now when she beckoned it, allowing her to sink into its scarlet fog and disappear into the battle.

Rumors were already spreading of the clanless woman who fought like a she-devil, and many of the clan warriors desired to spar with her. But the hjars and skals didn't allow it, not yet. They wanted everyone fresh for the fight at the border.

She didn't care. Her sword gently thumped against her thigh with each step, and her round shield was firmly attached to her back along with her pack, waterskin, and cloak. Her hair was pulled away from her face in a handful of braids, each ending with a bead and feather. Marta chattered next to her, waving at the crowds and joining the chant when one of the old battle songs started.

Johan walked on the other side of her, distant and silent. In those quiet moments when Brighid studied her companion, she felt a twinge of unease. That wasn't him. This wasn't her. What had happened to them? But then those thoughts would sink into a deep, dark oblivion and she would go numb again.

They marched for hours under an ever-warming sun. The scent of pine trees and earth filled her nostrils, and the constant thump of boots along hardened ground drowned out all other noise. They stopped the first night near a small village that held a celebration for them. Five days later they arrived in Udenhalla, the seat for the Stag Clan territory. The city was almost as large as Ragnbork with walls of stone encasing it. The Nordic army slept out in the adjoining valley but were allowed within the city during the day to replenish supplies.

For the first time since the oathbinding Johan showed warmth of affection. A small smile graced his face as he and Brighid approached the thick gates that led into Udenhalla.

"It's been years since I've been here," he said quietly. "My home."

Home. Brighid tilted her head to the side. What would she consider home? Her usual answer was Folkvar, but was that true? What about the Northern Wastelands? Ragnbork? She shuddered at the last place. No. Not Ragnbork. Too many bad memories. What would it be like to approach a place and feel like she was home?

There was a softness to Udenhalla with rounded architecture, thatched roofs, brightly colored clothing on the occupants, and springtime flowers for sale on every corner. Most of the citizens were clearly farmers and merchants, which made sense. Udenhalla was the breadbasket for the Nordic people. But if she looked closer, the clothing appeared worn, and there was a leanness to the faces she passed. Hunger thrived here. Hunger brought on by drought, harsh winters, and the south.

Soon one of those would be remedied. The south would no longer steal from them.

While others used the few coins they were given for drink or pleasure, Brighid followed Johan and used her stipend to fill her grain bag and even had a little leftover for some dried fruit. She still had strips of dried meat from the march and would combine everything together to make travel biscuits for the road.

Johan continued to smile and chat with her as they walked through the city, pointing out different places from memory, sharing stories from his childhood. "And what about you?" he finally asked as they approached the thick outer gates and headed for the army camped beyond. "I remember you saying you're from Folkvar and your mark is for your mother. Do you have any other family?"

Brighid paused. Being back in his home city had certainly made Johan more talkative. "No family," she finally said. "Only the woman who raised me."

"Your mother," Johan clarified.

"Yes." She wasn't about to explain her unique relationship with Elphsaba.

"I miss my family," Johan said with a wistfulness in his voice as they passed under the archway and left the city.

"I do as well." But where would she be now if Elphsaba were still alive? Certainly not here, marching toward the border and to war with the south. She had a hunch the moment she fought that first eljun for bread that her hands were made for fighting. Then knew for certain after the few times the red haze took over and left her opponents vanquished at her feet. What would Elphsaba say about that? She was no healer and never would be.

She and Johan walked along the dirt road that crossed the valley and toward the wide-open hills where the Nordic army camped. More companies had joined them overnight from across Nordica. There were thousands now, perhaps even tens of thousands, each of the companies grouped by their clans. The Eagle and Wolf Clan were by far the largest, the Bear and Stag Clans coming close. She could always tell where each clan was camped by what animals were present. There were only a dozen or so for each clan, and the beasts and birds were known to fight alongside their elite masters.

Once or twice she searched for Bard, the bear hjar's son she'd met on the road years ago, but she didn't recognize anyone but the silver-haired hjar. A few times she'd caught him staring at her from a distance, then he would shake his head and walk away. She'd bristled at his attention the first time, then ignored him the rest. She ignored almost everyone now, focusing only on her training and fighting, and staying close to Marta and Johan during their march.

The next day as dawn broke across the rolling hills, the Nordic army started south once again.

As they moved toward the Ari Mountains, the golden hills turned dry, and stunted pine trees replaced the fields. "There are multiple valleys and mountain passages between the southern countries and Nordica through the Ari Mountains," Johan said. According to him, it appeared they were heading toward Susfell Pass, a passageway through the mountains that would allow them to enter the coastal land of Avonai.

"I wonder why we aren't heading west toward the Rokr Valley?" Marta asked.

Johan shrugged. "Susfell Pass is closer."

"But it's not very wide. Perhaps they are going for a surprise entrance into the south. We'll end up near Mistcairn on the other side."

Johan and Marta continued to debate where they were going and why. Brighid listened. She had a limited understanding of the world outside the Northern Wastelands and Ragnbork. The thought of seeing new places rose slightly in her chest like a dim light, then disappeared, pulling her back into an inky emptiness.

It took two days to cross Susfell Pass. At the end of the second day, they camped within the pass with no fires or light. Brighid couldn't see it from her camp, but she heard that Mistcairn lay at the end of the pass. That would be their first fight. Tomorrow they would step into the south, and war would begin.

The next day, the sun rose over the valley where Mistcairn lay. The town was larger than most villages but smaller than a city like Udenhalla. Modest stone homes were scattered across the green valley with wisps of chimney smoke trailing up into the sky. Toward the center of the town, the buildings were closer together with dirt streets weaving through the stone structures. Merchants set up tents for trade, the smoke from a blacksmith drifted along rooftops, and greenish-blue banners fluttered in the wind from a couple of important-looking buildings.

These people had no idea what was about to descend upon them. Brighid touched the base of her neck. Why did she not feel something about that? Why was there no fear of the approaching death? Or despair over the fates of the people below?

Did it matter? She was a warrior for her country. And they were the enemy. She had taken an oath to fight. Even now, she could almost feel the words from the oath wrapping around her, binding her, helping her tighten her hand around the hilt of her sword, and leaving her strangely numb and empty. It was easier to fight when she felt nothing. The apathy would allow her to take another's life.

Horns blew minutes later. At the sound, forces of Nordica burst from the mountain pass and raced down on Mistcairn like an avalanche. The town's warning bells went off, but it was too late.

As she approached—one warrior among thousands—she gripped her sword and shield. She let out a yell at the gates, her voice joining countless others. As the first guard approached her, she drew on the red haze and sank into its embrace, letting herself be washed away by the scarlet numbness.

20

"Easy, Bein." Gurmund patted the shoulder of the enormous brown bear he rode as they descended the mountain. "Don't worry, my friend. You will see battle soon enough." He sighed as he tightened his grip on the harness. Not that he needed a harness. Bein listened to his words alone, but it made others feel like the bear was under control.

Bein loped down the hill along with a handful of other war bears and their riders—distant cousins of his. To his right, Volka led his wolf warriors, his own two wolf companions keeping pace with their master. To his left, the clanless company ran on foot with weapons raised.

In the past, the thought of the battle made his blood run hot and brought out his berserker spirit. But years had passed, and a more tempered spirit guided him now. He still fought—would still fight—for his land and people, but it no longer put a fire in his bones. Was this age? Or wisdom? He didn't know.

Alarms rang along the outer wall, but it was too late for the Avonain town. The Owl Clan had quietly taken out all the watchtowers along the pass, leaving Mistcairn open to this surprise attack.

Gurmund spoke the sacred words of his clan, and Bein responded with a burst of speed. He and the other bear riders reached the gates before they could close. Hardin and Asulf used their pikes and wedged them in near the massive hinges, sending the thick wooden gates to a shuddering stop.

Without pausing, Gurmund entered the city. The people were in a panic. Women ran ahead on the cobblestone street with children in their arms. Others dashed for the buildings on either side. Guards came running, but he could tell with one look they were inexperienced for real fighting. Maybe his warriors could take the city with little bloodshed.

Gurmund jumped from Bein. As he drew his sword, Bein let out a roar that sent the guards stumbling back. No doubt they had never seen a war bear. Gurmund readied his sword, shouted a command to his men, then dashed forward.

More horns sounded across the city as the Bear Clan and Mistcairn guards clashed on the streets. He was wrong; a few knew how to fight. And more were coming.

As he traded blows with a man near the age of his son, he saw a streak of grey and black go by. Volka and his warriors, along with a dozen timber wolves. Volka let out a war cry and rushed down the streets, taking out anyone in his way.

Including escaping civilians.

"Volka!" Gurmund roared when he saw the carnage the Wolf Clan was leaving behind. There was no honor in slaying innocents. But there was nothing he could do. The bloodlust was upon the Wolf Clan, and their hjar led the way in the slaughter.

He finished the fight with the guard and moved on. "Do not kill the women and children!" he yelled. "Focus your fight on those who are barring the way to the garrison. Hardin, take the right. Asulf, take the left."

A young blond woman ran past him, her arms pumping with a shield in one hand and a sword in the other. The woman from the clanless competition. The one who fought with the ferocity of a Bear Clan warrior.

Gurmund checked around him, then whistled for Bein to follow and chased after her down the street. For some reason, he didn't want to see her hurt. Not because she was a woman. There were plenty of women warriors among the clans. His own wife had once fought at his side. It was because he saw flashes of *her* in the warrior ahead. That young, wild, untamed daughter of his who had disappeared years ago.

And yet the young woman was different. Kalla was never a fighter. She hated fighting. And she did not possess the bear spirit. He watched the clanless woman smash her shield into her opponent, toppling over a man a head taller than her with unusual strength. She slammed him again when he tried to get up, then dispatched him with her sword and moved on.

He continued to follow, mesmerized. She never faltered, never stopped. Down the street she ran, dispatching her opponents until she reached the end of the block. No one could touch her. She fought with raw brute strength.

Then a little girl appeared around the corner. The girl froze like a deer, her eyes wide as the clanless woman approached. The two stared at each other. Gurmund waited for the clanless woman to dispatch the girl.

The clanless woman moved on.

Gurmund let out a sigh of relief. It seemed everyone but his own warriors had gone crazy with bloodlust. Except this young clanless woman. He watched her sprint another block, then clash with two guards. Something inside of him wanted her to be different. To be a true warrior. Not a savage like most of the Nordics had become under the oath.

He reached the girl who still stood frozen, watching the clanless woman fight down the street. "Get out of here!" Gurmund yelled.

The girl twisted around, her face growing pale at the sight of him.

"Run!" He swung his sword to the side. "Run if you want to live."

She stuttered a nod in his direction, then turned and fled.

He glanced back and found Bein lumbering toward him. "Come, friend. We need to get to the garrison ahead."

Bein huffed as Gurmund heaved himself up onto the bear's back. Then he shouted a command in the bear tongue, and Bein burst forward. Gurmund looked ahead, but the clanless woman was gone. Pity.

The garrison was a small structure in the middle of Mistcairn, just a square of wood and stone with a tower on each corner. The doors were solid wood and shut tight. That wouldn't stop the Nordic forces for long.

"Hjar Gurmund!"

Gurmund turned and spotted Adrian and the archers rushing in behind him. A single eagle with a golden ring of feathers around its neck flew high above. Haski, Adrian's companion. The archers spread out along the street that surround the garrison and prepared to fire. Adrian approached his side.

"Frieda is coming with the ladders. We need to hold out until her clan arrives."

Gurmund nodded.

Every time a head appeared above the garrison, the archers would shoot, or Adrian would let out a whistle and command his eagle to swoop. Gurmund and his warriors drove any guards away. The rest of the town was filled with smoke, shouting, and cries. He didn't want to think about the carnage that was spreading due to the Wolf Clan and those caught in the bloodlust. He sighed and readjusted his grip on his sword. Once again he was glad he'd assigned Bard and a handful of his warriors to stay back and protect the border. At least his son was safe from Armand and his mystical words.

A group of warriors appeared a block away—I clanless woman, a large man, another woman with fiery hair, and more clanless. The Stag Clan arrived shortly after with crude ladders they had built from trees in the pass.

"Protect the Stag Clan!" Gurmund yelled to the warriors gathered. Adrian gave a command to his archers. Then Frieda led the way with her warriors, while brawny stags pulled ladders toward the wall. An enemy archer went to take out one of the stags. As he lifted his bow, Adrian gave a whistle, and Haski swooped down, catching the man's face in her great claws. Gurmund heard the man's cry from his place on the street—a gurgled yell before he toppled over the wall and fell to the street, his face a crisscross of flesh, bone, and blood.

The dead man was ignored as the ladders were placed, and the Stag Clan scrambled up, followed by the clanless company. Gurmund and his warriors kept watch, taking down anyone who tried to approach the garrison from the outside. The clanless woman scaled the ladder and entered the garrison.

Minutes ticked by as the battle commenced inside. He heard

Volka's wolf cry echo across the city. His heart tightened at the sound. There would be many bodies to burn this evening. "Bolva," he growled. This war was inevitable, but he had hoped carnage would be kept to a minimum so a way of peace could be formed afterward. If they killed everyone in their path, neither the White City nor Avonai would be interested in surrendering. Both sides would fight until one could fight no more.

He and Adrian held the line around the garrison until the sun passed overhead and Frieda appeared at the top wall and motioned to them. At the same time, the gate began to swing open. They had done it. They had taken Mistcairn and now had a foothold in the south.

But at what cost?

21

The day after Mistcairn fell, Brighid and the other warriors gathered along the green plains outside the burning town. They were told Armand would be rebinding their oaths. Nobody asked why. They just did as they were ordered.

As Brighid stood in the sunlight, something seemed to be melting inside of her. A hint of emotion returned to her soul.

"Do you feel that?" she asked Marta who stood beside her.

"Feel what?"

Brighid frowned. How did she explain? "Like you're coming back to yourself?"

Marta turned toward her. "What do you mean?"

"Silence!" one of the skals shouted.

Brighid pressed her lips together, but still wondered at the feeling. Her gaze drifted toward the smoke rising from Mistcairn. A chill spread across her body. *Death.* It was like a whisper rising in the wind. *Death.* She sucked in a breath. She could feel it again. Death's presence. Her gaze darted from the burning city to Armand, who now stood before the massive crowd. Both seemed to be the source. Her body began to shake. *I don't want to feel this! I don't want to feel—*

Armand's voice reached her ears. His words floated on the air, twisting around her mind and body until a numbness stole over her. It was as if his words were a stifling cocoon, wrapping her as tightly as a spider would its prey, leaving her a husk that fought for the clans and Nordica.

After that, they marched across the coastal lands of Avonai. Village after village fell to the Nordic wave as they advanced west along the Ari Mountains. Sometimes a village would be empty by the time they arrived. Brighid thought about the strangeness of it once, then sank again into her stupor. Twice they met small pockets of resistance from the Avonains, but the sheer force and ruthlessness of the northern warriors wiped out any confrontation.

The Nordics arrived at the Onyx River a fortnight later. The Ryland fortress of Dallam stood on the other side. Unlike the battles before, which involved civilians and city guards, the fortress would be their first time against the military of the south. Without pausing, those clanless not serving as the vanguard were tasked to felling trees and collecting animal skins to create a pontoon bridge. The rest of the warriors prepared for battle while archers from the Eagle Clan kept the Ryland archers across the river at bay.

The job of building a temporary bridge went long into the night and the next day. As the sun rose on the second day, soldiers dressed in dark blue were spotted on the western banks of the Onyx River. Reinforcements had arrived for Dallam.

A couple of the Wolf Clan warriors jeered at the soldiers across the river. Brighid sat on a tree stump near the scoffers, sharpening her sword. She paused for a moment and watched the Ryland military prepare. She remembered Elphsaba's words. Her father had once been one of those men. A Ryland captain. Maybe he still was. All she knew was he never wanted her.

She snorted and turned away. How ironic would it be if she were to meet her own father on the battlefield? She resumed sharpening her sword. He would never know. He probably thought she was dead, left on a mountainside. No, he probably never thought once about the baby he left behind. A babe that grew up to be a warrior. A woman who now fought against his people.

She started to clean up. The idea of being part Rylander was as foreign to her as these tame and gentle hills around her. Nothing stirred her here in this country. Whatever Rylander blood she carried, it was overshadowed by her Nordic heritage.

The pontoons were ready early morning the third day. The archers provided cover, and the pontoons were dampened to help with any stray fiery arrows. Then the crossing began.

First went those with the scaffolds, then the clanless fighters. Brighid made her way across the makeshift bridge with Johan and Marta close by. The sun was hot and bright as they crossed the bridge and landed near the fortress. Both sides exchanged a volley of arrows, and one warrior fell with a cry behind Brighid. No one reacted. Instead, they moved as one unit, reaching the shore and running for the wall. They raised the scaffolds, then climbed like ants scurrying up a tree trunk.

At the top, Brighid went left along the wall and let herself sink into the red haze. Here, she didn't have to worry about civilians or innocents. Anyone who wore blue was her target. It was the only color she saw besides the red, and she made a path to the stairs in no time.

She felt nothing. Even the shouts and cries of her comrades and enemies fell on deaf ears. It wasn't until time passed and they stood in the center of the fortress that she emerged from the red fog of the fight. Within hours, they had taken the fortress. Nothing could stop them.

Then her body began to thaw from the battle. Every cut, every scrape stung. Her shield arm sagged, and blood ran in a thin rivulet along her other arm, across the back of her hand, and onto her sword.

A warrior let out a wolf cry behind her, and she turned.

"What a she-devil!" he yelled to his companions. She recognized the wolf symbol on his neck. "Did you see her fight?" Others nodded. "Hardly left a soldier for the rest of us."

"She's like the Stryth'Veizlas," one replied. "Swooping across the battlefield and leaving a feast of corpses behind."

"But aren't the ones from legend like carrion birds?" said a third. He stared hard at Brighid. "She's a lot prettier than a carrion bird."

More eyes fell on her. Brighid turned away. As she left, she could hear them saying more about her, but in this numb state, she didn't care. She made her way out of the fortress, bypassing the bodies and those gathering the dead, and toward the river. At the bank, with the fortress behind her, she laid down her weapon and shield, then dipped her hands into the icy water.

Stryth'Viezla. The fiercest fighters from Nordic legends. Ugly women with black feathers who fought with a ferocity that would put even a Bear Clan berserker to shame. Did the red haze appear like that to others who saw her fight?

"You should get that cut looked at," Johan said, breaking her reverie.

She blinked, then glanced at her upper arm. There was a deep gouge, the source of the blood across her hand.

He knelt beside her on the water banks and started cleaning his sword. "At least this time there were no women or children," he said quietly.

"What does the oath feel like to you?" Brighid asked as she rinsed her wound.

His head came up, and he gave her a questioning look.

"I . . ." she stared down at the tainted water where her hands had been moments before. "I feel nothing. I feel nothing when I fight. I feel nothing when I run. I feel nothing when I sleep. I'm numb. And sometimes I'm afraid that numbness will lead me to not care who I fight."

"Interesting." He scrubbed at a blood spot on the edge of his sword as he thought. That was Johan. A quiet, contemplative man. The opposite of fiery and opinionated Marta.

"Given what I've seen, I think the oath stirs up the bloodlust in some, gives courage to others, tampers down the inhibitions for some, and—in your case—takes away all feeling. Whatever the soul needs in order to fight." He let out a long breath. "But I'm not convinced this is the right way to motivate us to fight—or that it is truly the gift of the Oathmaker."

"What do you mean?"

"You asked what the oath feels like. Let me ask you a question: When Armand speaks, what do his words feel like?"

Brighid paused. "Like I'm trapped. Bound. I can't move."

Johan slowly nodded, then leaned in close. "I remember the old stories from bards who used to visit my village. Stories of the Eldarans and their gifts. The Guardians and Oathmakers. The Healers. The

Truthsayer." He continued to act as if he was cleaning his sword, but the metal already shone spotless.

"Eldarans?" The hairs prickled along Brighid's skin.

"Beings with power. Like Armand and the two others. And yet they are not the same. The mark on Armand's hand is not right. Eldarans carry light within their palm. Whereas Armand's looks like—"

"Rotting flesh," Brighid finished.

"Yes. Black and ugly. And their power seems off as well. A real oathbinding should feel free and empowering. A pure burning in the soul for righteousness."

"How do you know all of this?"

"Again, the bards. They would travel up from the Ryland Plains and tell tales from the olden times and the Great Battle."

"I never met a bard." Maybe the Northern Wastelands were too far for southern travelers. "So what do we do? I don't think I want this binding anymore."

"Here." Johan held out a small jar of honey. "For your wound."

She frowned until she saw a few of the Owl Clan warriors drawing close. Brighid dipped her fingers in the honey. Maybe that was why Johan had changed the subject. She rubbed the sweet concoction across her cut and winced. Johan passed her a small strip of cloth from the pouch around his waist. She wrapped it around her arm.

"I'll tie it off for you." Johan leaned close again and began to tie it. "I don't know," he answered quietly. "There was a group of men from the Bear Clan who no longer wanted to be bound a few days ago. I haven't seen them since."

"Maybe they left."

Johan snorted as he finished the knot. "I don't think so. I saw Hjar Gurmund's face the next day. He looked livid."

"He always looks mad."

"Nah, just gruff. But this time there was a real fire in his eyes—"

"What are you two talking so secretively about?" Marta asked from behind them.

Brighid jumped and Johan leaned back. A flush spread across his face.

"Johan was helping me with my wound." Brighid turned so Marta could see the wrapping.

"I see." Her gaze moved back and forth between the two, causing Johan's face to turn an even deeper red.

Brighid stood. "Thank you for your help. I'm going to go set up our camp," she said to both of them. Already camps were spreading around the outside of the fortress and the smell of meat roasting filled the air. She headed down the riverbank to find a good spot, her mind revolving around what Johan had said. If this wasn't what the oathbinding should feel like, then what was the real one like? *A pure burning of the soul,* he'd said. And beings with a mark of light upon their hand. Not like Armand's or his companions'.

So why were they following these people—these beings? Why were the hjars aligning themselves with them and not the Eldarans Johan spoke of? Or were the Eldarans like the southerners, seeing the Nordics as brutes and barbarians?

"Do I really want to feel again?" Brighid murmured as she placed a fist over her heart. The one benefit to the binding was the numbness that followed. But it didn't just numb her to the presence of death. She no longer felt love, joy, or anger. Johan was right in one sense. The binding had given her what she needed to fight. She couldn't imagine what the battlefield would feel like if she could sense death. It would be worse than birthings. She sighed and dropped her hand. Maybe it was better this way.

Brighid found a spot to camp near the river and collected wood as Johan, Marta, and a couple other clanless joined her. They laid out their bedrolls and cooked food over the fire. The sun sank behind the hills, and songs broke out over the vast camp. Johan and Marta talked quietly near the fire as Brighid lay down and turned her back to them and the fire.

There was no moon tonight. Just a thousand twinkling stars, each one a tiny, brilliant pinpoint of light. Light. Like how Johan described the mark on the hand of the Eldarans. Perhaps their marks appeared like they were holding a star in their hands.

Brighid closed her eyes and let her aching body relax until she succumbed to sleep's embrace. That night she dreamed of a man with a mark on his hand that shone with piercing white light.

22

Kaeden dropped onto the makeshift bed inside one of the small tents that housed the mineworkers who worked the quarry just outside Luith. He let out a long, slow breath. His muscles ached from a full day of labor, and his right hand felt raw under the glove he wore. He wanted nothing more than to shut his eyes and fall into a deep sleep, but his body was filthy and sweaty from work. With a groan, he sat back up. Best to wash up now and grab a bite from the food tent.

Outside, the bare hills turned gold beneath dying sunlight. Men lined up along the trickling stream that ran through the rocky valley, splashing water over their bodies and hair. Kaeden joined them, pulling his sweaty tunic off and throwing it to the side while keeping his one fingerless glove on his right hand. Better to keep the strange mark on his palm covered than answer questions. He washed his body, then hair, then his shirt. His pants were already wet from the washing. Good enough. Everything would be coated in dust and sweat again tomorrow.

As he wrung out his faded tunic, a short young man made his way along the stream. He wasn't one of the laborers or foremen. He was skinny, and his clothes, though faded, were clean and showed signs of age, not hard labor. He appeared uneasy as he seemed to search for somebody.

Kaeden flicked the water from his hair. He would need a haircut soon.

"Are you Kaeden?"

Kaeden glanced over. The young man stood a couple feet away, holding a small rolled message. Kaeden stood to his full height, towering over the young man, who shrank under his stature.

"Yes, I am. Who's looking for me?"

"I-I have a message for a Kaeden."

Kaeden sighed. No matter what he did, his presence intimidated people. Most of the time he appreciated that fact. It kept people away. But at times like this, it aggravated him. What did the young man think he was going to do? Pummel him?

He held out his gloved hand. The young man stared at it for a moment, then dropped the message into his palm and quickly backed away. Kaeden fought the desire to growl. Instead, he broke the seal and read the words in the dying light. It was from Mathias. He hadn't heard from Mathias in over a year—and hadn't seen him in two.

> *Please come home. I am in great need of you here.*
> *When you arrive in Avonai, seek out The Seagull along*
> *the outer port and have the tavern keeper alert me to*
> *your arrival. Leave as soon as you can.*
> *Mathias*

Kaeden turned the note over to see if there was anything else, but that was all that was written on the small piece of paper. *I need you.*

"Why?" Kaeden muttered. Mathias knew Kaeden couldn't use his Eldaran power. Not that he wanted to. He had no desire to help humans. Not after what they'd done to his family. "I'm no good, old man. You know that."

He turned and headed back toward his tent, which was currently empty. His tentmate had left a couple days ago after receiving an apprenticeship in Luith with a blacksmith.

Once inside, he lit the small lamp on the table that sat between the beds and lay down, his hands folded behind his head. He stared up at the canvas ceiling, his hunger forgotten in light of this message from Mathias.

When he'd first arrived on Mistsylver Island, he had given up on life. After watching his parents brutally killed during the Khodath uprising, it had taken what little strength he had to escape across the sea with Mathias, and even longer to accept the fact that they had died . . . and he had not.

Mathias had stayed with him for two years on the island before heading back to Avonai and the Lands of the West.

It was Mathias who helped him not succumb to the darkness. Mathias who nursed both his body and his soul back to health during those two years. Mathias, the oldest and wisest of their people, and the Truthsayer of this world.

His mentor and only friend.

Come home. There was a strange pull inside his heart at those words. They conjured images of a simpler time when it was just him and his parents living in the Tieve Hills, before they crossed the Illyr Sea, before the uprising, before—

He shook his head. Home. Where the trees turned to gold in the fall, and the water ran cold from the Ari Mountains, and life consisted of working the land and eating its fruits. Perhaps peace could be found there.

Kaeden sat up and tugged his glove off. His mark glowed dimly in the tent. It was all that was left of his Eldaran blood. Just this mark. He narrowed his eyes. Mathias couldn't possibly be calling him back to serve as an Eldaran. His power had died the same moment his parents did. So why did Mathias need him?

Only one way to find out.

Maybe it was time to go home.

Three weeks later Kaeden breathed in the strong salty air as he stood along the bow of the ship, the *Waverunner.* Ahead the city of Avonai rose along the eastern shores beneath a bright-blue sky. Sand-colored buildings nestled together between rocky cliffs and towering evergreen trees. The port was a maze of wooden walkways with ships of every size and color moored inside the coastal haven.

The *Waverunner* followed the narrow entryway into the harbor and made its way to the right. Hundreds of people worked on the piers, from fisherman offloading their catch to merchants whose ships were filled with crates of goods.

Kaeden took in another deep breath, happy to almost be on land again. Weeks at sea had been more than enough for him. He wasn't an Avonain and preferred solid ground beneath his feet. But at least he didn't get sick like the other passengers on the ship. He could still hear the retching of his bunkmate inside his head. Poor man. No doubt Roger would be happy when the ship made landing. Which, given how swift the *Waverunner* approached the docks, would be soon.

He took one last look at the nearing coastline, then turned to retrieve his pack. It had been eight years since he left this port with his parents to work across the Illyr Sea. And six years since they died at the hands of those they were helping.

Kaeden squeezed his gloved hand shut. Witches they had been called. Unnatural. Once he was safe in Mistsylver, he'd never revealed he was an Eldaran. He might have stayed there forever and remained anonymous, save for the message from Mathias.

Well, here I am, old man. Answering your summons.

Kaeden made his way down the narrow hall with his head bent and his wide shoulders brushing both walls. The first time the captain of the *Waverunner* saw him, he'd asked if Kaeden was a berserker from Nordica. He'd grunted and said no.

He reached the lower deck and headed for the hammock where his pack had been stored for the last few weeks. It was supposed to be his bed, but it was clearly made for a person much smaller than him, so he had taken to sleeping in the corner and safely away from Roger on his bad days.

He hefted the pack over his shoulder. All his worldly belongings in one canvas bag. Both Roger and his pack were gone. The young man must already be preparing to disembark at the first moment. Kaeden chuckled and silently wished Roger a safe journey.

As he reached the top deck, he felt the ship stall beneath him and heard a shout for the anchor. The walls of the city now blocked his view of Avonai, leaving only the port and taverns visible. Crates half the size of a man were stacked along one pier while fishermen worked on their nets on another. Women with their hair pulled back in off-white scarves inspected the daily catch for their dinners. Seagulls stood on posts, letting out loud cries that blended with the surf of the sea.

He reached inside his pack and pulled out the letter Mathias had sent him. The ink was fading, but the linen pulp from which the paper was made still held up. He might even be able to reuse the material. He was to head to The Seagull, a tavern along the pier, and have the tavern keeper send word to Mathias.

Simple enough. Kaeden gently folded the note and placed it back in his pack. The sailors had already secured the ship, and he spotted Roger disembarking along the gangway. Kaeden thanked the captain for the journey and headed for the dock.

The Seagull. A dozen buildings lined the city wall. Some were warehouses, others were stalls for selling and one was a shabby inn. He headed along the walkway toward the city, taking in the feel of Avonai. Not much had changed in the last eight years. It almost felt like . . . home.

How strange. His brows furrowed as he passed a ship unloading its cargo. When was the last time a place felt remotely like home? Not even the Mistsylver Islands had felt like home, despite his living there for over four years. Maybe it was because he was always on the move, searching for work.

Once he reached the main walkway, he made his way along the wall. There, just beyond the shabby inn was a sign over a small establishment: The Seagull. It appeared new, unlike the building next to it, with clean windows, fresh oiled lumber and brick, and a door with no dings or gouges.

Kaeden approached the tavern and pressed down on the handle. The door opened silently with ease. The inside was cheery and clean. Wrought iron chandeliers hung from rafters high above over a room filled with small round tables. A wooden counter stood on the left with a handful of pewter mugs turned upside down on a white cloth. The place was empty, but that was to be expected in the middle of the afternoon. Bright sunlight poured in from the large window, and a sudden waft of fresh bread tickled his nose.

He followed the scent to the counter. A doorway beyond led into another part of the tavern, and the clang of a pot echoed on the other side of the wall.

"Hello?" Kaeden said.

"What the—" More clinks and clangs, then a short, thin man came from the back, wiping his hands on the apron draped across his body. His dull brown hair was pulled back at the nape of his neck, and the sleeves of his tunic were rolled up to his elbows. He craned his neck to look up at Kaeden and let out a low whistle. "Well aren't you a big one. Just arrived in Avonai? Here to join the war?"

Kaeden had begun to open his mouth to inquire after Mathias, but the man's words stopped him. "War?"

"Yes, the war. I assume you're a mercenary here to answer King Erhard's summons?"

"I haven't heard anything about a war."

"Oh, well . . ." The man appeared sheepish as he grabbed for a cloth under the counter. "Given your size, I thought . . ."

"I've never fought in my life."

The man's head shot up, and his eyes went wide. "Really?"

Kaeden knew he resembled a warrior. With unusually wide shoulders and neck, and thick muscles that left his tunic tight when he moved, he probably did look like a mercenary. He sighed and dropped his head.

"Could you send a message to Mathias and let him know I'm here?"

"Mathias? Master Mathias?"

"Yes." Kaeden was already done with the man's questions and hoped he wouldn't notice the glove on his right hand.

"Oh yes, right away. He said he was expecting a visitor from across the sea. Would that be you?"

"Yes."

"I'll send my boy right away. Toby!" he hollered over his shoulder. "Aye! Boy, I need you to run an errand. Toby!"

There was a shuffle in the back, then a boy on the brink of manhood stepped through the doorway, his sand-colored hair sticking up all around his face. "What is it, fath—" He froze as he caught sight of Kaeden.

Kaeden fought the urge to run his fingers through his recently trimmed hair. It seemed no matter where he went he stood out. Toby's Adam's apple bobbed up and down as he stared.

"It's not nice to stare, boy," the man muttered. Toby ducked his head. "Go let Master Mathias know his visitor has arrived."

"Yes, Father!" Toby dashed to the other side of the counter, then across the tavern and out the door.

"He's a good boy," the man said as he hung the mugs on hooks along the rafter above the bar counter. "I'm Finn, by the way."

"Kaeden."

"Kaeden . . ." Finn gazed up at him again. "Where are you from, Kaeden?"

"Across the Illyr Sea. I've been living on Mistsylver Island for the last couple of years. But I was born in the Tieve Hills south of here."

"Well, welcome home. Hungry?"

Kaeden's stomach growled in response.

Finn chuckled. "That answers that. Go ahead and take a seat at a table. Bread is fresh out of the oven. Afraid the stew isn't done yet, but I do have some cheese."

"Cheese is fine." Kaeden turned and moved toward the nearest table while Finn disappeared into the back. He dropped his pack beside the chair and sat down. War. What in the Lands had happened here in the west for there to be a war? And between who?

A minute later, Finn came around the counter with a wooden plate topped with a chunk of bread and cheese. "Anything to drink?"

"Just water."

"Water? You're a funny one," he said under his breath and went back.

Kaeden broke the bread and stuffed a hunk of cheese inside the soft interior and bit down. Drinking water in a tavern was probably strange, but he wasn't too keen on ale. Usually it tasted like dirty water. Maybe it was in the places he had visited.

"Here's your water." The liquid swished over the side of the pewter mug.

Kaeden swallowed. "Thanks. Could you tell me more about this war?"

"You really are from across the sea if you haven't heard about the war with Nordica."

"Nordica?"

"Started shortly after the Summer Solstice." Then he frowned.

"Actually, maybe further back than that. There were always skirmishes along the border. But then news came a month ago that the Nordics had appeared out of Susfell Pass with a monstrous army. They took Mistcairn in a day, then headed west and conquered everything to the Onyx River. Now they're heading south along the river. They might head here next. Hence the call for mercenaries. We don't have the soldiers to face the might of Nordica."

Kaeden blinked in amazement. "What about the White City? Has Lord Rayner sent troops?"

"No idea. I'm sure King Erhard has sent messengers, but I haven't heard anything more."

"So Avonai is attempting to bolster their own troops."

"Yes."

Kaeden frowned. "This doesn't make sense. Why would Nordica start a war? Aren't there treaties between our countries?"

Finn shrugged and turned back toward the counter. "Again, I'm just a simple tavernkeeper. And my son is too young to enlist, thank the Word."

Kaeden took another bite and slowly chewed, a frown settling across his face. Was that why Mathias had called for him? To help in this war? He finished the bite and scowled. He had no wish to participate in a war. Mathias knew he wouldn't fight. He'd vowed that long ago when his parents died. So what did Mathias think he was going to do? Ugh. Maybe he shouldn't have left the island. Then again, maybe he would just head south to the Tieve Hills.

You're just running away again.

Kaeden tore into the cheese. *I didn't sign up for a war,* he fought back.

Wars don't always need fighters. They also need healers.

Kaeden chewed angrily. Like his parents. And look where that got them.

I want nothing to do with humans. Let them fight their petty wars.

Deep down, he knew it was his bitterness talking. A cancer of the soul that was eating him alive. But he didn't want to fight it. Maybe he still longed for death.

Did Mathias know? He huffed and finished the last bit of cheese. Probably. After all, he was a Truthsayer.

As if summoned by his thoughts, the door opened at the other end of the tavern, and a man dressed in an ornate white robe trimmed in gold with a cowl over his head proceeded inside.

Weeks, months, or years, Kaeden would recognize those robes and the man who wore them. He stood to his feet and bowed his head. "Mathias."

The man drew his hood back and grinned. "Kaeden. It has been a long time."

23

"You've filled out since the last time I saw you." Mathias stopped before Kaeden and clapped him on the shoulders. "You are truly a man now." Creases covered Mathias's dark face, and his tight curly hair, once peppered with grey, was now like white wool. But his eyes still gleamed with an inner light, and his smile was as warm as ever.

Something shifted inside Kaeden's chest, and tears stung his eyes. He swallowed the lump in his throat, then smiled back. "It is good to see you, too, Mathias." The powerful longing inside of him took him by surprise. A feeling that he was home.

"Finn!" Mathias called over his shoulder.

"Yes, Master Mathias?" Finn raised his head, a look of reverence on his face.

"Could you make me a cup of hot black?"

Finn laughed, his reverence melting away into mirth. "You and your strange drink. I'll get on it."

Kaeden smirked at Finn's reaction. No matter where Mathias went, he seemed to make friends, despite his awe-inspiring status as Truthsayer.

"Go ahead and sit down. We have much to talk about."

Kaeden sat. "Your message was interesting. I heard there is a war with Nordica."

"Yes." A shadow fell across Mathias's face. He took a seat opposite Kaeden with his back to the bar counter. "That's why I've called you here. We need help."

Kaeden's heart fell. "Nothing's changed. I still can't use my power."

"Let me see your hand."

Kaeden hesitated, then lifted his right hand. He pulled at each finger and removed the leather glove. His mark glowed with a dim light.

"At least the light still shines in your mark," Mathias murmured. "That means there is still hope."

"Still hope for what?"

"That your power can be rekindled. I've had a lot of time to think about your predicament and what could be causing this strange phenomenon."

Finn entered from the back room with a steaming mug. Kaeden grabbed his glove and hid his hand under the table. While Finn placed the mug in front of Mathias and the two exchanged pleasantries, he tugged the glove back on. Eldarans might be accepted in the western lands, but he still didn't want his heritage known.

Mathias took a drink of steaming black liquid and sighed as Finn went back to the counter. "I'm glad I found someone who makes my drink just right."

Kaeden wrinkled his nose at the smoky, bitter smell. "You said you think you might know what's stopping my power?"

"Yes. It's a theory. Despite all of my research in the White City, there is no record of an Eldaran losing their power. The light changing, yes. But not losing the power."

"Light changing?"

Mathias's face grew dark. "More like the light going out, leaving behind a black hole."

Kaeden sat back. A black hole? That sounded even worse than losing one's power.

"I was relieved to see the light still in your mark."

Kaeden let out his breath. "Yes. That has never changed."

"Good." Mathias took another sip. "I don't think you ever lost your power. Rather, your gift was suspended the day your parents died. Seeing your loved ones die so tragically created a knot within the flow of your power. I think this could especially be true since you were coming into your Eldaran blood at the time."

Kaeden slowly nodded. His mark had newly appeared when his parents were rounded up with a handful of other leaders and publicly executed in Khodath. The only reason he had not been with them was because he'd still been under the fever brought on by the change in his body, recovering in a small town nearby. He winced and closed his eyes as the bloody images resurfaced from the day he saw their bodies. He pushed the horrid memories back down until his mind was clear again.

"It still hurts," Mathias said quietly.

"Yes." Kaeden opened his eyes.

"Do you hate humans?"

Kaeden froze. A tightness filled his throat, making it suddenly hard to breathe. "Maybe," he said finally. He wasn't sure what this heavy emotion was. Fear, mistrust, maybe even hate. He didn't want to study it too closely. It was easier to ignore it—and humans.

"I think I know how to restore your Eldaran power. But you're not going to like it. And it's going to hurt."

Kaeden looked up.

"We were created to serve mankind. It is why we were marked and given power. I think by fulfilling your purpose as an Eldaran, your power will return."

Kaeden's heart beat faster. "What do you mean?" Both his mother and father were healers. Not only did they study the art of healing, their Eldaran power lent itself to healing. The thought of touching someone to heal them make his gut twist.

Mathias seemed to sense his reserve. He took another sip of his hot black while studying Kaeden over the rim. "You're still shielding your heart." He put his mug down. "I can see a wall around you, and you've yet to let anyone inside. I had hoped the last few years on Mistsylver Island had given you a chance to heal, but the wound is much deeper than I thought."

Kaeden shifted uneasily. Even without using his power, it seemed as though Mathias could see right through him. Maybe it was from years of living as a Truthsayer.

"I've called you back because I need your help. And you need mine."

"Does it have to do with this war with Nordica?"

"Yes. We are in need of healers."

Kaeden shook his head. "Then you've asked for the wrong perso—"

Mathias reached over and grabbed his hand. "No, I don't believe I have. You carry the same healing power inside you that dwelt inside your parents. And I believe by serving with your hands, your heart and power will finally unlock."

Kaeden's fist tightened under Mathias' grasp. "I don't know if I can." The thought made him feel nauseated.

"We will start small. You'll work alongside me. One patient. Then another. There is much potential inside you. I believe you might even surpass me in time."

Kaeden tried to pull away. There were many gifted Eldarans. And Mathias was the greatest of them all. And he . . . he didn't even have access to his Eldaran powers.

"I won't lie. It will hurt to heal. And when you come into your power, it will hurt even more. But becoming who you were meant to be will allow you to do more than you can as you are right now."

Kaeden swallowed as he studied Mathias. It did not take much imagination to see how much pain the old man had been through to help others. The physical scars attested to that. How much darkness had Mathias seen as a Truthsayer? And yet here he sat, his face full of peace and love, with an inner strength of steel. Strength that had been born of pain and grief, of giving himself over to the Word, and letting the Word pour out His power through this humble man.

Kaeden peered down at the table. Hearing the conviction and power in Mathias's voice stirred him. Somewhere deep inside he wanted what Mathias had. Yet fear wrapped itself tightly around his heart, choking him until he could barely breathe. Could he do this? Could he move past the hurt inflicted on him by humankind? Could he serve humans, *heal* humans? Would it bring his power back?

Did he actually want that?

"Just one step," Mathias said softly. "One patient. And I will be with you."

Kaeden let out a long breath, then glanced up at his mentor and friend. "I don't know if I can do what you're asking of me. And I can't promise I won't leave."

Mathias stood, finished the last of his drink, and placed the mug on the counter. "That is enough for me. If you accept my offer, the Avonain camp is set up outside the main city gates. You will find me at the healers' tents." Mathias spoke again with Finn near the door, then departed.

Kaeden stared down at the table, tapping the rough surface with a finger. Should he do it? Would his power come back? Could he overcome his aversion of humans? It would take a lot of trust and faith for him to become an Eldaran again. And he wasn't sure if he had it in him to do it.

But what did he have to lose?

He stood and grabbed his pack. If things didn't work out, he could head to the Tieve Hills and start a life there.

But he would at least try, for the sake of his mentor.

24

Kaeden made his way through the city of Avonai. It appeared much as it had eight years ago. Long beige buildings lined the dark cobblestone streets. The only colors were white shutters placed on either side of small windows and a few flower boxes filled with bright-red blossoms. Otherwise, the city was as dull as the ocean on a cloud-covered day. Even the people wore dark-grey and blue clothing.

And yet, it felt comfortable. A hint of smoke permeated the air from numerous smokestacks, and the streets overflowed with conversation, squeals of laughter from running children, and happy yips from the dogs chasing them. Women sat on rickety wooden chairs outside their homes, repairing nets or catching up on the latest gossip. The center of the city grew even livelier with people moving in and out of shops, the clang of the blacksmith's hammer, and the cries of those selling wares.

Kaeden continued to make his way west toward the city gates. Occasionally a few people stopped to stare at him, and he heard one whisper about his size. He ignored the comment, shifted the pack across his shoulder, and kept walking. It seemed to be business as usual in Avonai, despite rumors of war. Was it because these people had never experienced such a conflict? Or was it out of sight, out of mind?

His thoughts turned dim. He had experienced war during the uprising in Khodath. If the Nordics were as powerful as the tavern keeper hinted at, war would be on Avonai's doorstep soon.

"Why am I involving myself in this?" he muttered as he approached the gates. He wasn't an Avonain. He wasn't a Rylander. This was not his battle. For one moment, he considered turning left after he passed the gates and heading south toward the Tieve Hills. The chances of war reaching that far were small.

No. I can't. He kept his route as he approached the thick wooden gates. Despite the grumblings of his heart, he couldn't shake this invisible thread that led him to Mathias. Deep down, he knew his future was bound to his old mentor. He'd heard of such a calling from his parents. It was what led them to cross a sea and live in Khodath.

Where would his calling lead him? And could he do it?

Kaeden took in a deep breath of the salty cool air and let it out slowly. Beyond the city gates, hundreds of tents dotted green fields bordered by towering evergreen trees. Avonai wasn't really a military-capable country. That was the White City's strength. Still, the sight of the enormous camp ahead boosted his confidence about Avonai's ability to hold out against the Nordics.

He headed toward the first few rows of tents. Past the canvas structures, men and woman dressed in leather were practicing with various weapons. A line of archers let loose their arrows, followed by dull *thwaps* against the targets. Others trained with their swords. A soldier approached as he paused to watch.

"Here to join the war effort?" the young man asked. He wore a simple tunic and leather with a blue-green tabard, and his dull brown hair was swept back. He possessed the strange ever-changing sea eyes of the Avonain people. Those same eyes currently studied Kaeden, moving from his broad chest and shoulders, then up to his face.

Kaeden shook his head. "No. I'm searching for the healer's tents."

"Oh?" There was a look of confusion on the young man's face. "But I thought—"

"I'm a healer."

The young man's eyes widened until his eyebrows disappeared into his hairline. "Oh?"

Kaeden suppressed the urge to snicker. For once, he found the reaction to his size and position comical. "Can you point me to where they are?"

The man blinked. "Yes, yes, of course. Follow me." He turned and continued along the rows of tents. Kaeden trailed, taking in the sights and sounds of the camp. Once again, a shadow of doubt filled his heart. What was he doing here?

Then the tents parted to reveal three large canvas structures. The left and middle one had a blue star over the opening flaps. The one on the right appeared to be the military command.

"These are the main healer's tents. There are more in the back," the young man said. "Can I do anything else for you?"

"Do you know in which tent Master Mathias is serving?"

"Master Mathias? The Truthsayer?"

Kaeden fought the urge to hide his gloved hand. "Yes."

"He and the woman Eldaran are in the middle tent."

Another Eldaran? There were others here? His stomach tightened. He hadn't seen his own kind in over eight years. Before his change. Before his parents had died. This time he clenched his hand. He had no desire to reveal his lack of power to other Eldarans.

Before he could reconsider and leave, the young man entered the flaps and asked for Master Mathias.

Kaeden's mouth went dry as his body flushed with discomfort and anxiety. Did the other Eldaran know? Had Mathias told her? Or could he keep it a secret a little bit longer? After all, he wouldn't have to use his power anytime soon. Maybe it never needed to be said—

Mathias exited the tent and spotted Kaeden. "Kaeden! You came!" He smiled as he approached, his ornate white robes flowing behind him. A woman stepped out after Mathias. She appeared young, almost the same age as him, and wore white healer's robes. Her hair was long and black, and her eyes a pale blue. Wait. She seemed familiar . . .

Her eyebrows furrowed as she approached the two, almost as if she were having the same thoughts.

Mathias turned and motioned toward her. "Kaeden, this is Selma. She is also helping as a healer. Selma, Kaeden."

She glanced up, and he was sure he knew her from his past. Back when they were young.

"Kaeden?" she said. "Did you and your family live south in the Tieve Hills?"

"Yes." He answered in one breath, not trusting his voice.

"I think we knew each other once. And then you moved across the Illyr Sea."

"Yes." This time his voice was firmer.

She smiled. "Welcome back to Avonai."

He bowed his head. "Thank you."

"Are you gifted in healing like your parents?"

Kaeden glanced at Mathias. What should he say?

The old man seemed to pick up on his panic. "Kaeden is here to learn," Mathias said. "And I'm going to teach him."

Kaeden let out an internal sigh of relief. He wasn't ready to reveal yet that he was an Eldaran in name only.

"We can always use more healers. Especially Eldaran healers," she said.

He stiffened. Did it matter if the healers were human or Eldaran? For some reason, the way she said that made him bristle inside.

"Come, Kaeden. Follow us." Mathias motioned for him to enter. Kaeden readjusted his pack and followed them into the first healing tent. The inside was spacious with ten long rows of cots. At the back two tables groaned beneath wooden boxes, small glass vials, mortars and pestles, and other healing equipment. Next to the tables was a partitioned area. The cots were empty save one near the tables. Two healers dressed in white robes attended a man who appeared to have been injured during practice.

"We're getting ready to pack everything up and move, but for now, I think it's good to familiarize yourself with the layout, how we plan to handle the needs of the battlefield, and with whom you will be working." Mathias motioned across the tent. "Most of the tents are set up like this one with beds for those seriously injured and tables to hold our supplies. The closed-off area is for the healers to use or if we need to place someone apart from everyone else."

The interior of the healing tent sent a familiar ache across his heart. The beds, the table full of herbs and books, the healer's white robes . . . even the briefest hints of mint and lavender in the air. It was all the same.

"It's just like my parent's tent," Kaeden said softly. "Back in Khodath."

A compassionate look came over Mathias's face. "Of course. If you need to step out for a moment, feel free."

"No. It hurts, but it also brings back good memories."

Mathias smiled softly. "I was hoping it would. Your parents were some of the best healers who ever lived."

Yes, they were. Sometimes he wondered if his Eldaran power would have been one of a healer. But healing meant touching, and touching meant close contact with a human, and taking on the wound or sickness. Even now, the thought left a sour taste in his mouth.

Selma watched him from nearby. He didn't know if she knew his story, or what had happened to his family. But she didn't ask any questions, and for that he was thankful.

Mathias continued their circuit around the tent and introduced him to the human healers. "We'll have to see about getting you some robes." He eyed Kaeden's form as they stepped back outside. "You're a lot bigger than the last time I saw you."

"I grew, and my time in the quarry bulked me up," Kaeden said, feeling Selma send an appreciative glance his way. He ignored it.

"I imagine those you've met so far thought you were here to fight."

"Yes," Kaeden said.

"And were shocked to find out you're a healer." Mathias grinned.

"Yes."

"You still grapple, right?"

Kaeden thought back on those nights when the men would make wagers down at the quarry. He'd never lost a contest. It was the only time physically touching a human didn't feel repulsive. Maybe the competitive nature of grappling and the will to win dulled his senses. "Yes, I do."

"Might be fun to see you take down a few of these Avonain soldiers." Mathias chuckled.

Selma eyed Mathias and Kaeden laughed inside. Mathias might be the revered Truthsayer of their people, but he also enjoyed life, which meant cups of hot black, small wagers for fun, and a good story at night. Maybe that was why he'd always liked Mathias. He was real and authentic.

"I hope I don't disappoint," Kaeden replied with a smile.

"I'm sure you won't." As they started for the smaller collection of tents at the rear of the healing-tent section, a young man emerged from one on the right. He wasn't dressed like a healer or a soldier. Instead, his clothing was of fine quality, with a blue-green cloak over a dark tunic and pants. His hair was a dark sandy blond, his mustache and beard neatly trimmed. When he looked up, he bore the strange sea eyes of the Avonain people. In his hands he held a beautiful leather-bound book.

Mathias spotted the man and waved. "Treyvar!"

Treyvar glanced at the three of them and waved back. After tucking the book under his arm, he approached them and bowed his head. "Master Mathias. It is good to see you."

"It is good to see you too. I believe you know Selma?"

Treyvar lifted his head. "Yes, we've met."

"Let me introduce you to Kaeden, my new apprentice."

"Pleasure to meet you." He held out his free hand. Kaeden brought up his own gloved one and shook it. Treyvar didn't comment on the covering. Instead, he smiled. "Are you also an Eldaran like Master Mathias?"

"Yes." He quickly withdrew his hand.

"What is your gift?"

"I am . . . a healer." That seemed to be the best answer at this point.

Treyvar tilted his head to the side. "A healer? I would have thought an Eldaran your size would be a fighter or a Guardian."

Kaeden's body stiffened as Mathias answered for him. "Kaeden's strength and size will help him as an Eldaran healer. It will allow him to take on more hurt and wounds."

Kaeden blinked at Mathias's response. He hadn't thought of that before. It made sense. That was, if he could actually use his power.

Treyvar nodded. "I see."

"What are you reading?" Selma pointed at the book he held.

Treyvar held up the tome. "It's a collection of accounts from the

Great Battle and the Word. I've been studying while waiting for the order for the troops to move out."

Mathias turned toward Kaeden as Selma and Treyvar discussed the book. "Treyvar is a gifted scholar," he said quietly. "He is here to learn and to help. I've never met a more brilliant mind. I think you two might get along."

"He will be working with us?"

Mathias hesitated for a moment. "Yes. As another healer. He wishes to learn."

Kaeden narrowed his eyes. Mathias was hiding something about the young man. But it wasn't his place to ask.

"I see." He glanced at Treyvar, who now carefully turned a page and showed it to Selma. If this man held Mathias's esteem, that meant something. Interesting.

25

Mathias wasted no time in acclimating Kaeden to the life of a healer. Most things were familiar to him, such as the various herbs and process of creating medicine, as well as a basic understanding of human physiology, tools, and methods for healing wounds. Memories of his parents working together at a table like this one brought a sad smile to his face. They had loved this work and helping people.

As for him . . .

Kaeden held up his hands, one currently covered by a fingerless glove. They were rough and scarred from his time in the quarry. He huffed softly. He looked nothing like a healer. And without the typical glow and power his mark should have, he wasn't an Eldaran either. So who was he? *What* was he?

Who am I, Word?

The prayer caught him by surprise. He hadn't prayed in years.

He took a step back and dropped his hands. He'd never stopped believing in the Word. Rather, the same knot that muted his power seemed to reside in his soul. He could no longer hear the Word, see the Word, feel the Word. Like perpetual storm clouds forever hiding the Word's presence from him.

Kaeden swallowed the sudden lump in his throat. Maybe his time with Mathias would heal what was broken inside him.

The next day the Avonain army prepared to march.

Kaeden pulled on the robes Mathias had acquired for him as the sun rose outside his tent. They fit . . . barely. He tightened the cord around his waist, then sat on his cot and pulled on his boots.

Treyvar stepped inside the small tent they shared. "Good morning, Kaeden."

"Morning, Treyvar."

Treyvar placed his book inside the chest at the foot of his cot. "A wagon is coming for our things."

Kaeden glanced at his own chest, which held only a few essentials. "I'm ready."

Together, the two men carried out their belongings. The rest of the camp bustled with activity: storing tents, packing wooden crates and loading them into wagons, acquiring last-minute provisions, and checking weapons. Mathias and Selma gave directions to those assisting with the healer tents.

Kaeden helped place the larger crates onto the wagons, garnering a few glances as he easily picked up what otherwise took two men. It felt good to be using his body again. Sweat collected along his back and neck as he breathed in the salty air from the Illyr Sea.

By noon the Avonain army started their march west. According to the most recent scout report, the Nordics already held Mistcairn and the Dallam Fortress and were now moving south along the Onyx River. It appeared they planned to cut off the White City from Avonai by use of the river that naturally divided the two countries. It was a risky venture since it opened the Nordic forces to attack from both the east and the west, but it also weakened the southern countries since they could not unite.

The Avonain commanders wanted to reach the Tamrath Bridge that crossed the Onyx River before the Nordics could take it. If the coastal army could hold the bridge, they could hold the Nordics in check and keep the pathway between the White City and Avonai open.

Kaeden walked quietly alongside the other healers, his thoughts on the upcoming battle, his mind churning over the Nordics. He knew very little of the northern people and their land. They usually kept to themselves and were considered barbaric by many in the south. He'd met a northern traveler once—a man with gruesome tattoos across his body. They were known fighters but lacked any sophisticated equipment or battle strategy.

What had changed? Why were they attacking the south? And how had they become powerful enough to take Dallam, one of the White City's strongest fortresses, and Mistcairn?

Nobody seemed to know the answer—and no one seemed to care. Except Mathias. He was puzzled by it all as well. And Treyvar. Kaeden heard the young man muttering to himself as he pored over a book with a pen and parchment at his side at night while taking notes.

Treyvar walked quietly a few feet away. Was the young man truly a scribe? There were few this side of the Ari Mountains. Most lived in the city of Thyra and dwelt in the famous Monastery. Maybe Treyvar had traveled here to learn from Mathias. No, that wasn't right. He had sea-eyes. Which meant he was an Avonain and his blood was connected to the sea.

An Avonain scribe?

But why would Mathias hide that fact?

Kaeden chewed over these thoughts until the army reached its first stop for the night.

No one raised a tent. Instead, groups gathered around fires for a quick meal and rest. When the sun rose, the army rose as well and continued their trek west. They traveled through forests, using wide roads that allowed passage for such a large group. Sunlight flickered through the evergreens and broadleaves. The smaller Ascana River nearby provided water.

The goal was to reach the bridge and cross before the week was out. But as the fifth day dawned, scouts reported Nordic troops were nearing the Tamrath Bridge. Alarm spread across the Avonain forces. If the Nordics crossed, not only would they block the main bridge to the White City, but they might also turn their sights on Avonai itself. Kaeden felt a shadow of fear. He'd seen war before. He knew what could come.

As they approached the bridge and the trees gave way to the view, the vast Nordic army appeared, advancing on the other side. Their forces spread along the sloping hills and into the trees beyond the river. A distant roar grew from the Nordics, accompanied by drumming that echoed across the river valley. It took Kaeden a moment to realize the drumming sound came from weapons being thumped against shields.

Then a long bellow filled the air as a cavalry of war bears emerged on the left. A flock of crows rose into the air from the trees as if sensing death and prepared for the upcoming feast.

"Word, be with us," one of the healers nearby whispered. Kaeden caught the words and agreed. His own heart thumped harder. This was more than the uprising he had experienced in Khodath.

As the two forces converged near the banks of the Onyx River, the Avonain commanders and captains shouted instructions to their troops. The river was too wide and deep to forge. Crossing by either would be a death sentence. And the bridge was constructed from stone. Unlike one made from wood, this one could not be burned. Whoever held it at the end of the battle would have access to the other side.

Kaeden glanced at the Avonain army. Could they do it? Could they hold it? They had the advantage of defending their home. But even as he watched, faces paled around him as the Nordics shouted and raised their weapons in preparation for the fight. Avonains were not fighters. They were sea-people. And the Nordics knew it. Even now they jeered at the southerners from across the river.

Kaeden clamped his mouth shut and turned away as Mathias instructed the healers to set up their tents. In Khodath, he'd learned that the first fight in war wasn't physical, it was mental. So far, the Nordics were winning.

As he helped Mathias and the others, he heard nothing more of the battle plan. He wasn't a soldier, and this wasn't his fight. Instead, he found himself in the same place he'd been six years ago: preparing for the aftermath. After the tents were raised, he moved inside and unpacked the crates while flags were hung on poles so those on the battlefield knew where the healers were. His fingers moved without a thought, preparing the herbs, checking the bandages, setting out honey, water, and wine for washing the wounds. A fire was prepared outside to heat water and rods for cauterizing.

The camp was oddly silent, save for the distant shouts of the

Nordics. In the quiet, a sick feeling pooled in his gut apart from the upcoming battle.

As if sensing his unease, Mathias appeared at his side. "One patient at a time," the older man said quietly. "You will only need to touch someone if you feel comfortable. Otherwise, I will have you assist me and the other healers. You remember what is needed for what, correct?"

"Yes." The sick feeling lessened. He could assist. He could do that much. But his hands still trembled.

Mathias placed his aged, wrinkled one over Kaeden's. "Healing comes with pain. It will be difficult to overcome what you've seen and been through." He sighed and looked down. "Sometimes I wonder if I should have left you on Mistsylver or brought you back here. But what is done is done." He patted Kaeden's hand. "Open your heart a little today. Then a little more tomorrow. Open your heart to the Word and to humanity. It won't come all in one day. But if you keep at this, you *will* change. You will heal. And when you need to take a step back, rest. Your healing is a journey from this point on. But you're not alone."

Kaeden nodded, not trusting his voice. There was still a part of him that didn't want to be here. His life at the quarry had been simple and unobtrusive. But another part of him—a small part—wanted to overcome this hurt. To be free. To live and laugh and love like Mathias did. He clenched his gloved hand. *Healing comes with pain.*

Well, he wasn't a stranger to pain.

26

Screams penetrated the tent walls. Familiar sounds. Shouts, cries, clashing. Kaeden leaned forward and pressed his palms across the wooden table and took in deep, measured breaths. Had the Nordics crossed the bridge? Or were the Avonains leading the charge?

Treyvar stood nearby, dressed in the same white robes as the rest of the healers. He raised his head and glanced at the tent flaps behind them.

"So it has begun." A flash of anger rippled across his face before he schooled his features.

Kaeden lifted his head. He agreed with the man, but there seemed to be more to his anger.

Selma finished recounting the bandages and came to stand beside the two men. She appeared calm and collected.

"Isn't this your first battle?" Kaeden asked her.

She looked up at him. "Yes. But I've been healing almost my whole life. No matter how the wound happens, it's still the same. Do everything you can to save the person."

"Have you used your Eldaran power to heal another?"

This time she paled slightly. "Yes." She rubbed the mark on her palm. Traces of light from her mark glowed through the gaps between her fingers. "As you know, it hurts to take on the wound of another. I do it rarely, and for a very good reason."

No, he did not know. He had never healed another person. But he had watched his parents heal. They'd used their gifts to restore many, and he remembered the numerous scars they carried on their bodies because of their healings. He frowned. What constituted a good reason for Selma?

Time ticked by and shadows moved across the tent as the sun made its path across the sky. Both Treyvar and Selma left the tent to watch the fight, but Kaeden had no desire to join them. He'd seen enough fighting to last a lifetime.

Then came the words he had waited and dreaded to hear came. A healer stuck his head inside the tent flaps. "Runners are bringing in the first wave of wounded!" Then he was gone. Moments later, Mathias appeared, already rolling up the sleeves of his robe. His mark shined through the gaps of his glove in the shadows of the tent likes beams of light.

"Are you ready, Kaeden?" he said as he secured his sleeves.

Kaeden took in a deep breath. "Yes."

But doubt filled his heart when the first handful arrived crowding the cots. The smell of blood, sweat, and vomit permeated the air. Only the most critical were brought in. The rest were treated outside or were already on their way to the Celestial Halls and beyond help. Two human healers joined Mathias and Kaeden. Leon and Darry, if he remembered correctly.

Leon started on a man with a gash across his thigh while Darry helped another who held his arm close to his chest. Others were left to cry and moan across cots until someone could help. Mathias moved to help two runners carrying a bloody mess of a man between them. The soldier had taken a pummeling, and Kaeden found it hard to believe he wasn't crossing the veil already. Selma stood outside the tent, directing runners and deciding whether or not those brought had a chance. If she'd sent him in, he'd been given that chance.

Mathias directed him to be placed near the table in back and immediately assessed the damage. Kaeden grabbed items as Mathias called for them. A knife for cutting away cloth. Wine and water for cleansing. When he called for Kaeden to hold the man down, he hesitated. This was it. Time to take the plunge. Neither Mathias nor the man had time for his waffling.

Mouth dry, Kaeden reached for the soldier. He shunted away all thoughts save one: listen to Mathias and do whatever he asked. With his eyes still on Mathias, he gripped the man's shoulders. There was nausea, but nothing came up. He pushed through. *I'm here to heal*, he kept repeating to himself. *I'm here to help.* The man thrashed, but Mathias was able to quickly clean out the deep wounds, pack them, then bandage everything up.

"You did good," Mathias said quietly as the man fell unconscious.

"And the soldier?" Kaeden asked, finally peering down at his patient.

"His body needs to do the rest. But we've given him a fighting chance."

"Oh," was all Kaeden said. But he felt a release of tension across his body. He'd done it.

That feeling, however, was short lived. With so many needing help, Kaeden eventually grew numb to the cries that filled the tent as he followed Mathias and did whatever the older man told him to do. Those who could be moved were taken out to make room for more. As the afternoon dragged on, the healers took a few moments to rest and drink before working again. He never saw Mathias remove his glove. So far, they hadn't needed his Eldaran healing power.

Evening fell and the troops regrouped. Kaeden caught only snatches of conversation as he finally stepped out of the tent into the cool night air. Nordics had crossed the bridge at the beginning of the battle, but the Avonains had pushed them back just as evening fell. More words were spoken as he made his way to one of the feeder streams on their side of the river to wash and fill the buckets. A half moon lit his way.

If the wounded that came in were any indication, the Nordics had proven powerful and skilled, much more than had been anticipated. There was talk of men dressed in the pelts of wolves, eagles swooping down on their troops, and the famed berserkers who battled alongside their bears. And a woman who fought like a she-devil. Yet the Avonains had held the bridge in the end.

Safe within the tree line, Kaeden stared across the river as he knelt at the water's edge. In the distance, Nordic campfires glowed. He dipped his hands into the icy water, then proceeded to wash his face before filling the buckets. How many had the Nordics lost? Was it as many as they had?

Kaeden filled the buckets and headed back to the healing tents. Oil lamps lit the workspace so the healers could see. He placed the buckets down and retrieved more. The rest of the night was spent snatching a few hours of sleep in the partitioned area in the back of the tent or attending to those who woke up.

He no longer hesitated to touch a human. There was no time for vacillation. Whether he was overcoming his revulsion or was simply numb because of the job he wasn't sure. But maybe Mathias was right. By plunging him into the midst of healing with no other option than to help others, he might start healing his own internal brokenness.

The second day brought more injured. The Avonains held on to the bridge, barely. But Nordic archers were proving to be formidable, sending many southerners to the healing tents. Then a shout went up from outside the healing tents. The Nordics were crossing again.

Groans filled the tent and a few gasps sounded from those waiting for healers. Leon swore as he held a cloth to the shoulder of a man from whom he had recently pulled an arrow.

"Why don't we just destroy the bridge? Then there wouldn't be a reason to fight."

Darry stood nearby, along with a woman healer, bandaging the leg of another man. "It's a stone bridge. It would take a boulder the size of a house to crush it. And if we lose it, we cannot recapture Dallam or convene with forces from the White City. The next crossing is far to the south."

"Who cares about retaking Dallam?" Leon answered. "It belongs to the White City anyway. And we don't even know if the White City will come to our aid. We should be focusing on our own lands."

Kaeden listened quietly as he replenished supplies and prepared poultices. Both arguments had a point. Each held risk. Defend one's homeland and hope it was enough. Or merge with the White City and take on the Nordics together. But failure either way meant possibly losing Avonai and the coastlands. The gamble was choosing the right strategy.

"Depending on the White City is a fool's hope," the woman said, finally speaking up.

"What?" Kaeden looked over at her. He hadn't met or worked with this healer yet. Usually she labored in the other tent. But at the moment it housed the critical, and those patients were under Mathias's and Selma's care.

"Hush. Don't say such things around the soldiers." Darry glared at his partner.

She pressed her lips together and continued to roll the linen around the man's calf. It didn't appear as though anyone had heard her.

Kaeden picked up the tray of supplies he had prepared and started around the tent, delivering poultices, bandages, wine, and honey. As he passed a cot, a hand grabbed his wrist just above his glove.

The tray fell.

He reacted without thought and wrenched his hand away, hard.

The young man went flying forward off the cot and hit the ground with a thud.

"What in the Lands?" Darry dashed across the tent to help the young man. The rest of the healers stared at Kaeden. "What'd you do that for?"

Kaeden stood frozen as a sick feeling pooled in the pit of his stomach. He hadn't meant to react to the touch. He hadn't reacted to any since the battle began. But this particular moment of feeling the skin of another triggered something inside him.

"He startled me. I didn't mean to do that." He flexed his fingers, angry and horrified at his reaction. "It was an accident."

"An accident?" The woman healer frowned.

Kaeden twisted around without even picking up the tray. "I need some air." He left before anyone could say another word. Outside, he leaned against one of the tent poles and ran a hand through his hair. He'd thought he was doing better. After all, he had been helping people all day yesterday. But a single touch today sent him reeling.

"Word, why?" he said through gritted teeth. "I want to be like my parents. I want to help people. And yet I hate them at the same time. How can both be possible?" Was it thoughts like this that kept him from realizing his Eldaran power? *How do I change? Do I even want to change?*

Flashbacks filled his mind, sending his heart racing. Watching the very people his parents had been helping only weeks before haul them to away to be executed. The sick feeling moved to his mouth. He placed a hand across his lips. He was going to throw up—

Horns blew across the battlefield. Kaeden took in a couple deep breaths. He needed to clear his mind. This was not the time to revisit past memories or to vomit. He took in another breath and raised his head. What was happening?

"Retreat! Retreat!" he heard shouted in the distance. The horns sounded again.

Retreat? As the words moved across the battlefield, soldiers started to run. Kaeden straightened, the bitterness from the last few minutes replaced by resolve and cool willpower. He might not be able to touch others at the moment, but he was strong and fast. He could help the wounded and healers get away from here.

Before anyone could react inside the tents, he called for the wagons and started gathering the crates.

"What's happening?" Selma emerged from the nearby healing tent.

"The commanders have called for a retreat," Kaeden said as he moved another crate. "Let the others know. We need to get the wounded into the wagons once they arrive and stow everything away."

Selma nodded and returned inside. Like a tidal wave, Avonain soldiers raced past. Kaeden used his height to look over the passing heads toward the bridge. At least not everyone was abandoning their posts. Some still fought to allow others to retreat.

But they didn't have much time.

The wagons arrived, and those unable to leave on foot were loaded, along with crates and supplies.

"Where's Mathias?" Kaeden asked Selma as the first of the wagons left. One tent remained, of which everything had already been hauled out.

"He had to use his Eldaran power," she said.

Kaeden let out his breath. "Oh."

The fact that Mathias used his power meant someone had been on the brink of death, and his power had come alive and guided him to save that person. At least, that was how it had worked for his parents. Even now he remembered how the marks on their hands would glow before they touched the person and took on their wound or sickness.

And how they would be unconscious for at least a day afterward as their bodies healed.

He entered the tent. Sure enough, Mathias was laid out on a blanket, appearing as though he was sleeping. But Kaeden knew better. What new scar had Mathias acquired with this healing?

And why hadn't Selma been the one to heal?

"Take down the tent," he told the two men who entered behind him. "I will care for Master Mathias."

The men nodded. Kaeden bent down and wrapped the blanket around Mathias's body. For a split second, Mathias appeared like a corpse, shrouded and ready for burial. Kaeden blinked, and the image was gone. Mathias was breathing evenly. He was simply in a deep sleep.

Kaeden let out his breath, then with one powerful move, he lifted the older man. A slight frown creased his face. Mathias felt unusually light.

He left the tent and stepped toward the last waiting wagon. The moment he exited, others tore down the tent. Selma climbed into the wagon alongside a couple of wounded. "Here," she said. "Lay Mathias in front of me. I'll watch over him."

He placed Mathias inside, and Selma adjusted the blanket around him.

It felt like a hand had reached inside him and was squeezing his heart. "You can't die on me, old man," he whispered and brushed the top of Mathias's head. "I still haven't healed. You need to help me."

Selma gave him a puzzled look. Kaeden turned away. Within minutes, the tent was dismantled and stored. The driver let out a yip, and the horses started forward with the wagon. Kaeden glanced back.

Most of the Nordics had returned to the bridge. A few dressed in leather and grey fur gave chase. One of the companies under a Captain Bertin remained behind, engaging the Nordic warriors and giving the rest of the Avonains time to escape.

Another long sigh escaped Kaeden's lips.

They had lost this battle. But there would be many more.

27

Brighid stood beside the bridge, panting. The sun beat down across her heated face, and the smell of sweat and blood drifted into her nostrils. In the distance the Avonain army retreated through the evergreen trees. A few of Volka's clan chased after them, but Hjar Adrian had given the command to let them go and for the Nordic forces to regroup. Yes, they'd won this battle, but they had also taken quite a few causalties.

She went to wipe her face with the back of her hand, only to find blood across her knuckles and thought better of it. Instead, she held her sword up and studied her fingers and the reddened blade. The blood was already drying across the surface, turning dark in the sunlight. Strange. She didn't feel anything toward the life liquid currently coating her body and blade. No, that wasn't entirely true. There was something deep within her that recoiled at the blood, but it was a tiny ripple on the lake of her otherwise stationary emotions. She flicked the blade and placed it in her sheath to clean later.

"Brighid, help me!" Johan shouted from her left, assisting a limping Marta among the Nordics moving slowly back to the bridge.

"What happened?" Brighid hurried to Marta's other side.

Marta laughed through gritted teeth. "One of those sons of Morrud thought he could take me out as he was retreating. When we clashed, I twisted my ankle. But I still got him. He should have run when he had the chance." She grimaced as she put her right foot down.

"Here, pass me your weapons so you can focus on walking."

Johan and Marta stopped so she could pass over her shield and sword. There were a few notches and splinters in the wood, proof of a fierce battle. Brighid tucked the extra shield under her arm and carried the sword with her other hand.

Marta wasn't the only one limping. Quite a few held arms close to their bodies, limping, or mopping blood away from gashes. Usually each person was responsible for taking care of their own medical needs if they were simple. Johan kept a small pouch with a few essentials he shared with those around him. If the injury was really bad, the deathkeepers were ready in the rear to heal, or if need be, assist the warrior to the beyond.

A handful of clanless passed them, carrying long hooks at the end of wooden rods. They were in charge of gathering the dead. Brighid paused and watched them go by, a shiver passing through that deep place inside where a spark of feeling still lived. She didn't raise her eyes to search for the bodies soon to be gathered. She might no longer feel death, but it was still here, and she didn't want to see it.

With a deep breath, she caught up to Johan and Marta. A line gathered to cross the bridge to the other side, where sleeping rolls and packs had been left around empty campfires.

"We sent them running," a young man snickered ahead of them. Brighid saw the faint tattoo of antlers along the back of his neck near where his light hair was gathered in a braid.

"They chose to retreat," Johan said under his breath. "It was a tactical decision."

The young man must have heard because he swiveled around, his pale-blue eyes bright and angry. "What did you say?" he asked, then flinched when he found himself looking up into Johan's face.

Marta turned her head, but Brighid caught her laughing under her breath.

"I said they chose to retreat. We didn't send them running. There were heavy causalties and injuries on both sides. Because of that, they pulled out first."

"What are you, a clanless coward?" The young man jutted out his chin.

Johan ignored him as he walked past him and onto the bridge while holding Marta by his side.

"Clanless coward." The young man spat on the ground, then glanced over at Brighid. "Are you a clanless coward too?"

Brighid rolled her eyes and followed Johan. The young man wasn't worth her time or words. He reminded her of a tiny rooster strutting about, seeking a fight.

"No, she would be the Stryth'Veizla, you son of Morrud," a deep voice said behind them.

Johan, Marta, and Brighid stopped and looked back to find a handful of Bear Clan warriors approaching the bridge. They were all brawny men and one woman. They wore dark leather jerkins across their midsections and bracers along their forearms. Marks of Remembrance crisscrossed their exposed skin.

The speaker was the largest one of the group, his black hair pulled back in a dozen braids and a beard that covered his face. One scar ran the length of his cheek from his temple down into his beard.

The young warrior's eyes went wide as his gaze bounced between Brighid and the bear warrior. "The Stryth'Veizla?" he asked as he considered Brighid again. "I-I didn't know." He pushed past the three of them and hurried toward his companions.

"Bonehead," the bear warrior said, and those around him laughed. He glanced at Brighid. "First time we're meeting. But I've seen you fight. Like a berserker. Where did you learn to fight like that, young clanless one?"

"The streets of Ragnbork," Brighid replied coolly. "The last few years were not kind to the clanless."

His eyebrows shot up. "I see. I'm learning how much we misjudged the clanless. Apparently there were many warriors lying dormant. Like the three of you. Perhaps when this war is over and you live, there might be a place within the Bear Clan for fighters like you." He bowed his head. "Stryth'Veizla." Then he bowed toward Johan and Marta. "Fellow warriors." Then he and the other Bear Clan warriors started across the bridge.

"That was some brave talk, Brighid," Marta whispered as the warriors passed. They followed a few paces behind. "Answering the right hand and skal of Hjar Gurmund like that."

"That was one of the skals for the Bear Clan?" Brighid eyed the broad back of the tall, dark man ahead.

"Yes, Skal Stein. He leads those who fight without bears."

She watched him as he walked and talked with his fellow warriors and felt nothing. Not brave, not anxious. Nothing.

"It was the truth," she said. "We all learned to fight in order to survive."

Marta looked at her. "Yes. But not all of us fight like you."

They finished crossing the bridge. Brighid had nothing to say. How did she explain the red haze? How it felt? Like this overwhelming need to fight. An adrenaline rush that allowed her to overpower anyone in her path. How it gave her the power to conquer. And without it she would have died at the hands of an eljun a long time ago. Brighid finally spoke.

"I'm not sure I like that name."

"What, Stryth'Veizla?" Marta asked.

"Yes. It makes it sound like I enjoy fighting. And killing."

"And you don't?"

"The first time I fought, it was to survive. And every time after. It is to survive or protect. But I find no joy in it. Especially not killing. It is something I must do." That, and she didn't want to die. Even though she couldn't feel death anymore, it still existed. And it could claim her at any time.

"Wise words," Johan said with a nod. "That is the true way of a Nordic warrior."

"Humph," Marta said. "It's not that I like killing. But there is a thrill in winning a fight." Marta glanced at Brighid. "Watching you fight is almost like watching a dance. A bloody, deadly dance. You're gifted, Brighid. It's a gift I wish I had."

Brighid didn't answer. Instead she mulled over Marta's words as they reached the other side of the bridge. Maybe there was a part of her that *did* like fighting. The competitive aspect of going head-to-head with another warrior. But not the crushing part. And definitely not the death part. Could one have the hands of a fighter and find honorable pleasure in that ability?

What would Elphsaba say?

My daughter, this is what you were made for. Use those hands to fight, to protect. And find joy in that.

She could almost hear Elphsaba's low voice in her head as those words came to mind. Perhaps there could be joy in protecting. And pushing oneself to the limit. But war meant death. So how did she reconcile the fact that protecting meant death? How many had to die to save others? Who made that decision?

"Ugh." Brighid winced as a sharp pain spread from her temple and over her head. Too many conflicting thoughts. It was giving her a headache.

"Everything all right?" Johan asked. "Are you injured?"

Brighid rubbed her forehead. "No. Just a headache coming on."

"I might have something for that. I'll check when we get back to our camp."

A small smile crept across her face. Of course he did. Johan was ready for anything.

The Nordic forces celebrated that night with fresh supplies brought down the river from Dallam. Kegs of ale were passed out, along with smoked meat and cheeses and hard rounds of bread.

"Who would have thought these southerners could actually brew a decent drink?" Marta lifted her wooden mug to her lips. Brighid laughed but did not partake. However, she found the smoked pork amazing. Johan and a few other clanless enjoyed themselves around the fire.

"Were all these supplies just hiding out in Dallam?" Johan asked as he broke off a piece of cheese.

"I heard they're from the smaller villages between Dallam and Mistcairn," one of the clanless warriors said. He was short and thickset, and an axe hung at his side.

"The villages? But we never took the time to take them out," Johan replied.

"Didn't have to. One of those strangers working with the hjars did it herself."

Brighid paused. "All by herself?"

The warrior finished chewing. "That's what I heard. Name's Hagen, by the way. Her power is different from Armand the Oathmaker's."

"What does her power do?"

Hagen shrugged. "All I know is she clears out a village, then a couple clanless assist her in bringing back the spoils. We would run out of food and supplies soon if not for her raids."

"All by herself," Brighid murmured again.

"I bet you could do that." Hagen lifted his mug toward Brighid.

Brighid huffed. "Hardly." She tore off a chunk of the smoked pork and popped it into her mouth, savoring the rich smoky flavor. She could eat this all day.

Hagen glanced up thoughtfully. "Maybe she's a real Stryth'Veizla."

"There's only one Stryth'Veizla, and that is my friend here," Marta said, a dark look coming over her face.

Hagen peered over at Brighid. "I think you're right, Marta. One of my comrades helped clear the first few villages the stranger Viessa took out shortly after Mistcairn. Said when he entered the entire village was already dead. Everyone was just lying around on the ground. But there was no blood, no wounds. Nothing. As if they had all collapsed in a deathly sleep. Very eerie, he said."

"I've never heard of such a thing," Johan said. "I know a bit about the Eldarans, but these beings working with the hjar . . ." he paused, then leaned forward. "They're not the same."

"Eldarans?" Hagen tilted his head. "I've heard that word before. A long time ago. But if they're not Eldarans, then what are they? Eldarans are the only ones I know who possess real power in this world."

Johan shook his head. "I don't know."

"And how are they taking out whole villages?" Brighid asked.

Everyone grew silent around the campfire.

"Ugh, we're supposed to be celebrating!" Marta held up her mug. "We won a victory over Avonai, and they retreated. Let's celebrate!"

Her words broke through the solemnity, and everyone laughed.

"You're right!" Hagen took a big swig from his mug. Then he broke into an old Nordic song and the others joined in.

28

Armand sat up with a groan. How long had he been out this time? The last thing he remembered was the Battle at the Bridge, then binding the Nordics again to their oath. He slowly lifted his hand and stared at his palm. The area ached with a burning sensation. Each time he bound the warriors to his words, his mark burned as if each utterance set his palm on fire.

He clenched his hand and grimaced as pain shot up his arm and into his shoulder. Yes. It hurt. And yet the power it brought was exhilarating. This ability to exert his will over such a large group of people. Like puppets on a string—and he was the master. So much better than the unassuming life he used to lead.

He glanced around. Peder snoozed inside the tent with his hands folded over his lap. Armand's lip curled. He didn't care much for the younger man. He was brash and wild. But he was also Viessa's brother, and she only agreed to accompany him across the Ari Mountains if they brought Peder with them.

Not that any of them had a choice. They had been exiled from the Eldarans. Called heretics because they had vocally declared the Word had no say in their lives and their powers were their own. He laughed softly and stood. What did that make the elders and those who followed them? The same? They claimed to follow the Word, but they lived for themselves. He was just more truthful about it.

Armand stretched his limbs. Peder might be wild, but he did have his place. His ability to absorb and transfer lifeforce was unparalleled, and he possessed inhuman strength. Both were useful in a guard. Armand opened and closed his hand. Despite the residual pain from the oathbinding, the extra life-giving energy Peder had given him coursed through his body. He'd keep the young man. Retaining Peder meant Viessa would continue to work at his side. He paused. He hadn't heard from her in weeks. Perhaps he should see if she had sent any word from Dallam.

Armand emerged from the tent to find the camp still asleep from a second night of celebrating. Dying fires sent swirls of smoke into the overcast sky. The hjars and skals were still in their tents while the rest of the Nordic warriors slept under an open sky around firepits. Thousands lay across the fields, sleeping off the ale imbibed the night before. They were a powerful people, but barbaric.

He carefully stepped around tents and bodies as he made his way toward the river. What he wouldn't give for a hot bath in a real tub. And a glass of red wine. Not a filthy river surrounded by drunks.

After minutes of maneuvering, he made it to the riverbank. The water was icy to the touch and took his breath away. He stepped into the flowing stream and washed. No matter if it was a battlefield or Wolf Clan hovel, he would maintain his dignity and way of living.

This was only temporary. Once the hjars, and particularly Volka, had what they wanted, he would have what he wanted: a life free of control and service. He snorted. The Eldaran elders preached humility and poverty, but they certainly didn't live by their words. Why should he? He'd seen their actions during the yearly journey to Thyra: the pleasure houses, the dishonesty and use of power during haggling, and their drunken ways. And yet he and his comrades had been the ones cast out.

He scowled as he climbed onto the riverbanks. No. He would not dwell on the past. The only path forward now was the future. He stood and let the sun soak through his chilled body as he cast a glance across the camp again. The Nordics weren't necessarily the people he wanted to work with.

When he'd arrived in Wolfvar, the living conditions of the Wolf Clan had been rugged and rustic. Not the castle and luxuries he desired. But when he'd heard about the skirmishes on the border and sensed the bloodlust inside the Wolf Clan, he'd realized how easy it would be to manipulate them into achieving his goals. And when he'd arrived in Ragnbork and seen Elding Citadel, he'd known he wanted it. He wanted that city. All he needed to do was give the Nordics their victories and he could have what he wanted: his own empire.

Granted, it would be easier if he had the power of the Truthsayer. With the truthsaying gift, he could have twisted their minds. But he and the other Eldarans had no idea who their Truthsayer was or where he or she could be found. The last one had left their assembly ages ago to serve humankind. But the oathbinding worked almost as well. A few words and people were addicted to his voice. He just had to keep rebinding them or else they would suffer. Not that he cared. He just wanted them obedient.

As he started back toward the tents, he spotted a few Nordics moving. Apparently not every Nordic had drunk themselves into a stupor. He was halfway across the camp when he spotted a young blond woman stoking the fire. He was about to walk by, then stopped. He recognized her. Something she said that first day had burrowed into his mind like a sliver.

You are death.

When she'd said those words, he realized she knew he carried death in his palm. The truth of it was in her eyes and in her tone. Fear of him. Revulsion. He'd let his emotions get the best of him that day, and he'd bound her more tightly than any of the other Nordics. Afterward, she'd appeared an empty shell with no seeming knowledge of what had transpired.

However, that one moment, and those few words, had broken through the veneer he lived behind and reminded him his mark was no longer filled with light. That he *was* death. And that his Eldaran gift had died a long time ago, replaced with something dark and hideous.

She glanced up. He held his breath as they stared at each other across a couple campfires. Then she turned away. For a moment, he wondered if she would remember again what he really was. But that woman was gone or buried deep beneath his words.

As it should be.

Armand straightened his clothes and held his head high as he reached the tents again. He swept back the flap and entered the temporary dwelling. Peder still slept in the corner, and there was no folded message left by his bedside. He would check later.

Later that evening a messenger stopped by with a note from Dallam. From Viessa. Armand entered his tent, stood by the light from a small lamp, and broke the seal. The letter was long and detailed. Viessa had been able to secure the entire region along the Ari Mountains from Dallam to the coast, using two shadows she had brought across the veil. After the shadows did their work, a small clanless unit secured the spoils.

A smile lit across his face. He'd known Viessa and her guardian power would be helpful. The shadow-wraith Mordra were perfect for silently entering small settlements and stealing away the lives within. No need for warriors, and the clanless who had been assigned to her were bound in silence.

> I can only control two right now. And I've been forced to take a life every few days to sustain myself. So far I've been using villagers. But most are gone. I might have to use a clanless soon.

Armand tapped his chin. Should he have her return the shadows to the other side? Keeping two Mordra under control in this world was taxing. But ripping the veil to bring them back and forth each time was also taxing. No, he would have her keep the two shadows for the time being.

"Is that a letter from my sister?" Peder asked as he entered the tent.

Armand folded it and placed it in the creases of his robes. "Yes."

"Is she doing well?"

"Yes."

"Will she be joining us at some point?"

Armand thought for a moment. "Maybe." Perhaps he would speak to Volka and have the hjar send reinforcements to Dallam and solidify their hold on the north. Then Viessa could come here and assist them by taking more villages within the Ryland Plains. Her shadows would provide more provisions, take care of those between here and Anwin Forest, and clear a path toward the White City. He would have to be careful not to reveal the shadows to the Nordics. Their superstitious religion in the old gods would not welcome the presence of the shadows.

"Yes, I think I'll see if she wishes to join us," Armand said. "Where were you?"

A vicious glint entered the young man's eyes. "Searching for someone to replenish my strength." He stretched out his hands. Armand caught sight of Peder's mark as he flexed his fingers. Black and scorched around the edges. Just like his own. "Volka said he would send someone to our tent. Do you also need replenishing?"

"No, the life you gave me yesterday was enough."

"Are you sure? You still seem pale."

"We don't want others to grow suspicious. Especially Hjar Gurmund. We have made progress with the other hjars, but the old man continues to be distrustful."

Peder settled down on the edge of his bed. "We should get rid of him. Old men like him are useless. I know Volka agrees."

"He still holds sway over Hjar Adrian and Hjar Frieda. His son would become clan leader, and I suspect his son is like his father. No, for the time being this is better. His suspicions work in our favor. The others lean on him instead of thinking for themselves. As long as we don't give the others a reason to suspect, his distrust is enough for them."

Movement came from outside the tent, then a low voice spoke through the flaps. "A gift from Volka."

Peder stood and smiled. He crossed the tent and accepted a bound and gagged young man inside. The warrior remained outside, his shadow barely visible along the canvas wall.

The young man tried to speak, then move, but the Wolf Clan had restrained him well. Peder held him by the arm with his unmarked hand and glanced at Armand.

"Are you sure you don't need replenishment?"

Armand shook his head. "He's all yours."

Peder grinned and grabbed the young man's throat with his marked hand. The sight was always the same during the exchange of life. First, the person's eyes grew wide, then the mouth opened in a scream, silenced by the gag. The body would begin convulsing until every drop of life was extracted. Afterward, all that remained was a corpse.

Armand watched in fascination as Peder finished and tossed the body to the ground. What was supposed to be a life-giving and healing ability they'd reversed and now took life instead. Every gift of the Eldarans had an opposite effect, and this was one of them. Sometimes in the darkest recesses of his mind he was puzzled as to why the Word allowed such a dichotomy.

"I'm done," Peder told the warrior outside. The man entered and took the body without a look or word. He had done this a half dozen times now. But Armand still wondered what the man thought.

The body was hauled away, and Peder had a glow of life around his face. "I needed that. Your oathbinding yesterday required much of your power, which required much of mine."

Armand bowed his head. "Thank you for your support. I couldn't bind so many people if it wasn't for you." Which was mostly true. But he grew stronger each time he used his words.

Peder held his hand up and stared at his palm for a moment, then dropped it.

Armand was sure he spotted a look of disquiet on Peder's face. They all felt it. The darkness inside. Sometimes he wondered if their marks were a reflection of their souls. If so, they needed to stay alive as long as they could. Forever if possible. He might not follow the Word, but he knew the One was real, and he suspected they would have to pay for twisting His gift.

But if they could cheat death, there would be no Word to judge them in the afterlife.

29

Kaeden sat beside Mathias's cot, waiting for his mentor to wake up.

The Avonain army had retreated east until the sun set, then continued east for another day until they reached the foothills where the forest grew thick and they could defend should the Nordics pursue. Kaeden and Selma had watched over Mathias as they traveled by wagon. Tents were set up for the wounded once they reached the forest while the rest of the army slept between the trees.

As the hours dragged by and Mathias still didn't wake from his healing, Kaeden had begun to fear the time had come for Mathia's departure to the Celestial Halls. Despite the gift of healing, even Eldarans grew old and their bodies weary. And Mathias was very old.

Not today, Kaeden pleaded. *Please, not today—*

Mathias sat up with a start. "W-where am I?"

Intense relief spread across Kaeden. He reached over and gripped Mathias's shriveled hand. "You're safe, old man." They were in a partitioned section of one of the healing tents. The sun had set an hour ago, and the oil lamps cast soft light over the area.

"Kaeden?"

"Yes."

Mathias fell back against the pillow. "Thank the Word." He gave Kaeden a sideways glance. "I see you're still disrespectful."

Kaeden grinned while inside he sighed. "You're the only one I call 'old man.'"

"Humph." A smile twitched along his lips.

He gave the old man's hand another squeeze, then stood. "I'm going to get you some food. And Selma has been waiting for you to awaken."

"And a cup of hot black if they have any," Mathias called out as Kaeden turned.

Kaeden grinned. Yes. Mathias was back.

Twenty minutes later, he returned with a bowl of broth and a cup of hot black. Where the supply officer had found the grounds to make the hot black, he didn't know. But he had a steaming cup of the bitter brew for Mathias. The stuff always seemed to perk him up.

Kaeden passed the broth to Mathias first. Mathias eyed the cup instead. Kaeden held it away. "Broth first."

Mathias growled but complied. He drank the small bowl of broth, then held it out to Kaeden. "Satisfied?"

"Very. Here you go."

Mathias held the cup to his face and breathed in the scent with a contented sigh.

Kaeden smiled at his reaction. "Selma is finishing her rounds in the other tent, then she will be here."

Mathias took a sip. "Always working, that girl," he murmured. "And what about you?"

"Me?" The happier feelings from moments ago evaporated.

"How did it go while I was unconscious? Were you able to help? Or did you find difficulty touching another person?"

It was as if Mathias could read his thoughts. Maybe he could. Kaeden leaned forward in his chair, crossed his arms over his knees, and looked down. "I hurt somebody."

"Accident?"

"Yes. I reacted. To his touch."

"I see." Mathias held the cup in one hand and used his other to cover Kaeden's shaking one. His fingers were warm from the cup. "It's all right. The Word understands your struggles. But you are here. And you are taking steps."

"Sometimes I don't want to help. I want to walk away from it all: humans, the hurt, life."

"Of course you do. We share the same feelings humans have." Mathias paused. "I'm sorry I wasn't there for you."

Kaeden raised his head. "What are you saying? You healed somebody. That is one of the greatest things an Eldaran can do." Which made him wonder again why Selma had not been the one to heal. Yes, her real power was in oathmaking, but every Eldaran could heal. Except him. And Mathias was getting along in years. Soon he would no longer be able to take on the wounds and sicknesses of others.

"You are doing that very thing. Except the person you are healing is yourself."

Kaeden let out a snort. Count on Mathias to turn his words on him. But maybe Mathias wasn't wrong. Kaeden had been able to assist Mathias on the first day of battle. So what had happened on the second?

Mathias took another sip, then studied him thoughtfully. "Maybe we should give you a different task. What if you became a runner? You're strong enough to assist those injured on the battlefield. You also have a strong constitution and are levelheaded. The sight of blood and carnage doesn't seem to affect you as much, and you can think on your feet."

Kaeden mulled it over. He would still be touching others, but it would be those in dire need, even more than those who lay in the healing tents. Deep down, he still possessed his parents' heart to help others. Maybe seeing those who needed him most would connect with that part of him, allowing him to move past his revulsion.

Maybe.

Kaeden lifted his head. "All right, I'll do it. In the meantime, I'll continue to help you."

Mathias smiled. "Remember the Word is near. The time you spend here will not be in vain. He never turns away those searching for light and healing."

"What about the times when I don't?"

"He knows your heart. Kaeden, if you really didn't want to change, you wouldn't be here. You are choosing the hard path, but it is the one that will heal not only you but others as well."

Kaeden narrowed his eyes. There was something cryptic in Mathias's words. Did the old man know more? Had he seen a vision of the future? Would his Eldaran power awaken?

Mathias lifted the cup and took another satisfying sip. "Are you sure you don't want a cup of hot black?" he asked, a twinkle in his eye.

Kaeden wrinkled his nose. "No. I don't know how you can stand the bitter liquid."

Mathias shrugged. "Each to their own." And he finished the cup.

The Avonain forces seemed to be at a standstill. While the commanders deliberated in the main tent, the soldiers bickered among themselves as to the best course of action. Even the healers hotly debated what they should do next around the cooking fire that night.

"If we head south, we leave Avonai vulnerable," Leon said as they ate a soup made from dried fish and spices. "We shouldn't have retreated. We should have stayed at the bridge and fought."

"Are you serious?" another healer asked. "Do you know how many wounded we have? Did you see what those Nordic warriors did to our soldiers? They overpowered us."

"I heard stories from some of our wounded." Treyvar spoke up next to Kaeden. This was the first time the Avonain healer had joined them for supper. "About fighters dressed as wolves. And bears who fought alongside their warriors. And a woman no one could take out."

"The Stryth'Veizla," a young man said quietly as he dipped his spoon into his soup.

Leon glanced at him across the fire. "The what?"

"I was one of the runners during the battle. I saw her fight. Like a golden flash of deadly light. That was what her comrades called her. I also had to bring back those who were mauled by the war bears." He poked at his soup.

The first healer piped up again. "We need the White City."

Leon's face grew dark. "So we run? What if the Nordic army follows us? What if they follow us all the way back to Avonai? Do we hole ourselves up in the city and hope we can defend it? And what if the White City doesn't come to our aid? Or they're too late?"

"Avonai isn't defenseless," Treyvar replied. "The Nordics would have to pass through thickets and forest to reach the city. And don't forget our walls."

Kaeden continued to listen while taking small bites of the fish soup. It wasn't his favorite, but it filled the belly.

"I heard there is a possibility of fighters coming to join us from the Tieve Hills," a young woman said nearby. Kaeden looked up in interest.

"I heard we might head south and try to cross again at the Tieve Hills," replied another.

Treyvar winced. "Well, I'm not sure about more fighters—"

"We should head north to Mistcairn," Leon grunted.

"No." An older man spoke, his voice loud and punctuated, causing every eye to turn toward him. "No," he said again, softer with a shake of his head. "There is something up north that is taking out the villages. Something not human."

"What do you mean?" the young woman asked.

He leaned in. "Shadow creatures. Like smoke, weaving through the villages and leaving everyone dead."

Kaeden froze, his spoon halfway to his mouth. Shadow creatures?

Leon scoffed. "If they leave everyone dead, how do you know about this?"

"I was in charge of delivering the captains their meals and overheard them speaking about it one night before the Battle at the Bridge. Apparently someone survived and told them."

"How did they survive?" Leon shook his head. "It sounds like a bard's tale."

Kaeden lowered his spoon back into his bowl, his appetite gone. He'd heard of the Mordra who stole the lives of those they came in contact with. But the Mordra had been sealed away after the Great Battle. It couldn't possibly be them. Still, he should tell Mathias about this. If there was even a small chance it could be the shadows, something worse than a war was facing them.

Kaeden gathered Selma and Mathias later that night in the small partitioned area where Mathias was still convalescing. He glanced at Mathias as the older man sat up and greeted Selma with a smile and silently worried that Mathias still hadn't fully recovered from the healing. How much longer did he have in the land of the living? And what would they do when he was gone?

Kaeden sat down. No. Now was not the time for those thoughts. Mathias wasn't dead, not yet. And they had a more pressing issue at the moment.

As if reading his thoughts, Selma looked at him. "Why did you call us together this late at night?"

"I heard something disturbing around the fire during dinner and needed to share it with the two of you."

The smile on Mathias's face slipped away. "What is it?"

Kaeden let out his breath. "What do you know of the Mordra?"

"The Mordra?" Mathias asked.

"They were all sealed away, right? After the Great Battle."

"Yes," Mathias replied. "The Word banished those shadow creatures from the Lands. He tasked the Eldaran Guardians to split the veil and send them away into the void."

"Is there any chance there could be a few left here in the Lands?"

"No," Mathias said firmly. "All were sealed away."

"Could a Guardian bring them back?"

Mathias pressed his lips together with a disturbed expression. Selma glanced between the two of them.

"What is going on?" she finally asked, her gaze landing on Kaeden.

"A man spoke of shadow creatures taking out villages up north."

"What exactly did he say?" Mathias asked.

"He said he overheard the captains talking about shadow creatures entering the villages and wiping them out. Creatures that moved like smoke."

"What were the dead like?"

Kaeden frowned. "What do you mean?"

"Any wounds, any blood?"

"The man didn't say."

Mathias shook his head. "This is very alarming."

Selma turned toward Mathias. "Do you really think this is the work of the Mordra?"

"Possibly. And if so, it would mean someone has brought them back."

"You mean an Eldaran?" Kaeden asked. "Is it possible there are Eldarans fighting with the Nordics? But how? And why? And where did they come from?"

"I've heard of a settlement far north of Kerre," Selma said quietly. "Perhaps a few crossed the Ari Mountains and formed an alliance with the Nordics."

Mathias folded his arms. "I know of this settlement. My father departed from it when he was young. He felt called to serve mankind, not hide away. So he left them."

"There are more of us out there?" Kaeden looked from Mathias to Selma.

"Yes." Mathias smiled sadly. "But you don't know about them because they chose to separate themselves from humanity a long time ago."

Kaeden blinked. Did his parents know of this group? Why hadn't they told him? He only knew of Mathias and a couple other Eldarans, including Selma. He glanced at her. She knew. How? And they still didn't have an answer about these shadows or where they came from. Unless . . .

Kaeden sat back while Mathias and Selma continued to discuss the other Eldarans. Guardians possessed Veritas, a sword that could pierce the veil between the seen and unseen world. They were the ones who had sealed away the Mordra after the Great Battle thousands of years ago. But what if a Guardian reopened the veil? And could summon and control shadows? A shiver went down his back. Was that possible? Could an Eldaran turn so far from the Word that they would act in opposition of their calling?

What did that mean for them? For this war? For this world?

"What if there are Eldarans working with the Nordics?" Kaeden said quietly. "And they have somehow altered their power?"

"It's possible they are Shadonae," Mathias responded.

"Shado—what?"

"Shadonae. It's the name given to Eldarans who have perverted their power."

"I've never heard of them before," Selma said.

"Because there are very few who ever cross that line. It is one thing to choose not to use one's gift for humanity and another to twist it against humanity. To hurt the very ones the Word asked us to serve with the power He gave us." Mathias shook his head. "What awaits the Shadonae is unfathomable. That is why hardly any Eldarans choose that path. Although choosing to hide away is not much different."

Selma seemed uncomfortable at Mathia's remark, and Kaeden wondered if she had thought about joining that reclusive group of Eldarans.

"So what do we do?" he asked.

"First, we need to know for certain that there are Eldarans working with the Nordics and if they really have turned away from the Word."

"And then what? Do we fight them?"

"No." Mathias sighed and stared at his mark. It glowed softly in the dim light of the tent. "If there are Shadonae, it is my duty as the Truthsayer to rebuke them. I'm not only the Truthsayer for humanity; I am also the Truthsayer for our people. To show all the truth of the Word. I am His voice, His mirror, and His hammer. I would need to travel to Nordica and place them under judgment."

Could the old man do that? Mathias appeared so much older now than he had before the battle. Did he have the power and energy to make such a journey and condemn his own people? And what if he didn't? What if Mathias passed away before then? Who became the next Truthsayer?

Eventually he and Selma needed to find out. Usually an Eldaran's power was passed down through blood. But Mathias had no children. Who became the Truthsayer then? There must always be a Truthsayer. If and when the Eldarans finally faded from the Lands, the Truthsayer would be the last to go.

Kaeden glanced at Mathias. He opened his mouth, then closed it. No. Now was not the time to ask. Gather the facts first. Then, if

Mathias needed to travel north, Kaeden would accompany him. He might not be a Guardian or Oathmaker or even have access to his own Eldaran power. But he was physically strong and could fight and protect his mentor.

30

In the end, the commanders split the Avonain forces. A third would stay and defend Avonai and the coastal lands while the rest would quickly travel south and cross the Onyx River near the Tieve Hills. There was no bridge, but the river was narrow in areas, and there were barges for crossing, a fact the Nordics probably knew nothing about. More rumors spread across the camp. Not only would additional warriors be joining them from the hill country, but the Temanin Empire would be sending elite fighters to help them with their cause.

Kaeden walked beside the wagons, his long gait allowing him to keep up with the caravan and attend to Mathias. They traveled on an old road that wove between towering oaks that lent their shade to the army below. Mathias laughed when he heard the rumor about Temanin soldiers.

"Lord Talon would rather burn Azar to the ground than help anyone here in the north. Remember, I was born and raised in Hont, next to the desert empire. They have no love for the northern countries."

"But what if the White City sent payment for help?" Kaeden asked.

"There hasn't been enough time for Avonai or the White City to negotiate a treaty with the Temanin Empire. It takes weeks if not months to reach Azar from here, even if the envoys travel by sea. And Lord Talon is a shrewd and spiteful man. I dare say he would love to see the northern countries tear each other apart, then march on all of us. No, those rumors are certainly false. But I can see why they would spread. It gives hope."

"But it's false hope."

"Yes." Mathias sighed. "But some may think false hope is still hope. It gives people something to believe in."

Kaeden pressed his lips together. "I don't like it."

"I don't either." Mathias scratched the side of his head. "I wonder who's been saying such things." The wagon gave a sudden lurch as it rumbled over roots. Mathias caught the side of the wagon and held on while Kaeden grabbed the edge, ready to catch his mentor. The wagon righted itself, and the driver yelled back an apology.

"I hate riding in this thing," Mathias said as he settled back down. "I would much rather walk with the rest of you."

Kaeden started to voice all the worries swirling in his mind, but then closed his mouth and kept moving forward. He would rather believe Mathias would fully heal and return to his old self.

A small voice whispered in the back of his mind: Was he also falling for a false hope?

It took over two weeks to reach the Tieve Hills.

Summer had a firm hold on the land, and each day felt its radiant heat and light. Kaeden's pulse quickened as he stared ahead toward the hills that lined the southern edge of the Ari Mountains. Towering deciduous trees with bountiful green foliage lined the rolling ridges. A bright blue sky hung above the deep green. Birds warbled their songs while the dim roar of the Ascana River could be heard from afar.

Home. He breathed in the word. After eight years, he was finally back. Mistsylver had never felt like home, and Khodath was a place filled with horrifying memories. But this place . . .

He took in another breath and smiled. For the first time in a long time, he felt free and unburdened. It was as if his soul had been searching for a permanent rest and he'd finally found it. A small ache entered his heart. If only he could stay here. He'd build a cabin, hunt for food, maybe take up carving like his father once had before they left for Khodath.

But that is not your calling.

He swore he heard those words on the wind. Maybe it was because of Mathias's perpetual reminders that Eldarans were here to serve. He lifted his hand, currently covered by a fingerless glove. Was he really an Eldaran? What good was an Eldaran with no power? He might as well be human.

He wrinkled his nose at the thought and dropped his hand as he continued alongside the wagons. No. He wasn't a monster like humans could be.

Shadonae.

The word rippled through his mind. They were monsters too. Anyone could become a monster.

Even he could.

The idea sobered his spirit. His thoughts turned again toward the Shadonae. If there really were fallen Eldarans working with the Nordics, what had made them turn? Hatred? Desire for power? Superiority?

He caught sight of Selma ahead, walking with the other healers, her white robes swishing with every step, her wavy dark hair glistening in the sun. She served as a healer of mankind, but once in a while he caught a glimpse of dislike on her face. Whether that was toward particular patients or humans in general, he didn't know. But he could see how subtly the thoughts and feelings of his people could shift. They possessed gifts beyond the human race. Attributes of the Word himself. His truth, His words, His strength, His healing. They were His representatives. If they forgot why they were here, it would be easy to claim that power for themselves. Perhaps that was why Mathias was always insistent about their mission to serve humankind. Because if they forgot, they could become monsters.

Was Selma on that sloping path? What about him?

"Your face is full of thoughts."

Mathias's voice broke through his reverie. Kaeden laughed awkwardly. "Just . . . thinking."

"Humph. That's obvious. Do you want to put those thoughts into words?"

Kaeden paused for a moment. "When you asked to see my mark back in Avonai, what were you afraid to see?"

Mathias let out a long breath. "That the light had disappeared."

"What does the mark of a Shadonae look like?"

"It's more than a mark disappearing. I was afraid yours was gone, leaving behind a patch of white skin. A Shadonae's mark is different. Darkness replaces the light."

Kaeden frowned. "You've seen a mark like that?"

"Once. When I was young. My father had to confront a woman who had fallen away. Her entire palm appeared as if a fire had burned away her light, leaving black, rotting skin behind."

"What happened to her?"

Mathias paused. Kaeden waited, listening to the sounds of the caravan: the footfalls of boots, the creak of turning wheels, the hum of conversation. Just when he thought the old man wouldn't reply, Mathias answered.

"There was a confrontation. A fight. My father was wounded during the battle. Just before he died, he passed judgment on her by the Word's command. She turned to dust."

"Oh." Kaeden turned away, his chest suddenly feeling full.

Mathias lifted his hand and stared at his palm, uncovered and brilliant even in the sunlight. "I became the next Truthsayer. I never forgot how much my parents loved the Word—much like yours." He glanced at Kaeden. "And I never forgot the sacrifice my father made to save mankind from a Shadonae. If there are Shadonae truly working with the Nordic forces, I have no choice but to hunt them down. Both for our sakes and for the Nordic people. Before they are consumed and lost in the Shadonae's power."

"You would help the Nordic people?"

"They are still human beings. And my mission is to serve all of humankind and protect them."

Kaeden felt a hint of awe. Not another living soul in the Lands—Eldaran or human—loved the Word and people like Mathias did. That awe turned into a longing as he glanced one more time at his mentor and clenched his marked hand.

I want to become like him.

31

After the Battle at the Bridge, the Nordic forces spread across the Ryland Plains like a wildfire. Villages fell, people fled, and strongholds were solidified under the green banner of Nordica.

Brighid walked along the perimeter of the camp in the early morning, making her way toward the stream where they had stopped the night before. Only the Stag Clan and Bear Clan traveled with the clanless. The Wolf Clan had been sent north to secure their holdings, and the Eagle Clan was tasked with destroying the bridge they had taken to prevent Avonai from crossing again. The Owl Clan had vanished, probably sent to scout. She'd heard whispers that the White City was finally marching on them, but no one knew when they would arrive.

A grove of aspens grew along the river, their stark white trunks a contrast to their green leaves. The area was quiet and the water sweet and cool. Brighid knelt and first washed her face, then used a rag for the exposed parts of her body. Some of the men had no qualms bathing in full view when thcy found a stream or pond, and once in a while a few of the women would find an alcove. But she had grown up with nothing more than a bucket of cold water and a cake of soap for both her body and clothes. That was enough for her.

As she finished up, she heard a loud sniff behind her. Snapping her rag to her chest, she stood and twisted around. A few bears and their masters had gathered farther down the sandy banks just beyond a handful of bushes and rocks.

She recognized the warriors, particularly Hjar Gurmund, who stood a couple feet away. She locked eyes with the Bear Clan hjar, who gazed back with an icy blue stare.

"I'm sorry," he finally said. "We didn't see you there. We usually do not bring our bears to water when there are others around—"

The large brown bear next to him took a step toward Brighid. Only a bush separated them. Brighid held the rag even closer to her chest but did not move. She was wary of the animal but felt no fear. Not because most of her feelings were numb from the oathbinding. Rather, she felt an odd bond with the animal.

"That's strange," Hjar Gurmund murmured, barely loud enough to hear over the trickling water. "Bein doesn't like most people. But he seems interested in you."

The other warriors watched while their own bears lapped up water.

Bein lifted his nose in the air, his ears pointed forward, and his bright eyes set on Brighid. Hjar Gurmund rubbed the side of the bear's neck. "What do you smell, old friend?" Gurmund peered at her again.

Brighid bowed her head. "Excuse me, Hjar Gurmund. I will be on my way."

Before he could answer, she turned and walked steadily back toward camp. The men murmured behind her, and Bein sniffed again. Only once did she glance back. Hjar Gurmund and his bear, Bein were still watching her, the bear's master with a puzzled look on his face.

Brighid hurried the rest of the way, feeling that same puzzlement. Why hadn't she been afraid of his bear? Or any of the bears? Most of the camp gave the bear masters a wide berth and for good reason. Anyone who watched them and their masters fight knew what one swipe of a paw could do, let alone their teeth and rage. She felt something different.

Felt.

Brighid stopped and held a fist to her heart. She *felt*. Why? She wanted to turn back again but changed her mind and headed for the camp where Marta and Johan and a handful of others sat. The oathbinding left her numb. So what was this stirring in her heart? This strange feeling?

The White City was coming for them. And this time it wasn't a mere whisper.

The camp buzzed with the news as the skals ran the warriors through drills. Preparations were made for the battle, and inside tents the hjars made plans and sent word to the other clans.

Over the last few months, Brighid's body had become lean and muscular and was now tan from hours spent under the summer sun. Running through a forest or for long periods of time with her sword and shield was as easy as breathing. And the red haze rushed over her the moment she entered into battle. She still hardly remembered the fights in the aftermath, but she no longer feared it wouldn't come when she beckoned. Perhaps she had finally unlocked whatever triggered it.

The only thing she feared was losing control. That during the haze, she would kill indiscriminately.

She wiped sweat from her face and took a long drink of water from her waterskin. Maybe if she wasn't bound by Armand's oath she could command the red haze more. But if she could feel . . .

She glanced up as a wandering cloud momentarily hid the sun. She hadn't felt death's presence once since her oathbinding. She barely remembered the sensation anymore. But if she could still feel its presence, would she be able to fight? Or would the battlefield overcome her?

Which was worse? Feeling death? Or the possibility of losing herself in the red haze?

I don't know.

The next day, Brighid tucked her gear in her pack, then rolled up her cloak and attached it to the bottom. Last, she strapped her shield to her back and placed her sword in the sheath around her waist. Word came that morning that they would be moving out to a more defensible location, and she was part of the first wave. Johan and Marta were also part of the first group.

"Once again it's the clanless who will be marching first," a young man grumbled nearby. Brighid couldn't remember his name. "They say we are one people, but why are we always the first ones sent in?"

"At least we have the Stryth'Veizla with us," Hagen said as he attached his axe to his side. "She's the reason more of us haven't died."

The man continued to complain, and a few others joined in.

"He's right," Marta said, joining Brighid's side. "The clanless are always the first to be tossed into the fray. And Hagen's also right—you're part of the reason more of us haven't crossed the veil."

"Maybe." Brighid didn't like so many eyes on her. Some fighters enjoyed accolades and recognition from the battlefield. She was simply doing what Elphsaba told her to: using the gift of her hands. But she had yet to tell anyone—even Marta and Johan—about the real power behind her fighting. The strange red haze.

One of the skals shouted that it was time to depart. The clanless stood, and minutes later, they marched. It was a day's walk through the hills and trees to a place that opened into a wide plain. The place they would make their stand.

Just as the sun reached its zenith, a cry went up. Then more. A roar of voices echoed through the ravine through which they were traveling, buttressed on either side with trees. Hagen swore and pulled out his axe.

"Get to the plains!" the skals shouted. "Out of the ravine! To the plains!"

"Looks like the White City reached us first." Hagen readjusted his grip on his axe, then plunged forward, following the mass toward the opening ahead.

"This isn't good." Johan jogged beside Marta and Brighid. "If we're caught in this ravine, we will be annihilated."

Marta bared her teeth. "How did our hjars miss this?"

"Perhaps the White City marched through the night. Or the Owl Clan misread the signs."

Marta joined the others in swearing as everyone raced to get out of the ravine. Just as they spotted the open fields, they were flanked by soldiers in blue, and the fight began.

Brighid didn't remember much after that. Only sinking into the red haze. The smell of sweat and blood. The screams of those around her. Fighting until somewhere in the back of her mind she sensed her arms aching and a half dozen cuts from the blades swift enough to get past her own.

She fought until her chest throbbed and her vision started coming back. The sun was setting as her mind returned, and at some point, she had left the ravine. She sucked in a breath. Every muscle spasm tore across her body. Water. She needed water. But she had no idea where she had dropped her pack. All around her lay bodies, packs, waterskins, and unrolled blankets.

She stared blankly at the scene. If she could feel, she knew she would be paralyzed by the view. Instead, she took stock of the situation.

Thirty feet away a group clashed. The Bear Clan had arrived at some point and battled on the other side of the field. One of the bears let out a mighty roar while on his hind feet and sent an enemy tumbling across the field.

She turned and found more pockets of fighting. But no one was near her.

She grabbed a waterskin close to her boot and drank, then did a quick survey of the dead. The complaining young man from that morning lay twisted and lifeless. Hagen's body was nearby, his axe still in his hand, a huge gash across his face, and his eyes wide.

Yes, she was very thankful she couldn't feel at the moment.

Brighid bent down, placed her sword on the ground, and closed Hagen's eyes. Then she moved to the young man. And a few others. She knew it was futile. The clanless who gathered the dead after the battles wouldn't care if their eyes were open or closed. But for some reason, it mattered to her.

The bear masters and their opponents drew closer.

With a deep, heavy sigh, Brighid grabbed her sword, gripped her shield, and sank into the red haze once again.

The fighting stopped when twilight fell across the plains.

The Nordics retreated to one side of the ravine while the White City occupied the hills and valley on the other side. Wounds were bandaged, rations consumed, and those who could fell into a fretful sleep. Brighid winced with every cry that pierced the night. Not everyone had been as fortunate as her. She had only a couple cuts and bruises. Same with Marta and Johan. Somewhere deep within her being, where that sliver of feeling still existed, she cried with them. And cried for those who had fallen.

When dawn came, the hjars roused the troops. Plans had been made during the night and were executed shortly after daybreak. Brighid entered the fray again as her unit led the front charge on the forces of the White City. Her targets were those dressed in blue, and not one survived an encounter with her.

She fought under the red haze, surfacing only long enough to drink or gobble something down. A shout went up near noon. The Wolf Clan had arrived. The clan rushed through the trees like wolves themselves, crashing upon the battlefield with howls of bloodlust. Seeing their comrades renewed the rest of the Nordic forces, and the day ended with the Nordics holding the ravine, plains, and first set of hills.

Brighid slumped to the ground near Johan and Marta that night. Johan was carefully wrapping a bandage around Marta's arm.

"Ouch." Marta glared at him.

He didn't flinch or look up. "I'm being as careful as I can. You should really have it cauterized."

Marta shook her head, her red hair flying around her face. "It's a scratch. I don't understand why you're so worried about it."

Johan glanced up. "Because a wound like this can lead to infection. And an infection can lead to a loss of limb or death." He went back to bandaging it. "And . . . I care about you."

Marta didn't seem to catch his tone of voice by the way she answered back, but Brighid did. She stared at Johan. Was he fond of Marta? She blinked at the thought and laid down, her back to them. She supposed those kinds of feelings could crop up even on a battlefield. But it felt odd to her. Was it because she'd never felt such a thing? Her main goal in life had always been to provide for herself. To survive. She'd never had a thought toward romance or bonding. As her eyes closed, she wondered if she would ever be interested in a man.

Fatigue settled into her bones as Brighid started the next day.

When would this battle be over? Not until everyone was dead? Until one side could no longer fight? Just as the Nordics stepped forward, ready to face another day of fighting, a rumble swept through the forces. Brighid tried to hear the words as they rippled across the camp, but she couldn't tell what was being said until Johan spoke up.

"The Avonains have arrived. From the south."

"How?" Marta asked through a flurry of cursing. "I thought our hjars had the battlefield under control. And the Eagle Clan destroyed the bridge we took weeks ago."

"They must have gone south, down by the Tieve Hills, then crossed there."

Marta cursed again as Brighid gritted her teeth. Many of their warriors were tired, wounded, or dead. How could they take on fresh enemies?

The hjars and skals were already shouting commands to counter this latest development, but before the Nordics could retreat east to a more defensible position, the White City attacked. And shortly afterward, the Avonains joined. The Nordics were now pinched between both forces.

Instead of fighting forward, for the first time Brighid found herself falling back. The red haze no longer colored her vision. Her movements grew slower, and a deep ache formed along her muscles.

How much longer can I do this? she thought desperately. She tightened her grip on her sword and shield. *No, I have to.* Johan and Marta battled blue-clad warriors a couple feet away from her. *I have to do it for them.* Her gaze spread across the battlefield before her. *For all of them.*

She let out a war cry and dove back into the fight. Without the full power of the red haze, her arms felt heavier, and she had to think more about each swing of her blade instead of relying on instinct. The sun's hot rays beat down on her and sweat stung her eyes. Each breath came hard and fast. Sometime during the fight, her opponents had switched from the White City to the Avonains. Blue and green colors everywhere.

Everywhere?

Even as she thought this, she heard Johan yell. She whipped her head around. Marta and Johan were surrounded, and Johan was barely keeping the Avonain soldiers at bay. Brighid approached from behind and took out the soldier in front of her, then fought to reach her friends. When she broke the circle, she found Johan holding Marta, her face pale and her hand pressed to her side.

"Go!" Brighid yelled. "Get Marta out of here! I'll protect your back."

Johan nodded.

One more time, she thought. *I just need to sink into the red haze one more time.* The haze came, drawing her in deep until all her senses were swept into the fight. She never looked back to see if Johan or Marta were able to escape. Rush after rush of soldiers tackled her. Somewhere through her muffled hearing, she heard them yelling, "Kill the she-devil! Take out their Stryth'Veizla!"

The red haze started to dissipate. From the corner of her eye, Brighid could see no other Nordic warriors. Avonain soldiers poured in from every direction. Somewhere deep in her mind, she realized they were coming after her. And only her.

Like a tidal wave, they finally overwhelmed her.

Her sword was knocked from her hand and vanished among the bodies surrounding her. Brighid held up her shield, but they kept pounding on it until she fell to her knees.

"We have her! The Nordic she-devil!"

Some laughed and jeered as swords rained down on her shield. Someone grabbed a hold of her hair and pulled her head back. She stumbled, then fell backward. Boots flew at her, kicking every part of her body. Someone stomped on her sword arm, and she felt the bone break.

Cheers went up around her as she was pummeled over and over again.

Then something shattered inside her. The oathbinding around her heart and mind snapped, sending invisible spider threads waving in the wind. And with that snap, her emotions came rushing back. She felt anger . . . and despair . . . and a deep chill.

Death. It was here, and it was coming for her.

A weight crashed down on her. She couldn't breathe. Her heart labored. A scream filled her mouth, but she didn't let it loose. With every ounce of strength she had, she twisted around onto her stomach.

"I can't die," she gasped as she clawed her way forward with her one good hand. Darkness spread across her vision. "I can't die."

"What's she saying?" someone asked.

"Who cares? Do you know how many of my friends she killed during the Battle at the Bridge?"

A boot slammed into the side of her head. Another kick sent her onto her back. She stared up at a dozen faces around her, each one moving in and out of her line of sight. Her heart pounded so hard her chest hurt, and fear gripped her throat until she could hardly breathe.

I can't die, she thought, terrified as death's chill spread across her body. A tear trickled down her cheek. She could feel death hovering over her, coaxing her spirit away with a bony finger.

Please, someone, anyone, save me!

32

Kaeden grunted as he hefted up the soldier. The man let out a cry. "We don't have far to go," he said as he bent forward and placed his shoulder beneath the man's midsection and hoisted him into the air. Around them the battle raged between the Nordics, the White City, and Avonain troops. This was the fifth soldier he had assisted today in his new role as a runner. So far, so good. His aversion didn't seem to trigger when helping the wounded back beyond the battle lines and to the hastily raised healing tents just over the hill.

The sun beat down on him and sweat clouded his eyes. Kaeden rubbed his face, then gritted his teeth and climbed the hill with the man slumped over his shoulder. His muscles—strengthened by years in the quarry—could handle the task. Down he went on the other side and brought the man to the front of the healing tents.

"Another one," he yelled as Selma stepped out of the tent on the right. Bright red blotches were splattered across her white robes, and her hair was pulled back in a haphazard braid.

"Ailment?"

"A broken leg at least. I was able to retrieve him before the fighting shifted."

"Take him into my tent. We have an open bed."

Kaeden hauled the man inside. He found the empty bed at the end of a long row. Carefully he placed the soldier down. The man's face was pale and sweaty, and both of them smelled like blood.

"Thank . . . you," he said weakly.

"I'm just doing my duty," Kaeden replied. He wasn't sure what more to say. The leg injury appeared severe. He wondered if Selma or Treyvar or the other healers would be able to save it.

Once outside, he drank from a bucket of water, then headed back over the hill. The sounds of the massive battle echoed across the plains and valleys. Yelling, screaming, the clash of metal and wood, whimpers, and crying. When he'd made his first run that morning into the battle fray, the sounds were like rocks hurled against his head and heart. They still hurt, but he was used to it now, focusing instead on what he saw ahead, who he could save, and who he had to leave behind.

He reached the edge of the field and shaded his eyes so he could see more clearly. A scattering of trees dotted the plains and more grew along the ravine to the far right. The grass was yellow and dry in the sun and flattened in huge patches by the battle. A long line of Avonain soldiers pushed a small group of Nordics back toward the ravine.

He watched, waiting for someone to fall. He caught sight of a head of gold, then three Avonains fell to the warrior's blade. It was a Nordic woman, with long braids the color of summer wheat swinging around her face as she fought. He could barely make out her features from where he stood, only a thin patch of black around one eye.

A runner came to stand beside him. "Looks like we might have three more to take back," he said, his gaze on the battle ahead. "Or maybe not. That Nordic usually leaves them dead."

"You know that warrior?"

"She's known as the Stryth'Viezla. I was a runner at the Battle of the Bridge. She took out an entire force. Not one soldier was left standing. Or alive."

Kaeden's eyes widened. Stryth'Viezla. He remembered that name mentioned around the fire. He turned his attention back on the battle. Despite continuing to lose ground, it seemed no one could take her out. He'd never used a sword or shield, but even to his inexperienced eyes, he could tell she was far superior to those around her. A burgeoning respect rose in his heart, despite the fact that she was the enemy.

"She fights like nothing I've ever seen," the runner said a moment later.

Kaeden inwardly agreed.

She disappeared over the ridge along with those fighting her.

The other runner sighed. "Let us see if she left anyone alive."

Kaeden nodded and followed. Just as the young man had predicted, the three were dead, with another one nearby. Usually when he approached fallen soldiers, he would find them in one of three states: wounded, very wounded, or almost dead. But rarely did he reach a body and find it dead so fast. He looked up, but there was no sign of the Nordic woman. She had been swallowed up somewhere in the massive battle ahead.

Mercy. He felt the word on the breeze, and it brushed his heated face. The way she killed was a mercy. It was fast, with no lingering pain or agony. He headed left where another fight had left two on the ground and one staggering around. Like a compassionate angel of death.

A half hour later, he and the other runner crested the hill. The battle was fierce along a patch of ground a couple hundred feet away. They checked the few bodies that lay nearby, but two were already dead, and the other one was fast approaching the veil.

Kaeden knelt beside the man. Blood covered his chest and face, and his eyes had a far-off look. He reached for the man's hand. It was already growing cold. Strangely enough, this kind of touch didn't bother him. It reminded him of the times his parents could not save someone with their power and instead would gently usher the dying into the beyond.

He spoke words from the old scrolls, the words of the Word, until the light vanished from the man's eyes. Then he sighed and bowed his head. His ears registered a pause in the sounds around him. He lifted his head, puzzled. The other runner stared at the battle nearby.

"What's going on?" Kaeden asked as he rose. He could see it now. A crowd forming. A crowd of soldiers with chortles and gloating filling the air. It didn't seem like a fight. More like a celebration. That struck him as odd.

"They caught her." The runner's eyes were wide with awe.

"Caught her? Who?"

The runner glanced over at him. "The Stryth'Viezla. By the Word, I can't believe they have her."

Kaeden looked over again at the gathering crowd, a feeling of unease filling his gut. The way the soldiers were acting reminded him of a pack of wolves ready for the kill. His frown deepened as the unease turned into a chill that ran down his spine. He could feel the bloodlust in the wind. They had no intention of capturing her. They were going to kill her—after they spent their rage and passion on her. He stepped forward, not sure what he was going to do. All he knew was he had to stop this.

He began to run. A thousand thoughts flooded his mind as he raced across the field. She was the enemy. She had killed many. She deserved this—

No!

No one deserved this. And as the Stryth'Viezla of Nordica, she would have information that could be vital to this war. And . . . she was human, worthy of decency. That was what Mathias had drilled into him.

Go to her, my son.

Kaeden stumbled as the words filled his mind. *Word?* The Word had never spoken to him before. Was he finally hearing from the One?

Go. Now. Before it is too late.

There was no time to ponder the whisper in his mind. Another roar went up from the crowd. If he didn't get to the woman warrior soon, she would be dead.

He reached the outer ring and shoved his way through. The farther in he went, the more packed it became. This was a spectacle.

"Who do you think you are now?" a man jeered ahead.

"Hit her again!" Someone shouted.

"Strip her!" Shouted another.

Where were the captains? Why wasn't someone stopping this? Then he saw Captain Bertin and realized those in charge were indeed here and wanted this as bad as the soldiers under their command.

I've got to stop this. I need to reach her before . . .

When he couldn't break through the crowd, Kaeden started to

shove and pull men aside. For once he was grateful for his size and strength.

"Healer coming through," he shouted, hoping a few would move.

Seconds later, he broke into the middle ring, and gasped.

Before him a woman lay on her back, her face toward the sky. Her countenance was so bloody he could barely see her eyes, and the way her arm lay, he knew it was broken. Her honey-colored braids were plastered with mud, along with the rest of her armor. Her jerkin had been shoved upward as if someone had tried to remove it. Blood pulsed from a puncture along her lower side, each heartbeat causing more blood to gurgle out of the wound. Kaeden held a fist to his mouth. Oh, Word. He wanted to turn away from the gruesome scene—

The man next to her kicked her in the side, and the woman screamed.

Kaeden's vision went red, and strength returned to his body.

"Move! Now!" he roared as he broke through circle and approached the woman. He wanted to curse and shout and call the men around him animals, but he was an Eldaran. "She is under *my* jurisdiction now. If any man touches her again, you will face me." He glared around the crowd. How could they do this to another human being? The simmering hatred of his youth bubbled up and threatened to choke off any bit of common sense he had left.

The woman moved slightly and moaned. That sound brought him back from his anger.

He crouched down in front of her. He'd seen the worst as a healer, but this . . .

She coughed and sent a splattering of blood into the air. When some landed on him, Kaeden didn't even bother to wipe his face. He feverishly assessed her body . . . and her chances. His gaze strayed back to the pulsing wound along her side. As a runner, when he found soldiers like this, he knew they were already crossing the veil and there was nothing he could do for them. She would be dead in minutes. He was surprised she was still conscious.

One eye tried to open amid the swollen skin around her face. Blue. Like the sky. Her mouth quivered. "I-I don't want . . . to die," she whispered. "P-please."

In that moment, something burst inside him. Searing hot, like a molten flame, so powerful it sent a shudder through his body. The power flowed from deep inside his chest, filling him with fire, rising to the surface until it reached his arm and raced down toward his hand. He could feel it before he heard the murmurs around him. The light of his palm.

His eyes widened. Heat continued to pour through his body.

It couldn't be.

But it was.

His Eldaran power was awakening.

"Is he Eldaran?" someone asked nearby.

"What's he doing?" asked another.

"He's not going to heal her, is he?" Captain Bertin made his way over, but Kaeden ignored the man. The captain should have stopped this mob.

He clenched and unclenched his glowing hand as he gazed down at the broken body of the Nordic woman. If he chose to use this power, he knew it would hurt unlike anything he had experienced before. It might not even be enough to save her.

Her other eye opened, and she stared up into his face. In that moment, he saw past the blood, the fierce battle paint, and the strange mark around her eye, and simply saw a young woman. A young woman who wanted to live.

I can do that for her.

Without another thought, he placed his glowing palm on her face and cupped her cheek. Her eyes widened slightly at the touch. It was coming, that torrent of heat. It blasted through his hand moments later.

She gasped, and her body jerked under the power.

Kaeden closed his eyes. *Word, I've hidden away too long from who I am. And I'm not sure I'm ready to embrace my Eldaran blood. But today I want to save this woman. So please, help me—*

He drew in a sharp breath and hunched over. It was coming. Every cut, every kick, every broken bone in this woman's body. Somewhere past the haze of pain he could heard murmurs around him, but then sounds were washed away as wave after wave of agony crashed through his body.

His face felt like it had been pummeled, and his ribs cracked along his side. His arm suddenly jerked and broke. He wanted to shout, but no sound came. Then his side ruptured, and he could feel his blood flowing freely from his body. And still his power poured out until it felt like his very life was flowing from his body into hers. Maybe it was. She was so close to death that perhaps the only way to save her was to give his life.

A deep darkness spread across his vision. His consciousness started slipping away.

"What's going on here?"

Treyvar. Since when did the Avonain healer step onto the battlefield? Had someone alerted the healers to what was going on?

Kaeden let out a sigh. Treyvar would have enough sense to help this woman. He had done what he could. His hand slipped away from her face. The woman would live.

"Kaeden?" Treyvar's voice sounded as if it were under water.

He groaned and slumped to the side, hitting the ground with a soft thud. The darkness overtook his eyes and ears. Everything hurt. If he had been a normal human, he would be dying now. But he wasn't.

"Help her," he whispered. "Don't let them have her."

Then he let out a gurgled gasp as he slipped away. How strange. And Ironic. It had taken a young woman from Nordica to finally awaken his Eldaran power.

33

Pain. And heat. Rushing across his body. A deep ache in his side. The jostling of his limbs as others carried him. Voices speaking around him. The bloody visage of a young woman—

Kaeden sat up with a start. His body was drenched in sweat. Stars popped across his vision, and he lay back down with a groan.

"Careful, now. That was quite an ordeal you went through."

A cold rag touched his fevered head, and he sighed. Mathias was here.

"How is he doing?" That was Selma's voice.

"He's fully healed. But his strength hasn't returned yet."

"And the Nordic woman?" Selma asked, a dark tone to her voice.

Nordic? Was it the young woman from the battlefield? Kaeden wanted to look, but fatigue pressed down on his body like a thousand hands.

A soft rustle of boots moved across the floor.

"Also alive," Mathias said a moment later. "And awake. How are you feeling, young one?"

"Where am I?" a young woman's voice spoke nearby. Soft and sweet. Nothing like that bloody face and battered body.

"In a healing tent."

Kaeden finally pried his eyes open. Familiar canvas walls surrounded him with a high ceiling held up by wooden rods. One of the healing tents. This particular area was partitioned off from the rest of the tent, but he could see shadows on the other side and hear the murmur of voices from the rest of the occupants.

"Who are you?" the woman asked.

"Mathias. One of the healers for the Avonain forces."

Pause. "Then I am a prisoner."

"You are a person under my care. That is all I'm concerned about."

So the woman nearby was the warrior he'd saved on the battlefield.

Selma huffed. Her displeasure was not surprising. Probably half the camp wouldn't be happy with him healing one of their worst enemies. But he'd had no choice. The Word had finally spoken to him. And when he saw the way she looked and heard her plea, he couldn't deny her. Not when his power had awakened so powerfully. Surely it had been the will of the Word Himself.

Kaeden slowly turned his head so he could see more. The rag across his forehead dropped at his movement. One other bed sat a few feet away in this closed-off area. A single lit lamp hung from one of the wooden poles that supported the partition. He could barely make her out in the shadows. Just a tiny figure buried under a mound of blankets.

Selma stepped from the darkness and knelt beside his bed. She placed a hand on his shoulder and blocked Mathias and the other patient from his view.

"Kaeden. Are you all right?"

His mouth felt full of cotton. "I . . . hurt," he finally said, his voice raspy.

Mathias appeared over Selma's shoulder. "That is to be expected. It was your first time healing."

He'd known it would hurt. But not like this.

"Do you want water?" Selma asked.

"Yes."

Selma stood and disappeared through the break in the partition.

Kaeden closed his eyes. Heavy fatigue was dragging him back under. But he wanted to drink first before falling asleep. Then he frowned. Why was the Nordic woman here instead of the prison camp? Not that he wanted her there. Despite her reputation and the fierce war paint and blood smeared across her face, she had seemed vulnerable to him. If this had been a different time and place, she would be like those young women in the cities, selling flowers they had collected from nearby fields or embroidered handkerchiefs. Not fighting in a bloody war.

Selma entered again with a jug of water and a clay cup. Her dark hair was pulled haphazardly back, and blood stained her white robes. She purposely ignored the Nordic woman as she knelt with the jug and cup.

Mathias helped Kaeden up to a sitting position. He hated how weak he was. Mathias must have realized what he was thinking. "It's going to take a full day at least to recover, Kaeden. You took on death itself. That's not something most can return from, even other Eldarans."

Selma's hand trembled slightly at those words as she held the cup out to his lips. He didn't respond. Instead, he gulped down the cool water. Strange how just a drink of water could bring back vitality and healing.

"I don't understand why you did it," Selma whispered as she pulled the cup back.

Kaeden was too tired to answer. He could hear the prejudice in her voice, and he didn't have the strength to deal with it right now.

"Would you like some water?" Mathias said nearby seconds later. "It's quite safe. I have no reason to poison you."

There was a long pause, then he heard the woman drink greedily from the cup.

"I'll bring some food later," Mathias said.

Kaeden closed his eyes. He listened to the shuffle of feet across the dirt floor.

"How long are you going to keep her here?" Selma whispered to Mathias. "She should be with the other Nordics."

"As long as we need to. You saw how they are treating the prisoners of war. And we both know she isn't safe with our soldiers. What good would it be to save her just to have her die the next day?"

"She doesn't deserve special treatment."

"Selma, I'm a healer. So are you. We heal, no matter who the person is."

"We heal for the southern forces. She is the reason we are needed. And I don't like leaving Kaeden here with her. What if she tries to kill him?"

Kaeden doubted the woman was in any condition to do something to him. And he was twice her size. He might be a healer, but he was still strong enough and skilled enough to hold his own.

"She won't," Mathias answered. "But I'll post a guard if it will make you feel better."

Selma huffed. "It's better than nothing, I suppose."

They left, leaving the small area quiet. The Nordic woman was breathing evenly and softly. The sound, coupled with the sudden light tapping of rain across the canvas, lulled him to sleep.

Kaeden wasn't sure how long he was out. The small, partitioned area was completely dark except for the faint light from the lantern that hung from the nearby pole. On the other side of the curtains, he could hear healers whispering to those they attended and the soft moans of the injured. He took in a breath, then glanced to his left. Was she still here? The Nordic warrior?

He couldn't tell. The bed was still there. And blankets were piled on top.

Slowly he sat up. He felt almost whole. He reached over and rubbed his arm. No longer broken. He felt his face. Nothing. Then he touched his side without removing his tunic. There it was. Through the material, he could feel the uneven skin. His first scar from healing. He turned his right hand over and stared at his palm, which shone with a soft light. It wasn't as bright as Mathias's, but it was no longer so dim it hardly shined. He was finally a full-fledged Eldaran, and now carried the power of his people.

"Who are you?"

A soft feminine voice carried across the space between the two beds. Kaeden twisted his head and spotted a face turned toward his. So she was still here. In the lamplight, the cuts, bruises, and swelling were gone. A young woman stared back at him with smooth skin and what appeared to be the tattoo of a half sun around her left eye.

"I am a healer," Kaeden replied.

"You are more." Her words were confident.

He hesitated. Should he share? There were probably Shadonae working with her people, so most likely she was familiar with his kind. "I am an Eldaran."

"Eldaran . . ." The way she said the word was almost wistful. "I've heard of you. With the mark of light upon your palm."

"Yes."

The rain started again outside with gentle thumps against the canvas above.

"What did you do to me?" she asked.

Kaeden turned his palm from side to side. "I healed you." He could still hardly believe that. It had hurt. It hurt almost like he imagined death would feel. But he'd done it. Like his parents had.

"How?" She stirred beneath the covers, then sat up. In the faint light, she appeared fully healed and perfectly healthy. No hint that she had been at death's door not long ago. The mark around her eye caught his attention. He'd heard Nordics tattooed their bodies, but for what purposed he didn't know. Some said it was a death count. But why would a mark for such a gruesome reason appear as a sun around her eye?

He realized he hadn't fully answered her question. "My people are able to take the wounds or sickness from others, then we heal ourselves."

"So you took on all that happened to me on the battlefield?" She lifted her arm and examined it, then touched her side. She raised her head moments later. "Why would you do that for someone like me?"

"Because you asked me to. You said you didn't want to die."

She frowned. "Do you know who I am?"

"Yes. I've heard you are called the Stryth'Veizla of the Nordic people. A fierce warrior."

Her eyebrows shot up. "And yet you saved me? Do you know how many of your people I have killed?"

"Yes."

She stared at him from across the shadows. He could see the faint glint of her golden hair and clear skin. Selma or someone else must have washed the blood and mud away from her face and body. With the mark around her eye and the dozen braids around her face, she held an exotic beauty in her appearance.

She let out a long breath and glanced down at her lap covered in blankets. "So what's going to happen to me now?" This was the first time he'd heard hesitation in her voice.

"I'm not sure. You're a prisoner of war."

"Of course I am," she murmured and threaded her fingers together.

"But you will not be beaten or killed."

She lifted her head.

"Mathias and I will make sure of that."

She let out a small sad laugh. "Are you sure? There are many who wish to see me dead."

"I didn't save you so you could be killed later. And . . ." He paused. Should he tell her the Word told him to? He would never forget hearing the Word's voice. Or how powerfully his Eldaran power had come alive the moment he'd seen her. There was no question he was supposed to heal her. For what reason he didn't know. But it was definitely the Word's will.

"And . . . ?" she asked moments later.

No, he wouldn't tell her. Not yet. He needed to speak to Mathias first and determine why the Word saved her. He turned his full attention on her. "And I will keep you safe."

34

Brighid narrowed her eyes and stared at the strange man—the Eldaran—across from her. She did not understand him. Nor why she was here instead of locked away with the other Nordic prisoners. Why had he really saved her? She wasn't sure she believed his words. *I healed you because you asked me to. And I will keep you safe.*

She cleared her throat and looked away. Wasn't Armand also Eldaran? She couldn't imagine him healing someone. He'd made her a tool, bound and used by his words. And she was sure after she had served her purpose she would be discarded.

So what made this man different? She glanced at him again. The light from his palm caught her attention. Armand had no such light. Neither did the other two who worked with him. Just a black patch of skin that appeared necrotic. Did that light make this man different?

He pulled the covers back from his body and swung his legs around, then stood. Her eyes widened. She hadn't realized his size as he sat in bed. But now as he stood, she discovered how massive he was—even larger than Johan if that was possible. Beneath his white robes his shoulders were broad like those of a moose with a middle that tapered down to his waist, currently bound by a cord. His upper arms were solid, as were the little she could see of his calves. Dark hair hung thick like a black bear's fur, and the lamplight illuminated his firm jaw.

She mentally shook her head as heat filled her face. He couldn't be a healer. No healer looked like that. He was more like one of the berserkers from the Bear Clan.

"Are you sure you're a healer?"

He laughed. "You're not the first one to ask me that. But yes, I am a healer. I'm going to step out for a moment. There is a guard posted outside this opening, and the combined camp of Avonai and the White City surrounds us. If you try to escape, your fate will be on you. If you stay here, I can assure your safety like I promised."

Her gaze moved toward the opening between the partitions. She hadn't forgotten how brutal the Avonain soldiers were or their hatred toward her. Mathias and this man might be kind to her, but she was sure the rest of the camp wouldn't hesitate to kill her. Her best chance of surviving was here. For now.

She glanced back at his face. "I will stay."

"Good." Seconds later, he left the small area. On the other side of the partition, she heard the murmur of voices.

She slowly laid back down. When she'd first awoken, fear had captured her heart and body. The Nordic clans kept no prisoners of war, at least not that she knew of. Villages were wiped out, and the Wolf Clan butchered almost everyone in Mistcairn. So when she found herself here inside a tent surrounded by Avonains, she was sure they would dispose of her, despite being saved by one of their own.

Then the old man had spoken to her. The one named Mathias. She had never seen anyone like him, with rich dark skin and hair white like newly fallen snow. His voice was soft and gentle, and his touch warm. Not like the woman with the dark hair. Brighid had felt her frigidness across the small space.

Wait. Brighid paused and listened. Yes. She could hear Mathias's voice now, outside the canvas wall. And the healer who'd just left. The Eldaran.

"How is she doing?" Mathias asked.

"She's awake and alert. And asking many questions."

"Like what?"

"Like how and why I healed her."

The canvas muffled their voices, but as long as she didn't move, she could hear everything.

"And what about you, Kaeden?" Mathias continued.

Kaeden. Brighid mulled the word over in her head. The large healer's name was Kaeden.

"There are a few scars, but otherwise I feel fine."

"There are always scars after a healing. Like the Word, we take on the ailment, and it leaves a scar. And your hand?"

There was a pause. "He told me to go to her," Kaeden said. "The Word."

"The Word spoke to you?"

"Yes. This was the first time I've heard His voice."

The Word? Brighid blinked. Elphsaba had sung a song that mentioned the Word during birthings. Was this the same Word they were speaking about? She strained to hear more.

". . . and when I saw her, that's when it happened. I felt the power awaken inside me. And this light appeared in my palm."

Mathias chuckled. "To think it would take a Nordic woman to awaken your power. Who would have imagined such a thing?"

"Why do you think the Word saved her? You know who she is."

"Yes, I do." Mathias's voice was more serious.

"Do you think she has information that can help us?"

"Possibly. But only if she is someone important within their clans. The Nordics highly value clan and status. She might only be a powerful warrior and nothing more."

"Why else would the Word save her?"

Brighid's mind drew away from the conversation. According to them, this Word saved her. But what would happen when they found out she was clanless? Then there would be no reason to hold her. In fact, it would be better to kill her in exchange for all the lives she'd taken from their side.

She rolled onto her side as fear crept back over her. *I did what I was meant to do. I possess the hands of a fighter. And so I fought. I fulfilled my purpose. So why did this Word let me live?*

She tried to hear more of their conversation, but they must have moved away from the tent because she could hear only a dim murmur of their voices.

A single tear formed in the corner of her eye. She curled her knees in close and hugged her arms to her chest. *I still don't want to die. Not yet. Maybe never.*

"Young woman?"

Brighid twisted her head around. The one named Mathias stood a few feet away with a steaming bowl of something in his hands.

"Oh good, you're awake. I brought you some food." He pulled a chair from the corner over to her bed and sat down.

Part of her wanted to ignore him, but she couldn't escape his warmth and kindness, so she sat up and turned toward him. He held out the bowl and spoon. "What is it?" she asked. Lumps of white meat swam in a pale broth. The smell was unfamiliar and salty.

"Fish stew."

She tried not to curl her lip. The only fish she had ever consumed was freshly caught from mountain streams, skewered, then cooked over an open fire. This neither looked nor smelled like that.

She took a tentative bite . . . and gagged. Disgusting. She spotted Mathias watching her, so she used all the willpower she had and swallowed. "It's . . . uh . . ." She shut her mouth before the fish could come back up. She stared down at the bowl, sweat collecting along her hairline. Months of training told her to eat the whole bowl to maintain her strength. Another part of her said if she ate one more bite, her body was going to rebel.

"You don't like it." She glanced up and found Mathias's smiling kindly at her. "It's all right. It's an acquired taste, like most Avonain food. But it's all I could find."

"Thank . . . you," she said weakly, glancing down again at the bowl. Then she tightened her grip on the bowl and spoon. This man had been kind enough to find food for her. She would eat it. Even if it killed her.

Before she could consider it more, Brighid took another bite, and another. She refused to think about the soup or take in the smell. Instead, that iron will that had seen her through months of winter, starvation, and the battlefields helped her down the fish stew.

Mathias stared at her with wide eyes. "Well," he said after a few seconds. "I guess it wasn't that bad."

She finished the last bite, paused and, demanded her body to take in the nourishment, then passed the bowl back. "Thank you for the food."

"Of course." He took the bowl and placed it on the ground beside him. "How are you feeling?"

At the moment, sick from the stew. "Fine."

"I'm sorry you're confined to this area. But it's the safest place for you right now."

"Why are you keeping me?" Brighid wanted to say she had no strategic value, but then thought better of it. She might be tossed aside if they realized she was clanless.

"Because here I can make sure you are safe from our soldiers."

She had overheard as much when they first brought her here. But surely they could fit another body wherever they were holding the other Nordics and still keep her safe? "Are you going to interrogate me? Torture me?"

His eyes went wide again. "What? No. Lands no. But I feel there is a purpose for you being here. And I want to find out why."

"Because I'm the Stryth'Veizla?"

He didn't act surprised at the title. "No, because there is more to you than I understand right now."

Brighid frowned.

He smiled and tugged on a leather glove he wore over his right hand. As he drew the glove away, a piercing light filled the small enclosure, even brighter than the other Eldaran's palm. "I am a Truthsayer and messenger of the Word. From what I can tell, there is a reason you are here. One that transcends this war or your capture. My friend Kaeden was meant to heal and save you. Which means you're meant to be here. But why, I do not know yet."

Brighid couldn't tear her eyes from the light on his palm. "What is your power?" she asked.

"I reveal the truth."

"How?"

"By touching you."

Brighid drew back. "What kind of truth?"

"Your past, your fears, your desires. The very soul of your being. The secrets only the Word knows."

She gripped the blanket to her chest and stared at him. "You would do that to me?"

"Not forcefully. And only if the Word directs me. In some ways, I am a looking glass. Or an icy lake. What you see when I touch you is who you are. I only reflect that."

Brighid stared at him, her heart pumping madly. Would he see her ability to feel death? Or what Armand did to her? Would he make her relive every life she took? Would she be forced to watch Elphsaba die again?

Mathias closed his hand, quenching the light. "You do not have to be afraid. I do not use this power to interrogate or hurt others. Only to help, when the Word directs me."

His words alleviated only a small part of her fear. At any moment, he could reach over and grab her. Armand's word binding was uncomfortable. She had a feeling this truth power would be terrifying.

Mathias let out a soft sigh. "I prefer to talk when I can. So let's start there. I am Mathias, healer and Truthsayer. Do you feel comfortable sharing your name?"

It took Brighid a moment to bring her gaze from his closed hand to his face. She studied the deep lines across his visage and the tenderness in his brown eyes. Sharing her name couldn't hurt, right? "Brighid."

"Brighid. Does it mean something?"

"Strength."

Mathias chuckled. "Your mother named you well."

For the first time in a long time, a small smile crept across her face as warm memories swept through her mind. "Yes, she did."

"Tell me more about her."

Brighid spoke with Mathias for over an hour. She was surprised how easy it was to converse with the old man. Perhaps in part because he reminded her a little of Elphsaba. He spoke of his childhood, his favorite memories, and all the places he had traveled.

It wasn't until he lifted his hand to place his glove back on that Brighid remembered what his power truly was. But it didn't seem so frightening now. Perhaps Mathias was right. By talking, they had already shared truth between them. Or at least she knew his heart more. Of course, he could be lying, but there was no hint of deceit in either his tone or his face.

"May I come back later with dinner and talk some more?" he asked as he rose.

Why was he asking her permission? She was a prisoner; he could do what he liked. But she had a feeling this was his way of making her feel comfortable. To see if she still wanted to speak. "Yes. I would like that."

"I'll try to find something other than fish stew." He winked, then left through the opening into the rest of the healing tent. Brighid stared at the opening, now blocked by a canvas flap, and frowned. From what she could tell, she had been here a day and a half. Some of her encounters had been filled with kindness, some with brutality.

What was happening with the Nordic forces? Were they still fighting? She ran a finger along the edge of the blanket. What about Marta and Johan? Had they escaped? Or had they been captured too?

She had no idea. Time seemed to have no place here in this small enclosure.

Mathias returned that evening with a crusty piece of bread. Hard and dry, but much better than that fish stew. They talked some more. He shared about his people and the Word he followed. Yes, Mathias reminded her a lot of Elphsaba, and she found his presence comforting.

After he left, Brighid curled up on the bed, alone now in the enclosure, with only a slip of lamplight that shone through the gap between the flaps. She listened to the healers and patients on the other side of the tent. Ever since that beating, she hadn't felt death again. Which was odd. She should in a place like this where many souls hovered between life and the beyond. Now that she was safe, were Armand's words affecting her once more? But she hadn't been bound since the start of the battle. How long did the binding last?

Raised voices filtered through the canvas wall from the outside. At first, she ignored them, until she heard "Nordic." Brighid sat up and leaned toward the wall.

"You cannot take her." That was Mathias.

"Under what authority?" a deep male voice she didn't recognize asked.

"As the Truthsayer of these Lands and by the will of the Word himself."

"Then use your truthsaying power on her. Find out what she knows."

"That is not the purpose of this power. It is to reveal truth for the benefit of the one touched. Not for the benefit of others. I will not use it to interrogate her."

"She is a prisoner of war and might hold vital information."

"What information? We won the battle, and the Nordics have retreated."

So they lost. Brighid sat in the darkness as the words sank in. Even if she found a way to escape, she had no idea where to go. Probably north, since her people held everything along the border. Or toward the Onyx River and follow it toward one of their supply posts—

Something dripped from her nose. What in the Abyss?

Brighid touched the area and held her fingers close to her eyes. She couldn't see very well in the dim light, but the liquid was dark. Almost like blood.

Wait. Blood? Why was she bleeding—

Agh! A sharp spasm tore across the side of her head, followed by painful throbbing. Nausea filled her chest. The pounding spread behind her eyes. She pressed her palm against her cheek and eyes and felt more blood drip from her nose. The pain soared until she cried out. Then she vomited. And vomited again. She began to shake, her vision going completely dark.

The small bed couldn't contain her quaking. She fell to the floor and continued to convulse. Someone knelt near her. Hands touched her. Garbled words were spoken. Then everything went black.

35

"What's happening to her?" Kaeden asked as he wiped the sweat, blood, and bile from the woman's face. He had returned to check on the Nordic woman only to find her on the floor convulsing.

"I don't know." Mathias cupped the top of her head with his marked hand and shut his eyes. Kaeden's own power had refused to enter the woman. Hopefully Mathias could help her. The old man looked up moments later. "My healing power has no affect."

Kaeden let out his breath. "Nor mine."

Treyvar burst through the tent flaps. "So it's happening to her as well."

Kaeden glanced over at him. "What do you mean?"

"I've been treating the Nordic prisoners the last few hours. Minutes ago, every single one of them started shaking and falling to the ground. I left the others to see if the same was happening to the prisoner here."

Kaeden and Mathias glanced at each other over the woman's body. Selma arrived seconds later and made her way into the small area. She bent down and reached past Kaeden and touched the Nordic woman's face, then let out a sigh. "I should have sensed it earlier. I can feel words wrapped around her mind. Or the fading residuals of them."

"What do you mean?" Kaeden asked, but it seemed Mathias understood what she was saying.

"An Oathmaker," he said quietly.

"Yes," Selma said. "They were bound to an oath. Violently. An oath that once it starts unraveling, places the person in great pain."

"I've seen something like this before." Treyvar folded his arms. "Sometimes sailors would show up in the healing ward in Avonai bound to strange substances from across the Illyr Sea. It was like they were dependent upon it, and once they couldn't get it, their bodies would go into convulsions."

"Can you do anything to help them?" Mathias asked Selma.

She shook her head. "I can't heal them. And this Oathmaker is stronger than I am. I can feel their words, but I can't undo them."

Kaeden put aside the dirty rag and held a clean one to the young woman's forehead. "What's going to happen to her? To the rest of the Nordics?" At least she had stopped shaking, but her breathing was fast, and her eyes moved in quick jerks behind her eyelids.

"The only thing I can think of is letting the unraveling run its course," Selma said.

"Will it kill them?"

"I don't know," she replied.

Treyvar spoke up. "From what I saw in Avonai, it depended on the strength of the person. Some survived, some didn't. I'm not sure if it's the same with an unraveling oath."

"What evil," Mathias said through clenched teeth. "I never realized our kind could do such a horrific thing to human beings."

Treyvar stepped toward the opening. "I'm heading back to the Nordic prisoners to help Darry and the others."

Selma stood as well. "I'll go with you, since I am no help here."

"You should go, too, Mathias. You might discover something." Kaeden readjusted the rag. "I'll take care of this one."

Mathias paused, then nodded.

All three left the small area. A few of the healers on the other side of the partition asked what was going on.

When it seemed like the woman had stilled, Kaeden moved her back on the bed. He was surprised how firm and muscular she was, despite the leather armor she still wore since the day he brought her in from the battle. Once she was settled, he washed her face again, thankful to find no more blood. Her breathing had slowed, but her eyes still moved behind her eyelids. Was she dreaming?

He knew very little of the Oathmaker's power, only that words were used to bind a person to their vow. Originally, the gift was given to a small group of Eldarans to help those fighting in the Great Battle and infuse them with the courage and strength to continue. He knew Selma possessed that same gift, but he hadn't heard of her using it. Not even on the soldiers of Avonai.

So what had this other Oathmaker done to these Nordics? Was that why they fought with more strength than the average warrior? Because they had been bound? Did this Eldaran know what would happen to those captured?

No. Not Eldaran.

Shadonae. The being that did this was anathema to their people and gifts.

The Nordic woman moaned and twisted across the bed.

"Word, I don't know what to do for her," Kaeden whispered as he took the clean cloth, spotted a half-empty jug of water, and dipped it inside. He wiped her face, then folded the cloth and let it sit on her forehead. It seemed to help a little.

He sat beside her bed and studied the strange mark around her eye. Like half a sun blazing across her face. It was beautiful, much too beautiful to symbolize a body count. He sighed. There was so much he didn't know about the Nordic people. And he was sure he wasn't the only one. Could that be one of the reasons for this war?

A healer came in later and filled the lamp with more oil. Every half hour, the Nordic woman thrashed across the bed or cried out. Once, her nose bled. She was pale and sweaty and fighting some hidden battle. All he could do was sit by her side, cool her fevered face, and pray.

Halfway through the night, Mathias stopped by. "Brighid's still alive?" he asked as he entered. Kaeden looked up. "Yes." So that was her name.

"Half of the Nordics in the prisoner camp have already passed away."

"Half?" His jaw dropped and his eyes went wide.

"Yes. I'm shocked from it all."

Kaeden glanced down at Brighid. "She's still fighting," he murmured. For once, she seemed calm and in a deep slumber.

"If I were a cursing man," Mathias sputtered as he raised his fist. "If I were a violent man . . ." He let out a long, hard breath. "But I'm not. However, I will pass judgment on those who have done this. This is a perversion of the gifts we were given as Eldarans. It is an affront to the Word Himself."

Kaeden thought the same. Maybe because he was raised by Eldaran healers who followed the Word, but the thought of purposely hurting another for power made his heart sick. "And there's nothing Selma can do for them?" he asked as he raised his head.

A strange expression passed over Mathias's face before he answered. "No. Apparently not."

"And your truthsaying power can't free their minds?"

"I tried. Our gifts are unique and different. I could no more tear the veil with the truth I see than an Oathmaker could use words to see inside the soul. It's the way of things. We were meant to work together, for the betterment of humanity." He reached over and touched Kaeden's arm. "Dawn will be here soon, and I dare say you haven't moved from this spot all night. Take a moment to rest."

Kaeden shook his head. "I want to be here if she wakes up."

"And if she doesn't?"

"I refuse to believe the Word had me save her just so she could die from an oath."

"What if her purpose was to expose this Shadonae's work?"

"You didn't witness what I did on the battlefield. She is perhaps the strongest woman I've ever seen, and I don't just mean physically. I don't know of anyone else who could have taken the pummeling she did and still be conscious like she was when I found her. She is tough, and I believe she will pull through."

"Well," Mathias stood slowly, "from your lips to the Word. I'm going to go back and try to help the few that remain. If nothing else, I can pray over those passing through to the other side."

Kaeden nodded and closed his eyes. He started his prayer vigil again.

Brighid convulsed one more time just before dawn, then she

appeared to fall into a deep sleep. Kaeden left her side only once, and for a short period. The rest of the time, he took care of the young Nordic woman, cooling her heated face, making sure she didn't fall or become twisted up in a blanket.

When she finally seemed to be in a peaceful sleep, he leaned back in the chair, folded his arms, and closed his eyes.

36

A hand touched Kaeden's arm.

He started awake.

"Kaeden?" Treyvar said next to him. "You're needed. Quickly."

Kaeden looked over at the bed where Brighid lay. In the dim light, the blanket rose and fell with each breath. She was still alive.

"You don't have much time," Treyvar said, a tone of urgency in his voice.

"What do you mean?" Kaeden stood.

"It's Mathias. He's asking for you."

Kaeden frowned as stood from the chair. "What's going on?"

"So the woman is still alive." Treyvar waved toward the bed.

"Yes." Kaeden glanced at Brighid. She lived, barely.

"Most of the Nordic prisoners passed away during the night. She is one of the few who have survived so far."

"What?" His head snapped back to Treyvar's face. A chilling tingle swept across his body as he followed Treyvar out of the partitioned area into the main healing tent.

"Mathias spent all evening with the Nordics, doing what he could for them."

"Of course he did." Mathias would help anyone with his dying breath. "But why is he calling for me? Did something happen?"

"There was pressure from the commanders a half hour ago for him to get what information he could before they all passed."

They reached the tent flaps and walked outside. Stars hung across the dark sky, and a sliver of light shone along the horizon.

"Mathias would never use his truthsaying power for such a reason." Kaeden rubbed his arms against the early-morning chill. He still couldn't believe so many had died.

Treyvar led the way between the tents. "Mathias said the same thing to Captain Bertin. The captain apparently did not like his response. He had one of the remaining Nordics brought before Mathias. When Mathias refused again, he had the prisoner stabbed."

Kaeden faltered. "He did *what*?" He knew Captain Bertin didn't like the Nordics and remembered how the captain had stood there while his men beat Brighid almost to death on the battlefield. "Was he threatening Mathias?"

"Yes, but it didn't work. Mathias went immediately to the young man and started to heal him."

A chill struck his heart. The last time Mathias healed someone with his Eldaran power, it almost took everything he had. This time it might.

Kaeden walked faster. "Where is he? Where were the Nordics being held?"

"Straight ahead—"

He didn't give Treyvar a chance to finish. Instead, he ran past the rows of tents toward the edge of the camp. Minutes later, he spotted a field where a couple dozen thick posts were set up, each one with five chains attached to the top. Each chain held a Nordic warrior like a fish tethered to a line. And every warrior was on the ground, dead.

He stared at the massacre in the misty morning light, his stomach clenching and bile rising in his throat. It took a couple of seconds for him to register voices to his right and to pull his eyes away from the scene. At the far end of the field he noticed a group of Avonain soldiers. He ran again.

As he approached, he spotted Mathias lying on the ground between the men standing there.

"Mathias!" he shouted, growing sicker with each step.

Mathias didn't move. Anger like a bubbling cauldron rose inside his chest, spreading heat across his cold limbs. "What did you do to him?" Kaeden shouted when he saw Captain Bertin nearby. He shoved his way between the men—the same men who had been at Brighid's beating—and paused at the bodies on the ground. Five chained Nordics. Five dead, including one still leaking blood from a gut wound. And Mathias . . .

"Oh, Word, no," Kaeden murmured as he knelt beside his mentor. Mathias's face was pale and sweat clung to his skin and hair. He held a hand to his midsection, a hand that should have been glowing. And a wound that should have been healing.

"No, no, no. Please no." Kaeden peered over his shoulder at the group around him, his eyes landing on Captain Bertin. "What in the *Lands* did you think you were doing?"

Captain Bertin stood above him with folded arms. "We needed information before all these filthy dogs passed away."

"So you stabbed one of them?"

The captain faltered slightly. "I didn't think Master Mathias would try to heal the man—"

"Then you know *nothing* of our kind or who we serve." All the pain, hatred, and bitterness from the last six years rose up inside his chest with such a fury that his whole body began to shake. "We chose to aid your people. To heal your wounded. And this is how you repay us?" It was just like Khodath. Just like his parents' death.

"He can heal himself. Isn't that what your people do?"

Kaeden turned away. No, this time Mathias would not be coming back. Tears prickled his eyes and he shut them tight.

"Kaeden . . ."

Mathias's sweet voice filled his ears.

"I'm here," Kaeden said and slowly opened his eyes again.

The old man reached for his hand. It was bloody and the light across his palm so dim it was almost gone. Just like his life. Kaeden swallowed hard and grabbed Mathias's hand.

"Don't let hatred take your heart."

Kaeden clenched his teeth. He could no more control the rage coursing through his body than he could stop the waves of the sea.

"Turn to the Word, instead."

How could Mathias say such a thing? Kaeden bowed his head

and swallowed again. How could he turn to the Word? Sometimes he wasn't even sure if the Word cared. Because if He did, He would take better care of His servants. He wouldn't have let his parents die, or Mathias now.

He felt Mathias's fingers grow limp. "Mathias?" He looked up. The light was fading from the old man's eyes. He tightened his grip, but he could feel the skin growing cold beneath his own.

"Kaeden," he rasped. "There . . . there must always be a Truthsayer."

He barely heard the words.

"There must always be . . . a voice for the Word. And you must save . . . the Nordic . . ."

Kaeden waited for Mathias to finish. But when seconds went by and Mathias failed to continue, he realized there was no breath in the man's body.

Mathias had crossed the veil.

Kaeden hunched over him as grief replaced the rage from moments earlier, piercing his heart more than any sword ever could. It hurt. It hurt so bad. He held Mathias's hand to his chest and began to rock back and forth. He didn't care about anything around him. He didn't care about Captain Bertin or the men nearby. He didn't care about the camp behind him or this bloody war. He didn't even care about life itself.

All he knew was his best friend and second father had just died.

Soldiers moved around him, taking down the bodies of the Nordics and hauling them away. Kaeden ignored them and remained next to Mathias's body.

"What do I do now?" he whispered. Part of him wanted to go back to Mistsylver Island and to the quarry and forget about this land. These people never deserved Mathias. Just like Khodath never deserved his parents. They took and complained and then abandoned them when they were done.

But he'd come too far. He let out a shudder and squeezed his eyes shut. By coming here, he had finally started to heal. To run away would be to lose everything he had gained. It would be as if his time with Mathias had been for nothing. He couldn't do that.

Mathias's hand was already growing stiff in his own. "It wasn't for nothing, old man," Kaeden whispered. He gently pulled the Mathia's hand away and folded it across his chest. Then he swept his fingers over his mentor's eyes and closed them.

He looked up and pressed his lips together as he watched the Nordics unchained from the poles and dragged away like beasts. If he had learned anything from Mathias, it was that all were equally human in the Word's eyes.

What did Mathias mean when he said to save the Nordic? Did he mean the Nordic people? The Nordic woman? And what would happen to the Shadonae who were working with the Nordics? Who would judge them now?

Ugh. He pressed his hand to the side of his face. A dull ache spread inside his head along with unusual heat across his body. Maybe his body was finally giving out from all the intense pressure from the last few days. His vision blurred.

Or maybe it was grief taking a toll on his already weary soul.

He fell to the ground.

"Kaeden!" Treyvar shouted.

Everything went black.

37

Dark. And hot. So hot. Kaeden tried to move, but his body felt ten times heavier. And he burned with an intense fire.

Voices sometimes spoke around him, warbled as if he were hearing through water. But he couldn't open his eyes. He couldn't move. All he could do was burn.

In and out of darkness his mind moved. Sometimes the darkness became a dim grey, then grew as black as night. Was this the veil? Would he soon pass as well, like Mathias? Like his parents? What brought him here? Why was he facing the beyond?

"Where am I?" He was finally able to speak, but he still didn't have the strength to open his eyes. He was lying on his back, and whatever cot supported him jostled as if in motion.

Cool fingers touched his forehead. "Treyvar, he's finally awake," a woman said. Selma. It sounded like her.

"Thank the Word," Treyvar said from nearby.

"Kaeden, can you hear me?" Selma asked.

Kaeden tried to open his eyes, but he was too weak. "Selma?"

"Yes, it's me."

"Where . . . what . . ."

"You've come through another change."

"Another change?" He finally managed to pry his eyes open. A late-afternoon sky filled his vision with sparse clouds and the beginning hints of dusk. He was in a wagon, which explained the bouncing. Selma stared down at him from his left. "What do you mean, change?"

"The Eldaran change."

"That . . . doesn't make sense." He closed his eyes. He was still so very tired. Eldarans came into their power when they reached adulthood. There was not a second change. Unless . . .

His breath quickened. "Selma." His eyes snapped open. "Where's Mathias? What happened to him?"

Her face fell. "He passed. His body has been cleaned and wrapped and is being brought to the White City. He will be interred in the Sanctuary."

Grief and pain roared through Kaeden, almost taking his breath away. A tear squeezed its way out of the corner of his eye. He turned his head toward the side of the wagon. He didn't want others to see his sorrow. It was still too raw and real to share.

He took in a couple deep breaths until he regained control. "What did you mean I went through another change?"

"Treyvar and I believe Mathias's power has been passed on to you."

"What?" He drew in a sharp breath and twisted his head around. "How? Why?" It can't be. *I don't want that. I never wanted that—*

"Because there must always be a Truthsayer," Selma said.

There must always be a Truthsayer. Mathias's words. Eldaran power was passed on through blood. Mathias had no children. No one to pass on the most sacred power of their people. So did that mean . . . ?

No. It didn't make sense. A week ago, he didn't even possess the power of his people. How could such a drastic change take place?

He glanced at Selma. "Why me? Why not you? Or someone else?"

She shrugged. "Maybe because you were always the one closest to him. Like a son. Or the Word simply willed it."

Kaeden stared up at the sky. "Why?" he whispered again. It would explain the darkness and heat. As if his body was being reforged. He remembered the same sensation when he went through the change the first time, during the time his parents were executed.

He brought his hand near his face and slowly opened his fingers. His mark looked the same with a bright light illuminating from his palm. He still wasn't used to this light. It had appeared only a week ago when he'd healed—

Kaeden sat up. The wagon continued to bounce beneath him, and he swayed for a moment.

A hand caught his shoulder. "I wouldn't recommend moving so quickly," Treyvar said as he steadied him.

Kaeden glanced around. He was in the middle of a long procession of soldiers and carts. Banners of dark blue and green fluttered above soldiers and horses. They were traveling across a wide-open plain covered with tall, golden grass. Far head, he spotted the edge of Anwin Forest, and above that, the towering peaks of the Ari Mountains.

"Where's Brighid?"

Selma peered over her shoulder. "What are you doing sitting up? You should be resting."

Kaeden ignored her. "Where's Brighid? The Nordic woman? The Stryth'Veizla?"

Selma scowled and went back to attending the other person in the cart. Treyvar answered him.

"The Nordic woman lived. She made it through the unraveling. She's currently ahead of us and bound."

"Did Captain Bertin do anything to her?"

Treyvar's face grew dark. "No." It seemed he was remembering what Bertin had done to the Nordic prisoners and consequently, to Mathias.

"So she's all right? And safe?"

"As far as I can tell. Our scouts say the Nordics went north after the Battle of the Plains. With fall here and winter fast approaching, most likely the fighting has ceased for now. Half of the Avonain forces are returning to Avonai. The rest of us are on our way to Mostyn and the White City. I don't know if those in position plan on questioning her once we arrive or if they will save her for a prisoner exchange. Not that there is anyone to exchange her with. The Nordics haven't retained any prisoners that we know of."

Kaeden stared ahead at the long line of soldiers. Hundreds marched before him in groupings of dark blue and green blue. He didn't see a head with golden-blond braids. "Did any other Nordic survive the unraveling?"

"No."

So Brighid was the only one left. The only one they could question, trade, or even take their anger out on. Kaeden pressed his lips together. Was this the reason the Word had him save her? So she could provide secret knowledge for the war?

That didn't seem right.

And Mathias hadn't thought so either.

Mathias.

Kaeden bowed his head and gripped his fingers in his lap. What would Mathias do? Thin beams of light escaped his closed hand. What should he do?

Truthsayer. There must always be a Truthsayer.

"Why, Mathias?" he whispered. "Why me? I never wanted this. I'm hardly an Eldaran myself. This is too much." Too much power. Too much responsibility. Someone else should have taken the mantle. Someone like Selma who had followed the ways of their people all her life. He glanced at her as she assisted the other man in the wagon. What did she think of all this?

His head grew heavy, his body still fatigued from the change. Kaeden lay back down and watched the wisps of clouds pass overhead. His body no longer burned. In fact, the air held a slight chill.

Selma finished attending the other man on the wagon, then turned toward him. "Do you need anything, Kaeden? Water? Food?"

He closed his eyes. "Just rest. I need rest." And time to think.

Kaeden woke again when the sky was dark and a crescent moon hung low along the horizon. The wagon was no longer in motion. He sat up and looked around. Camps were set up, lighting the plains with hundreds of small blazes. A fire burned nearby, and he could smell something savory cooking in the pot hanging over the flames. He made his way to the back of the wagon, carefully let himself down, and stumbled toward the nearest fire where a half dozen healers were warming themselves.

"What did I say about getting up too fast?" Treyvar appeared at his side and helped him to a blanket that was spread out.

"I'm almost back to my full strength," Kaeden said.

"You're more like a foal on wobbly legs."

"I can only rest for so long."

"You're just like Mathias," Treyvar said.

Kaeden's lips spread into a sad smile. "That's true. The old man could never sit for long."

"Here." Darry, one of the healers sitting by the fire, ladled out soup and passed him the bowl. Some kind of pork and bean stew. He took a bite. Palatable, like most of their rations. Kaeden finished the soup, then ate another bowl.

"Good to see your appetite back," Treyvar said.

"Treyvar told us what happened," Darry said. The other healers nodded. "And that you have replaced Master Mathias."

Kaeden's throat tightened. "Yes." He could no longer deny it or wish it away. The change had run its course, and he could feel a strange, warm power swirling inside his chest.

He raised his head and looked out over the rest of the camp. Selma sat by another fire not too far away. The rest of the fires were surrounded by soldiers. He raised his chin even higher.

"Searching for the Nordic?" Treyvar asked.

"Yes."

"They have her tied up over to the far right."

Kaeden craned his neck but couldn't see any sign of her.

"She is under guard and appears to be tired from the walk. But I don't think they've done anything to her. Not yet."

Kaeden turned his attention to the fire and watched the flames flicker and dance along the logs. An urgency started to fill him. *Not yet.* He didn't like the way Treyvar said that.

They were on their way to Mostyn, one of the main military outposts for the White City. No doubt once they arrived, the commanders would want information from her. And would do whatever was needed to find out what she knew. Which, according to Mathias, might be very little. Then they would imprison her or discard her.

He shook his head at these thoughts. The urgency grew stronger until he found himself on his feet. "Where are the commanders?"

Treyvar also stood. "Why?"

"I need to talk to them.

"About the Nordic?"

"Yes." He didn't know what he was going to do, just that he had to go. The light across his hand flared for a moment. He stared at it. Was this urgency coming from the power inside him? Was it . . . the Word?

"I'll take you. But first, you should put on your new cord." Treyvar headed to the wagon and a minute later, returned with a golden cord. Kaeden felt a fresh wave of grief at the sight. Mathias's cord and symbol of his status as the Truthsayer.

"You'll have more clout with this." Treyvar held it out.

Kaeden's lips trembled, but he knew Treyvar was right. New robes would come later, but this cord would remind everyone that although Mathias was gone, the Truthsayer was not, and the authority and power of that position still remained.

Kaeden pressed his lips together as he untied the rope around his waist and passed it to Treyvar. Then he took the cord. It felt heavier, thicker. Like a mantle being placed on him. He brought it around his waist and secured it in a simple knot in the front.

Treyvar nodded. "Now you're ready to see the commanders."

With a deep breath, Kaeden followed Treyvar through the camp, bypassing fires and soldiers, until they reached the center where a handful of tents were set up for those in charge. In the middle of the tents glowed a single large fire. The men around it were older with a more polished air to their essence and attire. He spotted Captain Bertin, and his body stiffened.

A couple heads turned their direction as Treyvar approached. "Good evening, commanders and captains." The rest of those gathered glanced up. The three dressed in Avonain colors went stiff, and the oldest one stood.

"My pr—I mean, Treyvar, why are you here?" Commander Warin asked.

"Commander Warin, this is Kaeden. He is one of the Eldarans who have been assisting us in the healing tents. He has also taken Master Mathias's place as the Truthsayer of the Lands."

All eyes focused on the cord around Kaeden's middle. Then one by one, the rest of the men stood, including Captain Bertin. "Master Kaeden," they murmured together.

Their sign of reverence, whether real or pretend, reinforced the fact that Mathias was gone and he was now the Truthsayer. Kaeden's stomach tightened beneath the golden cord as he raised his hand. "Please, be seated."

As the men sat, Bertin's gaze never left Kaeden's face. He returned the look with an unwavering one of his own. "I am here for the Nordic woman."

"What do you mean?" Commander Warin asked. "Has the Word spoken to you?"

Before he could answer, Captain Bertin leaped to his feet. "You can't have her! She is being taking to Mostyn where she will be questioned—"

"I'll do it," Kaeden said.

Captain Bertin glared at him while the other men frowned.

A third man spoke, this one with a regal air. His brown hair and beard were neat and trimmed with a sprinkling of grey, and he wore the dark-blue colors of the White City. He bowed his head.

"Captain Reginar of the White City at your service. May I ask what you mean?"

"I will do what my predecessor did not. I will search the Nordic woman's mind. I will look for the information you seek."

"You can do that?" one of the younger captains asked, his eyes wide.

"As the Truthsayer, he can see everything," Captain Bertin replied stiffly.

The young captain balked and drew away. Kaeden bit back a snort. The power of the Truthsayer was coveted and feared. Others wished to possess it but were terrified of having that same power turned on them.

"Why would you offer this?" Commander Warin asked. "Why would you do what Master Mathias refused to do?"

"I am not like my mentor." Which was true. He was nothing like Mathias. Mathias was so much more. He was someone Kaeden hoped to be like someday. "But I am bound to this new power and the will of the One who gave it to me. It cannot be forced. So I will need her permission before I touch her."

"Then what good is that to us?" Captain Bertin asked. "What if she says no?"

The urgency inside Kaeden stirred again. Like a wind moving within his soul. He had to do this. As if he was on a trajectory he could not budge from. A course that led right to Brighid.

"I don't believe she will."

His answer surprised the captains and commanders by the way they glanced at each other. But he wasn't doing this for them. It was for her. It was to save her. He didn't care about them. He wasn't even sure how much he trusted the Word or what it meant to be an Eldaran. But he did know the Word had spoken to him that one time to save her. If he could find a way to help her again, he would.

As Mathias had said before, this power was never to be used to interrogate, but to show the truth.

Captain Bertin huffed. "Well, what have we to lose? Take him to her right now and see what he can do."

38

Brighid slumped against the wagon where her hand was chained to the side, careful not to move her raw and bloody wrist too much. A guard stood on each side of her, both silent and unmoving as they kept watch over their prisoner. No one had offered her food or water all day, and her lips were parched and cracked. Evening fires had been lit, and the smell of food cooking almost made her faint from want.

No. She struggled up along the side of the wagon and gritted her teeth. She would not pass out from such a simple thing. She had known hunger all her life. This was nothing. If these soldiers thought she would break under deprivation and neglect, they were in for a surprise. She had been forged by such things. And she wouldn't succumb now.

But she did miss those few days she spent in the healing tent, and the kindness and tenderness of Mathias and the bear-man healer, Kaeden. She brought her knees up to her chin and stared up at the star-studded sky.

When she'd woken up days ago after being on the brink of death, she had been dragged away from the healing tent and brought to a field filled with poles, chains, and dead Nordics. She could still see their bloated bodies in her mind and smell the putrefying decay. She'd been chained to one of the poles, then questioned over and over again, with beatings in between.

Why was every Nordic dead?

Why was she still alive?

What were the Nordics planning next?

What had she done to Master Mathias?

She'd never answered them. Whether because of stubbornness or shock, Brighid had remained silent. She had a feeling she knew why they had died. Armand had not bound them again to their oath. But why she'd lived through it, she didn't know. And she had no idea what the clans had planned. If the White City and Avonai realized she was nobody—despite the name her comrades had given her—they would kill her on the spot.

The last question was the most puzzling and worst of all. Rumors said Mathias had died shortly after the battle, and many claimed the Nordics had something to do with it. She wasn't sure how anyone had come to that conclusion if they had seen how the Nordic prisoners had been chained like beasts. And she had been detained in the healer's tent. But whispers had spread across the camp that the Nordics had taken their beloved Eldaran healer, and since she was the only one left alive, the brunt of their grief and anger was taken out on her.

With no way to defend herself, she endured the questions and beatings until the camp was packed up and they started journeying westward.

Her hand tingled from where it hung above her. With a groan, Brighid struggled up to her feet and leaned against the wagon. A cold wind blew, sending a chill over her skin. Summer was gone, and fall was already settling in across the country. If the cold nights were any indication, winter might come early this year.

She watched the fire closest to her, about twenty feet away, and listened to her captors talk. Their voices carried much bitterness and grief. Although they had won, they had lost many. One of them peered over his shoulder and pointed at her.

"Why do we keep her? Better she had died with the others."

"I lost my brother to her," another man said as he stood. The first one stood as well. Then the others.

"She's a dirty Nordic. All of them are." The first man approached her and spat. His saliva hit her near the eye and ran down to her chin. Brighid pressed her lips together and ignored him. Her guards did not react.

"Too good for us, eh?" a second soldier said. "Look at her. Apparently the beatings Captain Bertin has been giving her haven't been enough. Maybe we should finish the job. After all, the only good Nordic is a dead Nordic."

A stone flew from the shadows and grazed her cheek. Another barely missed her leg.

"Why are you throwing stones?" the first man shouted. "Who has a sword? We should execute her here and now!"

"No," the second soldier said. "A swift death would be too good for the Stryth'Veizla. Make her suffer." Shouts and cries filled the air. More stones flew before Brighid could react, one hitting her ear and leaving a trail of blood down her neck. Another caught her shoulder, and she instantly felt a bruise form.

The guard on her right stirred and took a step forward while lifting his hand.

"Are you going to defend her, Jerod?" the second soldier yelled. "You know what she did to your regiment."

Jerod paused.

"She deserves this and you know it."

He lowered his hand and took a step back without saying a word.

"That's right," the first soldier said. "She should have died with the rest of her kind."

Brighid turned her head and tried to hide her face. A few stones went off course, hitting the wagon or bouncing across the ground. But another one met its mark, striking her in the midsection.

Then the stones stopped. Brighid slowly turned around. A hush had fallen over the soldiers, as fast as the mob had formed.

"It's him," a young man nearby whispered as they backed away. "The Truthsayer."

Someone cursed. "And the commanders are with him."

Truthsayer? Brighid peered past the mob, her heart skipping a beat. Had the rumors of Mathias's death been lies? But then why had they accused her of killing him?

She caught a glimpse of a man who towered over the others, with dark hair and wide shoulders, wearing a white robe. She frowned. That wasn't Mathias. That was Kaeden.

As he drew closer, the soldiers parted like a stream around a boulder, their heads bowed in reverence, including her guards. What in winter was going on? She hadn't seen Kaeden in many days and heard whispers he was sick. Had something happened to him during that time?

"Truthsayer," the soldiers murmured with bowed heads.

The healer Treyvar was among the captains and commanders. He separated from them and approached the soldiers who had been tormenting her minutes ago.

"What were you doing? Especially you two?" he asked her guards.

Kaeden stopped before her, blocking her view of everyone. Brighid ducked her head. She spotted a golden cord around his waist. It was different from the usual rope. More ornate, more elegant, more . . .

More like Mathias's attire.

She sucked in her breath. Kaeden was also a Truthsayer? Like Mathias?

"If I use my truthsaying power on her, will you be satisfied?" he asked above her, his focus on those who had been throwing stones minutes earlier.

Brighid cast a glance in their direction. The soldiers appraised her while Treyvar watched with arms folded and a cold scowl on his face.

"We want the truth," they said. "And justice."

Justice. Bolva. They wanted flesh, not justice. Her flesh. And the flesh of every Nordic.

"Free her," Kaeden said.

Captain Bertin sputtered. "What?"

"She will not be a prisoner under my watch."

Before anyone else could object, Treyvar reached for the key, and the guard named Jerod passed it to him. He walked over and undid the manacle around her wrist. Her hand dropped and feeling rushed back in. The cool air soothed her raw skin.

"Brighid." Kaeden's voice was so quiet she barely caught his words as he bent down and leaned his head near hers. "I'm so sorry. If there was any other way to protect you . . ." Then he began to pull the glove off his hand.

She watched, unable to speak. As he drew the glove away, light shone from his palm as if he held a ball of sunshine. Bright and pure. Like the intense flames of the blacksmith's forge. The kind of heat used to purify.

She couldn't tear her eyes away from the sight. Had his palm always been radiant? Why had she never noticed? It was so very different from Armand's.

Wait. If he was a Truthsayer . . . A chill ran down her spine as she remembered Mathias's words and what his ability was.

"What are you going to do to me?" she whispered. Everything around them had faded away until it was just her and Kaeden and the bright light from his hand.

"This power will let me see everything inside of you."

Just like Mathias had said. Her heart pounded faster. "Everything?"

"Yes. Everything."

"Will it . . . hurt?"

He hesitated. "Yes."

Her mouth went dry. Everything.

Voices murmured around them. "Is he going to do it, or is he stalling?"

"I was hoping the new Truthsayer would take a harder stance."

"I want to see this."

"Brighid."

She looked up into Kaeden's face.

"I will only do this if you say yes."

She stared into his eyes. "This will save me? This will prove I had nothing to do with Mathias's death? Or the other things they are accusing me of?"

His eyes went wide. "What? What do you mean—"

"Do it. Do it now."

Before he could change his mind, Brighid grabbed his hand and squeezed her eyes shut. She would rather be at the mercy of Kaeden and his power than anyone else in this place.

But she wasn't prepared for the searing light that invaded her mind or the way it swept her away into the beyond.

39

Kaeden was hurtled into Brighid's mind before he had a chance to breathe. They no longer stood on an open field, surrounded by the soldiers and commanders under a night sky. Instead, he found himself outside a tiny cabin clinging to a mountainside. An old woman sat on a rickety wooden chair beside the door, humming a tune while what appeared like a young Brighid sat at her feet, working on a woolen dress. The scene was one of poverty and want, but there was also peace.

Then the images changed. They were in a city of stone and wood with high walls along one side and the steep sides of sheer cliffs on another. Harsh voices yelled at an older Brighid and the old woman as they were forced down a worn street with filth and broken homes.

More images flew past his mind's eye as Brighid's life was laid before him. He felt her want and hunger. He knew her love for the old woman. He experienced the chill of death, almost as if Brighid had a connection with the ender of life itself.

The old woman died, and Kaeden felt Brighid's raw grief and despair like a punch to his midsection. He understood it all too well. It mirrored his own past.

More images danced across his eyes and mind. The funeral pyre. The day she received her first Mark of Remembrance. The red vision of bloodlust when she fought, and how it empowered her. The night a man tried to take her. The battle in the arena and her first kill, and her horror of it all.

Somewhere in the back of his mind, he felt his body fall to his knees, his hand still grasped between Brighid's. He couldn't break away. Some kind of connection had formed between them, the forging of a bond. Whether that was because she'd initiated the connection first or the Word held them together, he didn't know. But he didn't want to break away either. He wanted to know her more. This woman who had endured so much, fought like a warrior, and experienced hardship like his own.

He could see now why she was known as the Stryth'Veizla of her people. He could feel strength coursing through her body as she fought, and the fierce love she had for her friends and the woman who had raised her.

More memories blurred across his mind until he found himself on a field with hundreds of warriors. Three hooded figures stood in front of the crowd alongside what appeared to be the leaders of the Nordic clans. As they drew back their hoods, he sensed who they were. Two appeared young and related, despite their differing hair color. But it was the older one with silky black hair and skin seemingly untouched by the sun that held his attention the longest.

It was this one who walked among the Nordics and bound them using words. He was the Oathmaker. Kaeden pressed his lips together in disgust. No, not an Oathmaker. That would imply his power instilled honor and courage. Instead, he twisted his words, binding the Nordic minds and hearts with invisible chains.

As the Shadonae approached Brighid, Kaeden felt a moment of chill, the same feeling Brighid seemed to possess around death. Then a numbness stole over her as the Shadonae's words penetrated her entire being.

Kaeden recoiled from the sensation. Was this what every Nordic experienced? Was this why they could fight with such strength and abandonment? Like unfeeling warriors?

He watched as time passed and Brighid marched with her people south, fighting battle after battle. Although she killed countless Avonains, they were guards or soldiers. Instinctively she shied away from the innocent, even under the strange red haze she fought within. Despite the words of the Shadonae, she fought with honor, up until the moment she lay on the battlefield with a crowd of Avonains around her, raining blows with their fists and feet on her body with all their pent-up hatred and bloodlust.

Kaeden blinked as he saw himself through her eyes. He could feel death gripping her body as waves of mind-searing agony swept over her, the kind of pain that would have knocked out a grown man. But she held on. And she reached for him—an enemy—asking for the deepest desire of her heart. For her life.

I don't want to die.

Thump. Thump. Along the edges of his mind, he felt their hearts beating as one. His heart and hers. His mind and hers, connected. Their fingers intertwined. Her truth now his.

The rest of her memories flew through his mind. He already knew she had nothing to do with Mathias's death. It was a ploy conjured by those at the top to deflect the truth that one of their own had led to the old man's death. And now having experienced her heart and soul, he knew she would never do such a thing.

There were evil men and women in this world who lied, killed, and stole from others. They came from all backgrounds: rich and poor, Avonain and Nordic, even human and Eldaran. But Brighid was simply a woman trying to survive in a harsh world.

How many other Nordics were like her: caught in a war and the web of powerful beings? Used then discarded, as the Nordic prisoners of war had been.

Then the world around him faded into a dim fog. He could no longer feel or sense Brighid. He jumped to his feet and looked around. Where—where was he?

Well done, Son of Light.

The voice was deep and melodic, echoing across the fog-covered terrain like the rumblings of thunder after a flash of lightning.

Was that voice . . . the Word?

Kaeden's heart beat faster as he turned around, searching the fog for a figure. What should he do? Bow? Hide his eyes? The Word was the One who held the world in existence with His very words. One pause, one moment of silence, and the world would fall away into nothing. How did one act in the presence of such a being?

A figure appeared in the mist. Kaeden gulped in air and fell to one knee, his head bowed. He watched as bare, scarred feet beneath a robe of brilliant white approached him. A heady awe and fear filled him to such a degree that he wasn't sure if he would pass out from the feeling.

Then a hand touched his head, and he breathed again.

"You did well, my Truthsayer. You saw what others do not. You witnessed what I witness. The heart of humanity."

Kaeden pressed his knuckles into the ground on each side of his knee. "Why me? I am nobody. I didn't even have my gift until—"

"Because I chose you."

Kaeden raised his eyes until his gaze fell on a single golden cord wrapped around a waist. The same kind of cord Mathias wore, that he now wore as the Truthsayer.

"Why?" he asked again.

"You have many questions."

Kaeden could feel the Word's voice reverberating through his chest. "Yes."

"Some answers cannot be known. They are written in words so deep that your mind couldn't handle their utterance."

Kaeden wrestled with this answer. It didn't satisfy. Why did his parents have to die after giving so much to humanity? Why did Mathias have to pay for the actions of Captain Bertin? Why was there so much sorrow in this world?

"In time, you will realize the weight of such questions—a weight you cannot bear. And I will be ready to hold them then."

Kaeden finally raised his head. It took a moment for his eyes to adjust to the brilliance of light emanating from the figure's face, but as his vision cleared, his heart stopped. He had grown up with stories of the Word, of the scars He bore, but nothing had prepared him for what he saw now.

The figure standing before him bore ghastly disfigurements. Scars crisscrossed His face, some small and thin, others grotesque and deep. The scars disappeared into the hem of His robe, but Kaeden was sure they continued across the rest of His body. The hand Kaeden could see was also scarred, and so were the Word's bare feet.

Without thinking, Kaeden touched the side of his own waist where a raised scar had formed after he'd healed Brighid. He recalled the scars across his parents' and Mathias's faces and bodies. But they were nothing compared to the Word's. Was it worth it?

"Yes," the Word said softly, His voice now like a gentle rain.

Of course the Word knew what he was thinking; He knew all words.

"What do I do now?" Kaeden asked out loud.

"Save the Nordic woman. She will be my special instrument."

"How do I save her?"

"That is for you to decide."

"What if she doesn't want to serve you?"

"That is her choice."

If Brighid was so vital, why was the Word leaving such an important choice up to her? Shouldn't He do something more?

"The road will not be easy. I will not bind her to it. Just as I will not bind you to your own path."

His own path. Did the Word mean the fact that Kaeden would have to judge the Shadonae? And live out the rest of his life as the Truthsayer?

The fog faded into darkness. Kaeden looked up. "Wait, I'm not ready!" But the Word had disappeared, leaving behind only shadows. He clasped his face in his hands. "This is too much," he whispered. "I only wanted a simple life."

I will not bind you to your own path.

Did that mean he had a choice? But could he really live with himself if he let the world around him burn while he lived a simple life? In his heart of hearts, he knew he could not. He had seen the sacrificial example of his parents and spent too much time with Mathias. His heart had started healing. He couldn't go back to the man working the quarry. But he was fearful of the future.

Torchlight came into view as he emerged from his experience with the Word and Brighid's mind and soul. They were both kneeling on the ground, fingers still clasped. Her eyes were on his face, wide and dark.

"Did you do it?" a soldier asked from nearby, and someone hushed him.

"Yes," Kaeden said without taking his eyes off Brighid. *Save the Nordic woman.* How would he do that when she was a prisoner surrounded by an entire camp of enemies? And how would he know she wouldn't just go back to the Nordic army to fight them once again?

She will be my special instrument.

What did that mean? What if she chose not to?

He let out his breath and loosened his fingers from hers. In the end, it didn't matter what she did. It was her decision. All he could do was what the Word had asked him to do. As his fingers drew away from hers, he made his choice. *I will save her.*

He stood and searched those gathered around him. "She had nothing to do with Master Mathias's death," he said, making eye contact with each commander and captain present.

"Are you sure?"

"If you like, I can show you how my power works," Kaeden said, raising his hand and letting the light from his palm spill over the crowd. Mathias never would have said such a thing, but he wasn't Mathias. From this moment on, he would forge his own way as the Truthsayer of these Lands. He would protect those who needed protection and bring light to the hidden prejudices and hatred of others.

The man made a hasty retreat while shaking his head. "No, no need."

"Did you find out anything of importance?" Commander Warin asked. "Any plans the Nordic army may have? Any secrets?"

"Yes. I know why the Nordics we captured died. And who is secretly working with the Nordics." He would give them this knowledge to buy Brighid time so he could figure out how to free her. He lowered his voice. "But I don't think this is information you wish discussed in front of your subordinates."

"Then let's head back to the tents," Commander Warin said.

Captain Bertin glared at Kaeden before turning toward Brighid. "If she is no longer of any use to us—"

"If you touch one hair on her head, I will reveal nothing. Treyvar will stay here and watch over her."

There were some grumblings, but the expression on Treyvar's face silenced everyone. The man had quite the withering look for a scholar and healer.

Kaeden cast one last glance at Brighid before turning around and following Commander Warin. She was still on her knees, her arms limp at her sides as she stared into the darkness in a daze. He had never seen Mathias use his truthsaying power, but he had a feeling anyone who had their entire life laid bare would feel overwhelmed and vulnerable.

I'm sorry.

He turned and walked away.

40

He'd seen . . . everything.

Brighid stared into the darkness, her mind replaying all Kaeden had seen. She had watched him brush through her mind with the same ease as someone glancing over a tool set. Bare. Naked. Exposed. That was how she felt right now. No wonder he had apologized before entering her mind. To have every truth lifted from her life and revealed to another was one of the most intimate and jarring experiences of her life.

If she'd known what she knew now, would she have let him?

Brighid sucked in a breath and came back to the present. A handful of soldiers remained nearby, their backs to the fire, their shadowed faces turned toward her while Treyvar, the man Kaeden had asked to watch her, stood a few feet away. His gaze moved from her to the soldiers, then back to her, his stance motionless, his arms crossed.

She moved to stand but instead fell to the ground. She had no strength.

"Where do you think you're goin—"

"Step back," Treyvar barked, his piercing stare on the soldier who had spoken. "Even better, go back to your fire. You're not needed here." One of her former guards stepped forward. "Not even you. You failed to do your job."

The soldiers shuffled and looked at each other, then one by one they left Brighid and Treyvar and headed back to their fire. She heard them mutter under their breaths but couldn't catch their words.

Treyvar watched them retreat with a frigid expression. Once they were gone, he pulled something out of the inner part of his robe and turned toward her.

"Here." He held out a small jar of salve. "For your wounds."

Brighid hesitated, then dipped her fingers into the cold, slick substance. It had a hint of mint to it. She rubbed the salve across the cut along her cheek and ear, then worked it into the raw skin around her wrist and sighed in relief. Too bad it didn't work on bruises.

"I apologize, but I'm going to have to lock you back up."

She paused, her fingers still pressed against her wrist. She stared at the fire ahead, then the hundreds more around her. There was a small gap from here to the darkness beyond. If she had been at her full strength, she knew she could take him on and the other soldiers and disappear into the night. But she wasn't. Kaeden's power had sapped her of her own.

She dipped her head, a heaviness filling her chest as that glimmer of freedom vanished as fast as it had appeared.

Treyvar took her other wrist and clamped it into the single manacle. The cold metal reminded her she was a prisoner once again. The soldiers around the fire closest to her conversed once more, and no one turned in her direction. Only Treyvar stood like a sentinel, watching her without a sound.

A cool wind blew across the wide swath of prairie grass that seemed to silence the world around her until she was alone, kneeling on the ground next to a supply wagon, with an unending night sky dotted with a thousand stars.

She clenched her free hand and pressed it between her knees. Kaeden's power had dredged up precious memories, each one as fresh and new as the day they'd happened. Elphsaba and the hardships they had endured together. The unfailing love of her adopted mother. The pounding thrill of the fight, and her own fierce love for her friends. Death's chill, and the first time she had seen Kaeden's face and pleaded for her life.

They came, then faded until she was alone under the night sky once again. "Why am I here?" she whispered. Words. She remembered words. No. Not words. The Word. Was He real? Elphsaba didn't believe in the old gods, but she never spoke much about the Word. However, she'd sung about Him. Mathias had spoken of the Word during their brief conversations. Even Kaeden had mentioned something once or twice. Said something about healing her because the Word told him to.

She looked up at the star-studded sky. "Why am I here?" she whispered again. She had the hands of a fighter, so she had fought. In that sense, her life should be done. Why was she still here and still alive? *Although I'm thankful.* She squeezed her eyes shut. *I'm not ready, not yet.* Deep down, she feared death more than anything. Near the end, Elphsaba had confidence that when she shut her eyes and opened them again, she would be . . . wherever was next. But if death felt so bitter and frozen, could anything really be good on the other side?

I don't want to die until I know. So if You're real, and You can hear me, please show me.

It felt like hubris to say such a thing, but it was as honest as her heart could get. She raised her chin, still vacillating between what felt like irreverence for a being who allegedly ruled the Lands and a dogged determination to know if He was who others said He was.

"If I'm still supposed to be here, and there is still something left for me to do, show me." She bowed her head. "Please, show me."

The wind blew again, and for one daunting moment, she felt like she could hear words in the air. Her head shot up, and her eyes went wide. She strained to make out more, but she caught nothing. Still, she couldn't shake the feeling that she had definitely heard words.

A tremor ran down her back. Maybe she should have watched what she said, even in her mind. After all, if beings like Armand, Mathias, and Kaeden existed with unnatural power, the One who gave them that power had to exist too. And if He existed . . . Maybe, just maybe, He'd heard her.

41

Kaeden followed Commander Warin through the camp.

I need to save her, but how? Walking among thousands of soldiers and fires was a reminder that he was in the middle of enemy territory, and she was the adversary. *Word, if You want me to save her, show me how.*

Minutes later they arrived back at the commanders' personal tents. Commander Warin led them past the fire where Kaeden had first met them and into one of the middle tents. As the flaps fell behind them and the captains and commanders gathered around the single table in the room, the questions started.

"What did you discover?" the first officer asked, a White City leader, by the dark-blue color of his uniform. Others echoed the same thought.

Kaeden took a deep breath and placed his palms atop the table. Beams of light escaped between the fingers on his right hand. What to share . . .

"First, there is more at work here than this war between the south and Nordica. There are beings assisting the Nordics in their war effort."

"You mean those shadow things that have been wiping out our villages up north?" one of the captains asked, glancing from Commander Warin to Kaeden as if to see if he could speak of such things.

So it was true. There were Mordra in the Lands. "More than that," Kaeden continued. "There are Shadonae working on their side."

"Shadonae?" Commander Warin asked. "What are 'Shadonae'?"

"They are Eldarans who have twisted their power and walked away from the Word."

Silence fell over the tent. "So they have the same power as you, Master Mathias, and that healer Selma," Commander Warin finally said.

"Yes."

One of the other commanders cursed, and a few faces paled in the lamplight.

"Did you see this when you searched the Nordic woman's mind?" one of the other captains asked.

"Yes," Kaeden replied. "But Mathias suspected before tonight. I don't think the young woman fully understands the powers at play among her people. Mathias was the one who first told me. We know one of the Shadonae is a former Oathmaker and has bound the Nordic army. That is why they have proven to be a formidable enemy. It is also why the Nordic prisoners of war died. Their binding unraveled."

"Why did Master Mathias not tell us?" Commander Warin asked.

Kaeden glanced around with a hard glint in his eyes. "He never got a chance. He was still investigating when he was called to use his power on the soldier Captain Bertin was interrogating." He glared at Captain Bertin. "Instead, he gave his life."

Bertin seemed to have enough sense to glance away.

"What do we do? Do you have a power that can make us as strong as the Nordic army?" the first captain asked.

Kaeden curled his fingers across the table. "That is not how we serve."

"You mean you can, but you won't," another man said.

Kaeden cast a dark look his way. "Like I said, that is not how my people serve."

"But it would be helpful if we could have access to the same kind of supernatural power the Nordics possess. We could win this war."

The others around the room agreed.

Kaeden straightened to his full height. "You would have me take away your will and mind? Force you to obey whatever command I give you?" He raised his hand, letting the light from his mark illuminate the tent. "You wouldn't even know I was doing it. You really want me to become like these Shadonae?"

Those gathered shook their heads with murmurs of *no*. Commander Warin lifted his chin and crossed his arms.

Kaeden didn't care if the commander or others disapproved of his words. They needed to know what they were asking for. He slowly lowered his palm. "That is what would happen if I forced my gift on you. But that is not the way of the Word. When I arrived in Avonai, I offered my services as a healer. And I will remain a healer."

Silence fell again across the tent. Commander Warin cleared his throat seconds later. "So how do we deal with these Shadonae?"

"I am new to my role and still have much to learn, including the responsibility my people have toward those of our kind who have turned away."

"In other words, you don't know."

"Not yet."

"So we are on our own, with such an enemy in front of us."

The others began to grumble, and Captain Bertin said something under his breath, but Kaeden didn't catch his words. All he knew was that as the new Truthsayer, it now fell on him to judge the Shadonae. But how was he supposed to confront them when there was an entire army of empowered Nordics between him and them?

One of the Avonain captains spoke up. "Then nothing has changed. And that Nordic woman has proven useless."

Kaeden pressed his lips together. That wasn't true. The Word Himself had designated Brighid as His special tool. However, there were some here who might take that statement as the Word siding with the Nordics. Men like Bertin. No, he couldn't mention that. Not yet.

"Is there any reason to keep her now?" another officer asked. "The Nordics have no prisoners to exchange her for."

"We certainly do not want her back on the battlefield. She killed many of our soldiers," another retorted.

The commanders and officers debated Brighid's value. Kaeden stepped back from the table until he blended in with the shadows near the flaps of the tent. The longer they spoke, the more a fire burned inside his middle. Unlike these men, he had seen inside Brighid's soul. He knew her: her fears, her sorrow, her hope. She was a human, not an object of war.

Captain Bertin casually lifted his knife and stared at the tip of the blade. "I say we kill her. We have no need of her." He looked around at the others. "She is a liability and a mouth to be fed."

Some of the men nodded in agreement. Others disagreed, and the debate started again.

Kaeden turned toward the flaps. He couldn't stand there and listen to them anymore. "Please excuse me," he said to the young man standing near the exit. "I am fatigued from using my power. If the others ask, explain that to them."

The young man bowed. "Yes, Master Kaeden."

Kaeden ducked through the flaps and stepped outside. It was true. He was tired. Mathias had never said how much it took out of him to peer into the soul of another. But he still had one more thing to do before he retired.

Save Brighid.

Now was the time—while the commanders and officers were busy.

A plan started to form inside his mind as he hurried away. It was daring and simple. He would free her. If he let her go now, she had time to get a head start and disappear into the night. He would have to convince Treyvar, or maybe he would just overpower the man. Then he would face whatever consequences came afterward. What was important now was getting her away from here before the commanders and captains could enact whatever decision they came to.

As if led by an invisible thread, Kaeden first made his way through the camp to the wagon where he had awoken hours earlier. A few healers encircled the dying fire with those they were caring for. Darry changed the bandages of an Avonain soldier nearby. No one seemed to notice him.

He reached over the side of the wagon. First, he retrieved his cloak and pack. As the air grew colder, she would need his cloak more than he would. He placed it in the bottom of the pack, then added his waterskin. He found a few travel biscuits and tossed them in as well and swung the pack over his shoulder. He had no idea where the Word would lead Brighid, but she would need the essentials.

He made his way silently around the camp. Most of the encampment slept now, fatigued from a full day of marching. There would be more marching tomorrow as they continued west. If he freed Brighid now, she could escape north through the Rokr Valley into Nordica. She would have to bypass Stelriden Fortress, but as long as she stayed along the eastern side of the valley, she would make it.

Kaeden nodded. Yes. It could be done. Especially as a Nordic woman who knew the ways of the forest and mountains. And with the Word watching over her and protecting her.

He reached the wagon again and found Treyvar still guarding Brighid. There was hardly any light, just a subtle red glow from the dying fire twenty feet away. Her wrist was held above her head, chained to the wagon. She seemed to have dozed off. That surprised him. He would have expected her to be wide awake after everything that had happened that evening. Perhaps the last few days and the truthsaying had taken all her energy.

"You're back," Treyvar said quietly.

"Yes."

"Did you tell the commanders what you learned?"

"Yes."

"What do they plan on doing with the woman?"

"They're still debating."

"I see."

Kaeden let out his breath. "I won't lie to you. I'm here to free her." He could have just knocked the man out, but they had already been through battle after bloody battle together. That had earned Treyvar at least a chance to hear him out.

Treyvar didn't respond. Kaeden relaxed slightly and took the man's silence as at least partial compliance. He held out his hand, his palm glowing with a soft gentle light.

"Did the Word tell you to do this?" Treyvar finally asked.

For some reason, he didn't hesitate to answer. "Yes."

"And you're sure? Do you really want to go against Avonai and the White City?"

Kaeden snorted. "What are they going to do? Kill me? They wouldn't try, not after what I shared. I'm the Truthsayer now. I am not under anyone's authority but the Word's, and the order to free her came from Him."

"They're not going to understand that." Treyvar passed him the key.

"I know. And I don't care. There is more at stake than this war."

Treyvar shook his head. "In this way, you are not like Mathias."

Kaeden placed the key inside the manacle. "No, I'm not. And I don't plan to be. Mathias was Mathias, and I am me. But I serve the same Word he did, and I will fulfill the command He has given me."

Treyvar sighed. "Then I will do what I can to cover you."

Kaeden frowned at his words, but before he could ask, the key let out a soft click, and the manacle opened. Brighid's hand dropped, startling her awake.

"Wh-what's going on?"

"Shh." Kaeden knelt and reached for her wrist. She would need to be in perfect health if she was going to escape. She hissed in pain as he wrapped his fingers around the area and closed his eyes. It took only a moment to transfer her wounds and fatigue to his own body, but it was not enough to faze him.

"Why are you back?" she whispered as he opened his eyes and found her staring at him. "And why did you heal me again?"

"Because I am setting you free."

She leaned back. "What?"

"The Word sent me to save you." He held out his hand to help her up. "Your future does not end here."

Brighid stared at him for a moment, then glanced at the fire where the soldiers slept. He could see thoughts flitting across her face and wondered what they were. Then she looked back at him. His hand glowed in the darkness between them.

"All right." She clasped it, and he pulled them up together. "What do I do?" she asked quietly.

"Head north." Kaeden offered her his pack. "Go back to your people."

"And then what?"

"You know the truth and what happened to the Nordics here. You have witnessed what will happen to your people if they continue to work with the Shadonae, the one who bound you to your oath and his comrades. Death. Not by our hand nor by this war. In the end, they will destroy you all. Find a way to free your people. And I will find a way to stop the Shadonae."

"How do you know you can trust me? What if I go back to the Nordic army?"

Kaeden shrugged. "You might. I have done what the Word asked of me. Now you must walk your own path."

"My own path," she murmured as she placed the pack on her back. A small part of him wondered if she really would go back to the Nordic army. But from what he had seen of her memories, he didn't think so. She was an outcast among her own people. His heart clenched at the thought. How would she convince the people of the north?

Maybe he should go with her. He had no allegiance to Avonai or the White City. He wasn't an outcast, but he certainly didn't belong to any people group. He never had. Not to the Eldarans, not to any nationality. And now as the Truthsayer, he stood alone.

A second later, he let those thoughts go as she adjusted the pack on her back. His presence wouldn't help her. And he had his own road to walk, one that would eventually lead to the Shadonae.

Brighid glanced at Treyvar. He gave her a small nod as if to say *go*. Then she looked at Kaeden one more time. He watched the fire dance across her face and felt something shift inside his soul.

"Will I see you again?" she asked.

His insides twisted at her question. "I don't know."

"I hope so." She turned north and disappeared a minute later into the darkness.

Treyvar came to stand beside him, his arms crossed as they stared into the night.

"I think we just released one of the most powerful women to walk the Lands."

"You can still stop her," Kaeden replied.

"No, I don't think I will. After all, the Truthsayer saw fit to free her. Who am I to stand in his way?"

Kaeden continued to stare into the darkness. She had seemed

alone and small as she walked away, but he knew better. He had *seen* her. All of her. He knew her strength more than anyone.

"Do you know what you're going to say when the commanders of Avonai and the White City come after you?" Treyvar asked.

"No." But he had a feeling the Word would give him the words when he needed them. And even allies for the days ahead.

42

The moment Brighid left the glow of the fires, she ran. Beneath the moonlight and beyond the grasslands, she could see hills. She needed to reach those hills before dawn.

With each step, she breathed out words of thankfulness to Kaeden. He had renewed her body and spirit with his power. Without that, she wasn't sure she would have the stamina to flee. Every cut and bruise was gone. Amazing.

The pack thumped against her back. The grass bent and broke beneath her boots. That would be a problem when she was discovered missing and search teams were sent out to find her. But she knew how to hide, she only needed to reach those hills ahead.

She set her gaze on the moonlit peaks. After she arrived, she would search for a brook or trees, something more than grass, a place where she could use a zigzag pattern and water to break up her trail. It wouldn't be perfect, but it would buy her more time to get away. Then she would continue north until she reached the towering trees of the Ari Mountains.

For one fleeting second, she glanced to her right. What if she returned to the Nordic army? She thought of Johan, Marta, and the other clanless. A thick lump filled her throat. She missed their camaraderie, laughter, and friendship. But if she returned, she doubted she would be allowed to rejoin the Nordic forces. She had been taken during battle and made a prisoner of war. She had also survived Armand's oath and knew what happened to those who were not bound again. She knew the truth behind his power and doubted Armand would allow her to live and tell the others.

She shook her head and kept on running. There was no future there for her there. And if Kaeden was right, there was no future for any Nordic. They had been manipulated and lied to by the hjars of their clans and the Shadonae, as Kaeden called them.

Her only choice was to go back to Nordica and find those not yet swayed by Armand. That was the only way she could rescue Johan, Marta, and the rest of her people.

Who is going to listen to me?

Brighid blinked. It was true. She was unknown, a clanless woman. Nobody outside the Nordic forces knew her as the Stryth'Veizla. And who would believe her story that the Nordics were being influenced by these beings?

She slowed her gait. *What am I even doing?* She breathed heavily but continued to jog. She glanced up at the star-studded sky. So many stars. One of those twinkling lights was like her: one in a thousand. No, maybe even a million. Lost amid the darkness, surpassed by those with brighter lights. Unwanted at birth, barely surviving this life. If she disappeared into the darkness forever, would anyone even notice?

The wind blew, and with it she swore she could hear words.

She stumbled across a root and caught her footing. She glanced around as she picked up her pace. The breeze brushed against her heated face like a caress.

The words were a song, and they filled her mind and soul. One moment they were in the voice of crickets, the next in the rustling of the grass. The wind's words almost sounded like her name. *Brighid.*

She focused on the hills. The sound changed to the beating of her heart and the constant whoosh of her breath.

I will be with you, warrior of the North.

A shiver raced along her skin. She peered over her shoulder, then the other way. Was she hearing real words? She could no longer see the fires from the southern camp, only pale light along the grass and the stars in the sky.

A gust of wind hit her from the back, rushing along her body and up through her hair, sending it flying around her face. And in the wind, she heard these words: *I am the past, the present, the future. I hold all things together. I am the Word.*

She slowed. This couldn't be. She pressed two fingers to her forehead. Was she really hearing a voice? The wind continued to roar across the vast plains, flattening the grass to the ground and whipping around her body. Then, as fast as the wind had sprung up, it tapered back down to a gentle breeze.

The words faded and the air became still. Not a blade of grass moved beneath the moonlight. Brighid came to a stop and looked around again. Had she really heard the Word speak? She wasn't an Eldaran, or a priest, or a scribe. She was Nordic, even if she didn't follow the old gods. Why would the Word speak to her?

She waited, expecting to hear more. After a minute, she let out her breath and looked up at the night sky. Everything appeared as it had before.

A cricket chirped, breaking the silence. Brighid resumed a slow walk, then a minute later picked up her pace until she was running again.

I will be with you, the voice had said.

Where? In her homeland?

Warrior of the North.

Was that her? What need did the Word have of a warrior? Especially a Nordic woman?

For some reason, Mathias came to mind. What would he tell her? Then her heart fell. He was gone. Death had taken him. She had known him for only a few days, but in a small, simple way, it was like having Elphsaba back.

Elphsaba. Did she follow the Word? Brighid scrunched her face. She couldn't remember.

Just as the sun started to come up and paint the sky around her in brilliant colors, she reached the foothills. She paused to eat and drink, then surveyed the land ahead of her. Over the first hill she spotted a brook weaving through the valley below. She would enter the water there and follow it for a while to erase her tracks. Then head into the forest.

The words from the night before flowed through her mind like a melody.

She held her hand up and made a fist. "I don't know what they mean or what my future holds." She looked at towering mountains in the far distance. "What I do know is my path leads north, and so that is where I will go."

With that thought firmly in mind, she started down into the valley, her heart and soul set toward Nordica.

43

"Did you feel that?" Peder stood motionless, his gaze toward the tent opening and his marked hand closed tight.

"Yes," Armand said as an invisible wave washed over them. Seconds later, another one came. Then another. Like ripples on a lake caused by a rock. Each time the ripple hit him, his mark burned as if his palm were being held to a flame. Sweat formed along his forehead, and he gritted his teeth against the groan rising in his throat.

Peder let out a huff and turned away as he clutched his hand to his chest.

Viessa ducked through the tent flaps, leaving the misty rain behind. She had arrived shortly after their defeat at the Battle of the Plains with supplies.

"Do you feel—ack!" She grimaced and her hand clenched. They all felt these waves. It could mean only one thing.

"There is a new Truthsayer in the Lands," Armand said between the ripples. Already the intensity of each wave waned.

Peder slowly turned back around, his face pale. "Is that what this is?"

"I believe so." He remembered one of the Eldaran elders speaking of the time when the last Truthsayer passed. It didn't matter where the Truthsayer was, when he or she died every Eldaran felt the passing and the transferring of authority to the new Truthsayer. Such was the power of the first of their people.

"What can kill a Truthsayer?" Peder murmured to himself.

"Do you know where the new Truthsayer is?" Viessa asked.

"No." What did these ripples feel like to the other Eldarans? The ones whose marks still held light? He doubted it was painful like this. Was it a warning? He lifted his chin. So be it. He could endure the pain. Better this burning than the hypocritical life the other Eldarans lived. If nothing else, he was true to himself.

The waves seemed to have disappeared, and all was still again. Peder let out a sigh of relief while Viessa walked over to one of the beds and sat down.

"Do you know anything of the previous Truthsayers?" she asked, looking at Armand.

"No."

"So no idea where they went when they left the assembly over a hundred years ago?"

He shook his head.

"Is there a chance the last Truthsayer was with the southern armies?"

"Possibly." The thought had occurred to him.

"Is it possible the new Truthsayer is also with the southern armies?"

"Maybe." He could tell Viessa was thinking the same thing. The Truthsayer might be closer than they thought.

"How does a new Truthsayer come into being?" Peder asked.

"The power is passed down through blood, like any of our gifts," Armand said.

"What if there isn't a direct blood relation? How is the next vessel chosen?"

"I don't know," Armand said slowly. "It's been a long time since the Truthsayer walked among our people. There is nothing recorded that I know of. Unless the writings are kept in the Sanctuary near the White City." And that was not a place they would be heading any time soon.

Viessa glanced up. "Is it possible the transference of the truthsaying power is as simple as proximity? That the closest Eldaran inherits the power?"

All three looked at one another while the rain softly tapped against the tent ceiling. "This is just hypothetical," Viessa continued, "but let's say the last Truthsayer had no blood heir, and the new one inherited the gift through proximity. There hasn't been time for a new blood heir to be born, so if the new Truthsayer were to die . . ."

"Or even if the new Truthsayer received the gift by blood, their offspring may possess other gifts, so the gift might be transferred anyway," Peder said.

Armand raised an eyebrow at Peder's response. So the young man could actually think.

Viessa spoke again. "What I'm saying is, could it be possible that one of us could become the Truthsayer?"

They glanced at each other again. Armand felt a sudden wariness in his heart as well as a craving in his soul. To be the Truthsayer and hold the will and mind of people in his control would be the ultimate power. Not just to bend them by words, but by truth itself. Or at least, his truth. But he could see a hunger for that same power blossoming across the faces of his comrades.

"This is all speculation," Armand said, breaking the silence. "What we need is information. We need to find out who the Truthsayer is and where they are located. And how this Eldaran came into the gift."

Peder nodded while Viessa narrowed her eyes and watched him. No doubt she was thinking the same thing. Only one of them could take this power, if it were possible. And he had a feeling she would like that power even more than her control over the shadow-wraiths.

"So how do we get this information?" Viessa asked.

"I'll meet with the clan hjars and see what I can find out. I'll also plant the idea that if the southern armies have a Truthsayer on their side, it is imperative that we capture that individual as soon as possible."

"And then what?"

"Then we will decide together what to do next."

Viessa held his gaze for a moment, then looked away. They both knew it was lip service. He would find a way to have that power for himself. He would just have to convince her to remain their Guardian and harness the power of the Mordra.

Armand turned away. The only question niggling the back of his mind was whether such power could be passed to him. What happened to a Truthsayer who turned from the Word? Not just walked away but became a heretic like him? Was it possible?

There was only one way to find out. To find and capture the new Truthsayer.

And then I will gain their power. No matter what.

ABOUT THE AUTHOR

Morgan L. Busse is a writer by day and a mother by night. She is the author of multiple series including The Ravenwood Saga and Skyworld series. She is a three-time Christy Award finalist and won the INSPY, Selah, and Carol Award for best in Christian speculative fiction. During her spare time she enjoys playing games, taking long walks, and dreaming about her next novel.

Visit her online at www.morganlbusse.com.

WHAT'S LURKING IN THE MIST
IS THE LEAST OF THEIR WORRIES...

THE SKYWORLD SERIES

Secrets in the Mist

Blood Secrets

Available Now!

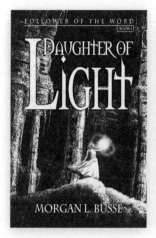 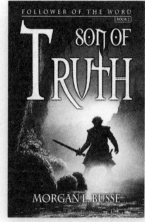